PRAISE FOR MARYBETH MAYHEW WHALEN

"Each character's voice is distinct and lived in as the reader gradually connects the threads tying everyone in this small town together . . . There's a lot here. An intriguing mystery filled with hearty characters."

—*Kirkus Reviews*

"Multilayered characters lift this elegantly plotted crime novel from Whalen (*The Things We Wish Were True*) . . . Loads of hidden love stories and small-town gossip will keep readers turning the pages."

—*Publishers Weekly*

"[*Only Ever Her*] will satisfy those who enjoy watching a community's underbelly exposed."

—*Library Journal*

"An inherently fascinating, page-turner of a read by an author with an impressively skilled narrative storytelling style."

—Midwest Book Review

"Marybeth Mayhew Whalen's character-driven suspense propelled me through the pages with a relentless need to absorb every word. Unputdownable!"

—Robyn Carr, *New York Times* bestselling author

THIS
SECRET
THING

OTHER TITLES BY
MARYBETH MAYHEW WHALEN

Only Ever Her

When We Were Worthy

The Things We Wish Were True

THIS
SECRET
THING

A NOVEL

MARYBETH MAYHEW WHALEN

LAKE UNION
PUBLISHING

Text copyright © 2020 by Marybeth Mayhew Whalen
All rights reserved.

Published by Lake Union Publishing, Seattle

www.apub.com

Amazon, the Amazon logo, and Lake Union Publishing are trademarks of Amazon.com, Inc., or its affiliates.

ISBN-13: 9781542019477
ISBN-10: 1542019478

Cover design by Shasti O'Leary Soudant

Printed in the United States of America

To the four most dangerous women in the world
Beaucatchers, all

Your beauty was theirs for the asking.

Ezekiel 16:15b

PODCAST TRANSCRIPT:

THE *NOSY NEIGHBOR*, EPISODE 108

BILL PARSONS, HOST: I'd like to welcome back all of my loyal listeners to the *Nosy Neighbor* podcast. I'm your host, Bill Parsons. If you're new to the podcast, well, then, welcome to the show devoted to asking questions and finding out details about some of the nation's most intriguing cases. For an hour each week, we invite you to be that nosy neighbor you don't want to admit you are. We delve into the gossip and peek behind the blinds. This week's show is no exception and one we've had requested for the past two years. It seems you all want to know the truth behind the arrest of the so-called suburban madam, Norah Ramsey, in Raleigh, North Carolina.

Rumors of Ramsey's ties to some pretty important men in Raleigh—a city known as a center for technology and the North Carolina state government—were rampant and relentless. And when news of the discovery of a body in the lake near Norah Ramsey's suburban residence hit, interest in this case reached a fever pitch. And I think in today's episode you'll find out why. Today we've got one of Norah Ramsey's actual neighbors with us. Bess Strickland, welcome to the podcast.

BESS STRICKLAND: Thank you, Bill. [*Clears throat.*] Excuse me.

BILL PARSONS: Would you like a drink of water?

BESS STRICKLAND: No, I'm fine. I'm just a bit . . . nervous. Talking about what happened can still be sort of . . . hard.

BILL PARSONS: But you felt it was important to come on the show.

BESS STRICKLAND: Yes. I did. Those of us who were personally affected by this case feel strongly that the true story needs to be told. There are a lot of rumors lingering that are just . . . inaccurate. There were people who were impacted by this case who did nothing wrong, and I think that's important to keep in mind. As someone who cares about my neighbors, I just want to make sure they're fairly represented.

BILL PARSONS: I'm sure. And don't worry. We'll make this easy. Let's just start with who you are in relation to Norah Ramsey.

BESS STRICKLAND: Well, like you said, Bill, I am—or I was—her neighbor. We lived on the same street. Our daughters were best friends and, well, once we were, too.

BILL PARSONS: Is there a story there?

BESS STRICKLAND: Not really. We just grew apart. It happens.

BILL PARSONS: Indeed it does. From what I've read, Norah kept pretty much to herself. Wasn't really close to anyone. Mainly just interacted with her daughter, Violet, who was, what, fifteen when all this occurred?

BESS STRICKLAND: Yes, our daughters are the same age. They were both fifteen when Norah was arrested.

BILL PARSONS: And you said they were best friends?

BESS STRICKLAND: Well, that friendship had actually tapered off, too. Both girls had started moving in different directions. No real falling out or anything. Just growing up, you know?

BILL PARSONS: But it was that friendship that prompted Norah Ramsey to send her daughter, Violet, to stay with you when she was arrested, am I right?

BESS STRICKLAND: Yes, that's right. Violet came directly to my house after the police allowed her to pack some things. They were searching the house, from what I understand, for evidence or whatever, so Violet had to leave while that was taking place. That went on for a couple of days, as I recall.

BILL PARSONS: I bet that was hard for the whole neighborhood. Cops everywhere. The press. Onlookers trying to get a glimpse of "The Madam's House."

BESS STRICKLAND: Yes, it was a stressful time for all of us. But, to be clear, Norah did not run a bordello out of her home. That was all run out of the spa used as a front. Our neighborhood was—well, it still is—a family-friendly community. It's not the place where something like that would happen.

BILL PARSONS: But it did, though. Didn't it?

BESS STRICKLAND: [*voice barely audible*] Yes, I guess it did.

BILL PARSONS: OK, we're going to take a short break to hear from one of our sponsors. But stay tuned because when we come back, we're going to hear more from Bess Strickland, giving us all that peek inside the home of Norah Ramsey, bringing out your inner nosy neighbor. Don't go away.

Norah

She was shopping online for luxury-brand anti-aging cream, about to press "Purchase" to spend more money than she cared to admit for the sake of her vanity, when her phone buzzed beside her. Lately, whenever that phone went off, she experienced a jolt of anxiety. It felt like a small seizure.

She could still recall when the sound of the ringing phone had meant creditors chasing her down, how her body had reacted the exact same way then. She could only guess it was like muscle memory: what to do in cases of severe panic. Back then she had thought that was as bad as it could get, owing money she didn't have to people who expected to collect it nonetheless. Funny how that time—those old phone calls—had led right up to this one, to these mini seizures every time the phone rang all over again.

When she saw that it was just Violet calling, she exhaled loudly, her breath making a whooshing sound in the otherwise quiet room. She needed to turn on some music, and fast. Music always made her feel better, drove the demons away. Quiet just bred anxiety. When baby Violet had cried, she used to turn the music louder than her wails. She would hold her on her hip and the two of them would dance away the tears.

She answered the phone. "Hey, baby," she said to her only child, hoping that the tone of her voice belied any wisps of lingering panic. She didn't want to alarm her daughter. Because no matter what happened, Violet would be fine. Norah would make sure of that. Norah always made sure of that.

She heard static on the other end, only pieces of her daughter's voice coming through, staccato syllables. Sometimes when this happened, she wondered if her phone was bugged. She glanced around the den, wondering if it was bugged, too. If someone was listening to her right now. Or, God forbid, watching her. She glanced down at the threadbare T-shirt and very old sweatpants she wore. She was just being paranoid.

"Vi?" she asked the static.

"Mom?" She heard her daughter's voice, then more static.

"Vi! Call me back!" she hollered into the phone. She ended the call, put the phone on her lap, and waited. A moment went by before it buzzed again. She smiled and picked it up. "Is that better?" she asked.

"Huh?" a voice said. She had not looked to see who it was. In that brief moment, as she'd waited for Violet to call back, she'd forgotten to be worried. Not that she wouldn't have answered her business partner's call if she'd looked first. She and Lois were in this together, after all. They were all each other had right now.

"Sorry, Lo," she said. "I thought you were Vi. We had a bad connection earlier."

"He was there again," Lois said, skipping pleasantries. Norah heard the anxiety in her friend's voice.

"Wh-what was he doing?" she asked.

"You know, skulking around like he always does. Looking with those eyes of his. Asking lots of stupid questions. He asked to use the bathroom, and Tessa said he had to be a paying customer. He said, 'Oh yeah, I'm sure I do.'"

"Tessa told you this?" Norah asked.

"Yes, she called as soon as he left."

Norah sighed into the phone because there was nothing else to say. "He's a cop," Lois said.

"We don't know that." Norah's words came out too fast, too desperate, to be reassuring.

Lois sighed too. "Yes, we do."

The two women sat silently on the phone, listening to each other breathe as they each weighed their options. They'd always known this day could come. But things had been going so well for so long, they'd almost forgotten about the possibility.

Lois spoke up. "I think it's time for plan B."

"I guess it is," Norah agreed. She'd been thinking the same thing but also wondering, was this panicking too soon, folding needlessly? She didn't know, but she wasn't willing to be at risk anymore. The infamous plan B was dreamed up the same night as plan A, a night of much wine and laughter, when success seemed like the only future they would have. Success, and money. Money to buy expensive eye cream to prevent the signs of aging. Money to keep creditors at bay forever. Money to provide a freedom neither she nor Lois had ever known. But the time for plan B had come. And who knew what would come after that? Certainly not Norah.

"So this is goodbye," Norah said.

Lois's voice in response was choked with tears. "Just for now."

Though Lo couldn't see her, Norah nodded. "So, then I'll just say, 'See you soon.'"

"Remember what we said? Remember what we promised?" Lois asked, and she sounded like a very scared little girl.

"Mouth shut," Norah intoned. "I remember."

"Mouth shut," Lois agreed. "Whichever one of us goes down, we go down alone. We take *no one else* with us. I'll do it for you."

"And I, you," Norah replied, the words from that long-ago night of plan-B scheming coming back to her like those verses she used to memorize back when her mother, Polly, went through that religious phase and dragged her to church every Sunday. Which of Polly's husbands had been the religious one? Norah wondered, more because thinking about the past was easier than thinking about the present. When she was little, she'd promised herself she wouldn't turn out like her mother. And she hadn't. She'd managed to turn out worse.

Norah heard the click on the other end that meant Lois had hung up.

"You think you're better than me," Polly used to say. "You'll see someday. You'll see."

And now, she did.

Violet

On Wednesday Violet's mother brought a pumpkin home, and on Thursday Violet's mother got arrested. When the student volunteer, a boy with a facial tic that only drew more attention to his terrible acne, came to get her out of class because the police were there for her, Violet followed him silently, thinking as she walked to the school office that she should've known something was up when her mother got that pumpkin so early. It wasn't even October yet. The damn thing would probably be rotten by the time they went to carve it.

A policeman drove her home, the size of the houses growing with each neighborhood they passed—big, bigger, biggest. He asked her inane questions throughout the drive, like they were just two people passing the time for no particular reason at all. He could've been an Uber driver, except for the uniform. He asked her name, even though he already knew what it was: Violet Ramsey. He asked how old she was: Fifteen. What grade she was in: Tenth. What her favorite food was: Sushi. If she'd lived in Raleigh her whole life: Yes. The officer probably thought he was getting her mind off what was happening, but it wasn't working.

Even as Violet answered his questions, a million questions of her own were running through her mind: Where is my mom? What did she do? What's going to happen to her? What's going to happen to me? She looked out the window at the familiar surroundings, keeping watch for their house to come into view, ready to spot that orange pumpkin sitting on the porch like a beacon.

The officer pulled in front of their house and put the car in park but didn't turn off the engine. A man stood on the front porch right beside the pumpkin, waiting for them. He was a policeman, too, but he wasn't wearing a uniform. Violet knew from cop shows on TV that that meant he was higher up in the police force, a detective or something.

Someone opened her car door, startling her. She looked up, expecting to see another cop, but instead she saw Mr. Sheridan, from their swim club. Just this summer Violet had helped his daughter learn to jump off the diving board, holding her arms up time after time as she coaxed the little girl to leap. She was four and scared, but, with time, she grew brave. By the end of the summer, she was jumping without Violet there.

Mr. Sheridan had addressed her exactly once this summer, marveling at how Violet had achieved something he could not. They'd stood side by side as they watched his daughter plunge into the water and come up grinning and shrieking, Violet, self-conscious in the new bikini Nicole had talked her into, and Mr. Sheridan, wan and paunchy in his beige swim trunks. And now here they were, blinking at each other as he extended his hand to help her out of the car. His hand was soft and meaty; her own hand disappeared inside it.

"Your mom asked me to come," he said. Then he cleared his throat, looking pained.

"M-my mom? Asked you?" She had never seen her mother speak to Mr. Sheridan at the pool, or anywhere else for that matter.

He nodded. "I'm her attorney." He handed her a business card as proof.

She glanced down just long enough to see "Jim Sheridan, Attorney." Then underneath it, the words "Specializing in Criminal Defense." She focused on just one word: *criminal*. He patted her back in an awkward attempt to comfort her, and she shoved the card in the back pocket of her jeans.

Mr. Sheridan pointed at the man waiting on the porch. "I think they want us to hurry this along," he said. He gave her an apologetic look.

"Hurry what along?" she asked. Her mother's car was in the driveway. Violet had thought they were taking her home to see her so she could explain what was happening. Obviously something was very wrong. She feared she was going to have to go inside and see her mom in handcuffs, because that was the worst thing she could imagine. But, looking at Mr. Sheridan's face, she realized that wasn't what they were there for.

"They're going to escort you in so you can gather some of your belongings—things you'll need for a few days, maybe even a week." Her eyes widened, and he winced. "Jeez, I'm sorry. I thought they told you this already."

"My mom's not here?" she asked, sounding stupid, sounding like a child. She pointed at her mother's car, parked right where she'd left it the evening before. Violet had suspected she hadn't parked it in the garage because she wanted to carry that big heavy pumpkin right up the front sidewalk and put it on the porch. Violet had watched from her window as her mother struggled under the pumpkin's weight and roundness. She could barely get a good grip on it and almost dropped it twice.

She'd laughed and knocked on the window at her, but her mother hadn't heard. She hadn't told her mom that she saw her carry the pumpkin, never even mentioned the pumpkin at all. She should've asked her about it that morning. She should've asked why she had bought a pumpkin so early. But her mom had been on her computer with her mouth pulled tight, which meant to leave her alone. Violet was thinking about the upcoming test in first period anyway. They'd barely acknowledged each other. It had been a normal morning.

"They didn't tell you at the school?" Mr. Sheridan asked.

She shook her head. "They just said that my mom had run into some legal trouble and I had to go home." She turned her gaze back to the pumpkin, ignoring the man standing beside it. She wondered who could carve it if her mom wasn't there to help. She doubted she could do it by herself. "Is she in trouble with the IRS?" she asked. "Did she get audited?" Her mom talked a lot about the IRS and audits. As far as Violet knew, it was her biggest fear.

"Sons of bitches," Mr. Sheridan said. Then he remembered who he was talking to and apologized.

"I go to high school," she said. "I've heard worse."

Mr. Sheridan grinned and clapped her on the shoulder like a buddy. The man on the porch motioned for them to come in. "They need for us to get a move on," he said. "So why don't you pack your things and then we can talk more."

"So my mom's not here?" she asked again. She asked it even though she knew the answer. For some reason, she needed to hear it.

Mr. Sheridan, attorney specializing in criminal defense, shook his head, his expression grim. "No, honey, she's . . ."

She needed to hear it, but he couldn't say it. So she said it for him. "In jail."

He squeezed her shoulder, just a light squeeze, meant to be a comfort, though nothing could be at that moment. "Yeah, honey. She's in jail."

They started to walk toward the porch, and that big-ass pumpkin, and the man who was waiting for them there. But she stopped one more time because she had to know. "Why is she in jail?"

Mr. Sheridan closed his eyes, thinking, she knew, of how he would answer. He looked just like his daughter did when she was mustering the courage to jump off the diving board. He opened his eyes again. "I might as well tell you, because you're going to find out anyway. What with all the social media you kids have these days."

She nodded encouragingly. She needed the truth, not some kid-friendly bullshit.

"She was arrested this morning on charges of money laundering and illegal prostitution." He said it like he was saying, *She got a ticket for running a stop sign.*

She squinted at him. It was the most ridiculous thing she'd ever heard. It was so ridiculous it was laughable, though laughing seemed wrong at a time like this. They had the wrong person. This would get straightened out in no time. She probably didn't even need but one change of clothes, because she would be back home that soon. Back home with her mom.

"My mother isn't a prostitute," she corrected him, straightening her back and giving him her bravest smile. "She owns her own marketing firm." She thought of all the times she'd written that on her school forms, on the line designated for "Mother's Employment": "Owner, Ramsey and Associates."

Mr. Sheridan didn't argue. He just started walking, expecting her to fall into step beside him. After a second, she did. The man on the porch got closer and closer with each step they took. He closed the file he was looking at—probably a file cataloguing all the accusations against her mom. Violet's eyes met his, and she narrowed hers. He gave her a little smirk. He was the enemy, accusing her mother of something she most certainly had not done.

Prostitutes do drugs and live in bad neighborhoods. Prostitutes wear hooker heels and leopard prints and push-up bras and hang out on street corners. Prostitutes have men hanging around all the time. Her mom was the boss of her own company, and other than Stanley, their lawn guy, Violet had never seen a man around. In fact, she had scolded her mother about it, told her she should go out on a date once in a while. Her mother was a beautiful woman, far more beautiful than Violet thought she, herself, could ever hope to be.

And her mom always answered the same way. "Honey, I've had enough men in my life. I don't need any more." Then she would smile and tickle her and suggest a movie they could watch or ask if they had any ice cream in the fridge. What the man on her porch and Mr. Sheridan and anyone else who would hear the news didn't know was, her mother was perfectly happy with her life. She wouldn't screw it up by doing something illegal. She would never do something that could take them away from each other.

Nico

Nico hated to be kept waiting, but he hated what he was waiting on even more. The scene on the sidewalk was clear: Norah Ramsey's attorney breaking the news to her daughter. Nico stood by and watched as the life the kid had known got blown to smithereens. His heart heavy, he tried to look at anything else but the girl, who looked a little like his own daughter, Lauren—same light-brown hair, same hazel eyes, same slim frame. One day she would be a beauty, but she didn't know it yet.

He checked the file he held in his hands, just to give himself something else to focus on while he waited. He flipped to the info about the daughter. Violet Ramsey was fifteen. His Lauren was thirteen, but looked fifteen. Violet Ramsey wore nondescript clothes—jeans, T-shirt, sneakers—ducked her head shyly if you looked at her, and her only makeup was some mascara and lip gloss. His Lauren thought "more was more" where makeup was concerned, wore loud colors to attract attention (preferably from boys), and encountered the world with her eyes wide and her chin jutted defiantly.

Nico tried not to think about Lauren, or his wife, Karen, or his son, Ian, for that matter, focusing instead on the job he was there to do. And that job was to first clear the scene so a proper search could be conducted. He was leaving nothing to chance, nothing that Norah Ramsey's attorney could use later. He'd been at the helm of this investigation for months, waiting anxiously for this day to come. And now it was here. He just had to get the kid in and out of this house quickly so they could get on with it.

She would need her things, and he was going to personally catalogue every item she took with her, making sure she took nothing but necessities and nothing that might possibly be evidence. Though the kid *looked* shell-shocked and completely daunted, she could've been coached. Her mother could've told her what to take with her if something like this ever happened. He'd seen plenty in his years with the force; nothing surprised him anymore.

He noticed movement in his peripheral vision, closed and lowered the file. They were on the move finally, the attorney guiding Violet Ramsey toward the house, her gait slow and wary. When their eyes met, the girl glared at him. Nico gave her what he hoped was a reassuring smile, though he doubted he had the power to reassure her. He was there as the enemy, the marauder. He understood that. He didn't like that part of his job, but he also didn't like what Norah Ramsey had done. For a moment his brother, Matteo, flickered through his mind, but he banished him from his thoughts. He couldn't afford to think about anyone from his family—his wife, his kids, or his brother—at this moment. It would only distract and weaken him.

As the pair climbed the porch steps to meet him, Nico rested his foot on a huge pumpkin that was there, an attempt to strike a casual, nonconfrontational pose.

"Don't do that," the girl said, then clamped her mouth shut.

He quickly removed his foot from the pumpkin and tucked the file under his arm. "My apologies," he said, feeling foolish. Violet Ramsey nodded once, then looked down.

"I'm Detective Rinaldi," he said. The girl nodded again but didn't look up.

Before going inside, Nico explained what was going to happen: He would walk with her through the house as she packed. He would make a list of each item taken, just for their evidential records. Jim Sheridan, the attorney, was welcome to be with them every step of the way. Violet Ramsey looked to Jim Sheridan, her eyes silently imploring him to do just that. He nodded obligingly. Nico wondered if the girl already knew Jim Sheridan and made a mental note to look into this. Just how much did this kid know? Nothing? Everything?

Nico kept his eyes on Jim Sheridan so he didn't have to look directly at the girl. She probably thought he was heartless. She probably assumed he was enjoying this. While he would enjoy putting an end to Norah Ramsey's business—and the people she was involved with—he did not relish evicting a child from her home. With any luck, he'd have the scene cleared quickly and she could return home. But with whom there to care for her? Because if he had anything to do with it, it would not be her mother. Surely there was family somewhere who could step in. He reminded himself this was not his problem. Norah Ramsey had put her daughter in this position because of choices she had made. He was just there to do his job. Because his job was all he had left.

Violet

After the detective from the porch followed her around her own house and watched her pack her things—even her underwear, so embarrassing—Mr. Sheridan drove her to Nicole's house, which was exactly seven houses away from her own. So it wasn't like she needed to be driven. But he insisted. He said he'd promised her mother. She thought of what her mother was accused of, thinking that—if it was somehow true, which it wasn't—Mr. Sheridan should be careful being associated with her. People might get the wrong idea about him. His wife might get mad.

Nicole's mother must've been waiting by the door when they pulled up, because it opened immediately to reveal her standing there, wearing yoga pants and a tank top that showed off her guns, as she liked to say. Nicole's mom was "practically perfect in every way"—at least that's what Violet's mom said about her. She had the perfect house, the perfect husband, the perfect kids. They were the perfect family, and she had the pictures to prove it, which she was only too happy to share on social media. It used to embarrass Nicole. Bess Strickland cooked the perfect meals and wore the perfect ensemble for every occasion. She exercised for the perfect amount of time to achieve the perfect physique. She was a role model, "a beacon of hope for all women," as Violet's mom liked to say.

Once upon a time, Nicole's mom and Violet's mom were best friends. Then they weren't. Kind of like Violet and Nicole, only the thing with her and Nicole was more recent. Violet's mom and Nicole's mom hadn't spoken in ages. She couldn't believe she had to go there of all places—not with things the way they were with Nicole lately—but Mr. Sheridan said that the arrangements had already been made. She couldn't stay with her father, because he was out of town. Her father was always out of town. Since he had married her witchy stepmom, he was basically out of her life.

On the Stricklands' porch, Mr. Sheridan told her he would be in touch as soon as he had any news. "You have my card?" he asked, and she nodded, patting her back pocket as proof. "OK, good," he said. "So you can call me with any questions." He produced another card seemingly out of thin air and handed it to Bess, who was standing there quietly, trying to act normal. "And here's one for you in case you need me as well." He and Bess looked at each other for a moment, both uncertain what to do next.

"Hey, Violet," Bess said. "Why don't you wait for me in the kitchen. I put out some fruit and some cheese and crackers in case you're hungry," she said. Violet nodded, happy to get out from under their dual gazes. She gave a little wave and headed off to the kitchen, thinking as she walked, Leave it to Bess Strickland to turn this into some wine-and-cheese party.

She wished Nicole was there so she could say that to her, so they could laugh about it. She wanted someone to talk to about all that was happening, but, though school was letting out in five minutes, Nicole would have play practice and wouldn't be home till dinner.

Nicole's new love of acting was what had caused the silence between them to begin. Last spring, out of the blue, Nicole had decided to audition for the school play. But Violet had terrible stage fright, so there was no hope of them ever having that in common. Lately, Nicole had been opting to hang out with her theater friends more than with Violet. The parting had been gradual but certain. They hadn't talked about it; they hadn't said anything at all. If any good came from this, Violet decided, maybe it would be that with her in the same house, she and Nicole would spend more time together. It would bring them closer.

In her head, she could hear her mom's voice: Look for the silver lining. There's always one. Her mom, though gone, was still there. She was in her head and in her heart, and no frowning detective or search warrant or criminal attorney could take that away.

She could hear the adult voices murmuring from the doorway—Mr. Sheridan's lower one in response to Bess's higher one. She half wondered what they were saying, if perhaps she should be listening in. She and Nicole used to spy on her family members all the time when they were kids, she knew all the good listening-in spots in this house. But she was suddenly so tired. She took a half-hearted bite of an apple slice. (Bess had artfully arranged the wedges on a plate.) But the act of chewing it felt too monumental, the chunks of apple in her mouth making her gag. She got up, walked over to the sink, and spit them out, then turned on the spigot and watched the pieces disappear into the disposal.

She headed back toward the foyer to tell Bess she was going to go up to Nicole's room to lie down for a bit. As she got closer, she heard Mr. Sheridan: "They're using intimidation techniques to try to get her to talk. They want that file, and they think they can get her to crack."

Bess gave a polite snort, if there was such a thing. "They don't know Norah, then."

When she approached, they stopped talking, both of their heads swinging around in unison as she came into view. They both looked guilty. "I'm pretty tired," Violet said. "I think I'd like to go lie down."

"OK," Bess said, nodding her head too eagerly. "You know where the guest room is, right?"

The guest room? When she spent the night at Nicole's, she had always slept in her room, in the trundle that attached to her daybed. It had been that way since they were seven years old. The only person who slept in the Stricklands' guest room was their grandmother from Michigan when she came to visit. Bess must've seen the confusion on her face, because she rushed to explain. "Since you'll be staying here over school nights, we thought it would be better for you girls not to be in the same room, so you can both get a good night's sleep."

We? Was this her and Nicole's dad's decision? Or her and Mr. Sheridan's decision? Or, worse, her and Nicole's decision? Bess and Nicole usually texted all during the school day, so Violet had no doubt Nicole was made aware of what was happening. That familiar feeling of panic she'd been having over the state of her friendship with Nicole came rushing back, but Violet tried not to think about it. She had bigger concerns than whether she and her BFF would in fact stay best friends forever. Concerns like investigation, evidence, and withholding information. If Mr. Sheridan sounded worried, did that mean she should worry, too?

She picked up the small bag she'd left just inside the front door— she'd refused to pack more than a few days' worth of clothing—and trotted up the stairs, past Nicole's sister Casey's door, which stayed closed all the time now that she'd gone off to college, toward the guest room just across the hall from Nicole's own bedroom. But first she peeked inside Nicole's room, inhaling the familiar scent of the place she'd spent so much time in. In this room they'd played Barbies and dolls, My Little Ponies and *Hannah Montana*. (She'd always had to be Lilly to Nicole's Miley.)

They'd made up dances to the latest songs and wore out the karaoke machine Nicole got for Christmas one year. They'd told each other's fortunes, played video games, and daydreamed about what life held for them. They'd sworn to be there for each other through thick and thin. Now she was in a thin place, and she hoped those little-girl promises would somehow, miraculously, hold.

She backed away from Nicole's doorway, walked across the hall, climbed into the unfamiliar bed, and fell fast asleep, hoping her absent mother would somehow come to her in her dreams and help make sense of all that was happening.

Casey

She took a taxi home from the airport, feeling very grown up and capable, yet childlike and afraid at the same time. She looked out the window as the cab driver navigated the vehicle through a part of the city she was unfamiliar with. Her life had primarily been spent in the suburbs, with the occasional trip into the city for various artsy events—a museum exhibit, a play, a concert. But mostly, she had existed within a much smaller space, with a select group of people. She wondered if that was why everything had happened the way it did. If her sheltered, small life had rendered her unprepared for the larger world.

Slowly, familiar street signs came into view, landmarks she recognized. There was the hotel where her senior prom had been held. (She'd gone with a boy she barely knew, one of her mother's friend's sons who had agreed to take her after she and Eli broke up so suddenly, the timing unfortunate with prom being weeks away.) There was the restaurant where they had eaten after graduation. There was the turnoff to the shopping center where she and her mom had bought the things she needed for college, most of which were sitting, abandoned, back in her dorm room. She wondered how she would retrieve it all, who would fetch it. Because it could not be her. She heard the condemning voice in her head, the voice of a sneering, jarheaded drill sergeant like the kind she'd seen in movies: *You didn't even make it two months. You're a wuss, running home to Mommy and Daddy.*

She felt the anxiety begin to build, tried to do what her roommate had said: Deep, slow breaths, redirect your thoughts. Think of something happy. She thought of her house in the fall, the way her mom made soup once a week and decorated with gourds and colorful leaves, lit pumpkin-spice candles, and put out mums on the front porch. In another few weeks her mom would buy their Halloween pumpkin and they would all carve it together, just like always. They would be together, and they would figure things out together. Yes, she had run home to Mommy and Daddy. But isn't that the place we're supposed to go when we're hurt? And she was hurt. She closed her eyes, blocked the memory of the night before, her embarrassing, very public breakdown, her roommate's hands pulling her up off the ground.

They turned into her neighborhood, and she scooched forward in the seat, her heart picking up speed the closer they got. What would her family say when she just showed up like this, so unexpectedly? They thought she was tucked away in college, happy, making friends, learning her way around the campus, joining clubs, doing exactly as she'd been meant to do. She hadn't had the heart to tell them any different, keeping what had happened a secret from her family, being the girl they expected her to be instead of the girl she was. But last night she had broken, and then she had run.

She'd charged the plane ticket on her emergency credit card at 4:00 a.m., booking a flight from Birmingham, Alabama, to Raleigh, North Carolina, that would land at 2:00 p.m. that day. Her roommate, a nice girl named Amanda, whom she'd been randomly paired with (what bad luck Amanda had—getting saddled with her), had helped her pack, then drove her the hour to the airport because she had a car. Casey could feel Amanda's sense of relief swell as they turned into the airport entrance and said their goodbyes. The sky was just starting to lighten as a new day dawned.

"I'll see you back here once you've got yourself sorted out," Amanda said, giving Casey her best, most affirming smile. Casey had agreed, but only because she was too exhausted to argue. Hungover, she'd bought herself a hot tea and a bagel at one of the airport restaurants, bided her time till she could board the plane, till she could go home. Unable to sleep in her dorm room, she'd slept like a baby on the plane, waking up to the announcement that they were beginning their descent and to return their seats to an upright position.

Now, in front of her house, she swiped her credit card (the emergency one again, because this was an emergency; her parents would know that eventually), added a generous tip, and stepped out of the cab. The driver hopped out, grabbed her luggage from the trunk, and handed the two bags over. Her parents had rented a U-Haul and driven for hours to move her into college, but she was coming home with just two bags. She'd learned what she could live without in the time she'd been away.

"Thank you," she said to the driver, who grinned back at her and wished her a good day. He hopped back into his cab and pulled away from the curb. She heard music come on inside the cab as he drove off. Then the sound of the music faded completely, leaving her standing on the driveway listening for something—anything—that sounded familiar. It was a weekday, and the neighborhood was typically quiet.

She stood in her driveway looking up the street in the direction they'd come from, then down the street, past her house. Her gaze stopped on the house across the street and seven doors down: her little sister's best friend's house. There were police cars parked in front of it, and men in uniform were buzzing around like flies who'd found a picnic. She left her luggage on the drive and walked toward the sight, her curiosity compelling her to investigate and providing an excuse to delay going inside her own house.

As she neared Violet's house, an officer posted by the mailbox stepped into the street, his arm up like a crossing guard. "Ma'am," he said, "I'm going to have to ask you not to come any closer." He was cute, in a cop sort of way. In her old life, she'd have flirted with him, pushed his buttons just because she could.

He was young and new at this, she could tell. Probably a recent graduate from the police academy. He'd drawn the crap job, guarding access to the house, keeping nosy neighbors at bay. He probably wanted to be inside the house, gathering evidence, guessing at the truth of whatever had happened there, doing the job he'd dreamed of instead of the one he'd been given.

She offered an explanation to try to sound concerned rather than plain old nosy. "I know the people who live here." She paused to give him a chance to speak, but he said nothing in response. She tried again. "I mean the girl who lives here—she's a friend of my younger sister."

He nodded dully, unfazed by her connection. But he didn't shoo her away, either. She thought of Violet: sweet, soft-spoken, shy Violet, who wouldn't hurt a fly. She hoped someone hadn't hurt her.

"Can I ask what happened?" She pointed at the house dumbly, as if he didn't know what she was referring to. She lowered her voice, feeling the familiar and unwelcome sense of panic returning. "Was it a murder?"

His official face lapsed into a momentary smile, and he shook his head. "I can't say what happened, but if you read the news, you'll find out." He raised his eyebrows meaningfully. "But it wasn't a murder."

"Oh," she said, feeling relieved, yet wondering just what it could be in her boring, quiet neighborhood, where nothing ever happened.

Another thought occurred to her. What if it had been a home invasion? There had been one—a robbery and assault—in a nearby neighborhood last year. It had sent her mother and all her mom friends running to a self-defense class. Casey swallowed, but her spit was suddenly made of glue. She thought of the news reports following the home invasion last year, the anchor intoning, "This is a violation."

"It wasn't a break-in, was it?" She couldn't keep the anxiety out of her voice. The cop's face changed as she spoke.

"No, no, trust me," he said, his voice kind. "It's nothing like that. You and your family are safe."

He gave her another smile, a real one complete with dimples, making him look younger and far less official. She guessed they were about the same age. He likely still lived at home. His mother probably posted the photos from his police academy graduation on her Facebook page, him smiling bravely in the face of his new, unknown future. Would he get shot in the line of duty? Shoot someone else? Would he know what to do when the time came?

It was hard to know what to do when the time came.

"OK," she said. "I guess I'll google it." She gave him a little wave and turned to walk back toward her house and her luggage still on the driveway.

"Have a nice day," he called after her. She could feel his eyes on her, watching her go. She felt the familiar panic begin to rise. She would have to figure out a way to not feel this way around men, seeing as how they were everywhere.

She turned back, forced herself to smile at him. This wasn't school; he wasn't Russell Aldridge. "You too," she said. As she walked quickly back toward her house, she realized that, at least for those few moments as she'd talked to the cop, she'd been so swept up in whatever was going on at Violet's that she'd forgotten about her own problems. It was, she decided, a start.

Polly

The buzzer went off on the oven, and her phone rang at the same time. Polly stood there frozen for a second, listening to both sounds echo off the kitchen walls in tandem, wondering which to attend to first. The timing really was remarkable. She wondered if this had ever happened to her in her entire life, and then she grabbed the phone. The casserole could burn, but she wasn't going to miss a phone call. She frowned when she heard Etta's voice on the other end. If she'd bothered to look to see who was calling first, she'd have let the call go. Etta Vandiver wasn't worth burning a casserole for.

"Polly?" She heard Etta's confused voice. "You there?"

"Yeah, hang on, Etta," she said, the heat from the oven slapping her in the face as she reached in to retrieve the casserole dish. Some of the sauce from the ziti had bubbled over and was sizzling on the bottom of the oven. It would harden into cement later. She'd have to remember to scrape it off before she used the oven again. If she remembered. It wasn't that she was getting forgetful. It was just that there was more to keep up with these days, so much on her mind.

She plunked the casserole dish onto the stove burners and dropped her oven mitts on the counter, then backed into a kitchen chair, plopping down with one exhausted heaving motion. It wasn't that she tired more easily, it was just that she was doing too much. She reached across the table for her cigarettes, lit one, and took a drag as Etta launched into the reason for her call. Polly's dog, Barney, asleep under the table, lifted his head momentarily, sniffed the air in case of food, then decided none was coming and lowered his head again.

"I'm just calling to make sure." Etta spoke in a rush. "Whether you're bringing the ziti and bread or ziti and a salad?"

"I only signed up for ziti," Polly said. She wanted to say *And you're lucky I signed up for that,* but instead she took another puff from her cigarette, then stubbed it out. She was trying to quit. Two puffs a day from one cigarette was all she was allowing herself. Just enough for the nicotine and her bloodstream to get reacquainted, however briefly. She usually waited till later in the day for her cigarette, but Etta's voice had brought out the need.

"Oh, Polly, we need bread and salad, too," Etta whined. "Is there any way I could get you to bring one or the other? Or maybe both?" She tee-heed like a little girl.

Polly sighed. She hated letting people down, and Etta Vandiver probably knew it. "I guess I could pick up some rolls on the way."

"Well, OK," Etta said. She didn't seem as mollified by Polly's offer as Polly hoped she'd be. Now she was going to have to leave even earlier to get by the store, then to the animal rescue fundraiser to deposit her contributions (baked ziti *and* rolls) on time. "I best be going," Etta said. "Lots of calls to make!"

"OK, then, see you there," Polly said, doing her best to sound pleasant.

"Don't forget that handsome husband of yours," Etta said, then gave that annoying little-girl giggle again. "You're so lucky, landing a catch like him."

Etta, who was older than Polly, was always making comments about Calvin like that. It made her sound like a lecherous older woman, like one of those cougars they talked about on the TV. Polly didn't know if she herself qualified as a cougar. Though Calvin was quite a bit younger than she was, to be sure. But Polly didn't know what the age difference had to be to qualify, and, frankly, at this point she didn't care.

"Speaking of husbands," Polly said, "he's pulling up now, so I better go greet him."

"Oh, give him a kiss for me," Etta said. Polly hung up while she was still giggling.

She put the phone down on the table and stared at the ziti, the steam curling up over the top of it, doing a little dance. She'd lied to Etta. Calvin wasn't home. She had no idea when he would be home or where he was. She knew only that he was out somewhere, likely spending the money he'd stolen from her and pretending to be the catch everyone thought he was.

"Oh, Barney," she said to her sleeping dog. "What am I going to do?" But Barney didn't hear her, or if he did, he didn't bother rousing. She shrugged, then reached for another cigarette. It was as good a day as any to break the rules.

Violet

She woke up disoriented, uncertain where she was or what time it was. She thrashed around until she found her cell phone and looked at the time, anxious to orient herself to something measurable. It was light outside, so it was daytime. But what day? Her phone told her it was 4:37 p.m. and it was still Thursday. She'd slept for only about forty-five minutes. It felt like she'd been asleep for days.

She looked around at the guest room with its plethora of throw pillows she'd tossed on the floor, its green-and-yellow color scheme, its dresser featuring a large arrangement of fake flowers that had never changed and were covered in dust. Slowly, everything came into focus and she remembered. Her mother was in jail. And she was at the Stricklands', even though she and Nicole hadn't been on the greatest of terms lately.

She'd kept that detail from her mother, certain it would blow over and her mother didn't need to know. Now Violet rolled over and punched the pillow, regretting that decision. If she'd told her mom, maybe she would've arranged for her to go somewhere else. Maybe, Violet thought, she should find out when her dad would return home from his trip. Though she didn't exactly love his new wife, he was family. And the Stricklands weren't.

She got up and went to the door, intending to open it and find Nicole, or her mom, or someone who might know something she didn't, new news that had happened as she slept. But voices on the other side stopped her in her tracks. Angry voices. She lowered her hand and stood frozen as she tried to figure out who was speaking and where they were standing on the other side of the closed door. After a few minutes of listening, she decided that it was Nicole and her mom, arguing about something. But she couldn't understand why they kept mentioning Casey's name, seeing as how Casey was away at college.

Casey Strickland was a triple threat. As in she was gorgeous, popular, and smart. Nicole had long ago given up trying to measure up to her; Violet and Nicole had had many conversations about that. Though Violet didn't envy Nicole's struggles with her sister, she did envy her having a sister at all. Standing there alone in that room, she longed for someone to go through this with, someone to talk to, to be by her side when her mother could not be.

Instead she just listened to Nicole and her mom arguing.

"They can't both be here. It's too much. I've got my first term paper due in Shupe's class, not to mention rehearsals starting," Nicole grumbled. "I don't need this right now."

"I know, honey," Nicole's mom said soothingly, "but how was I supposed to know that Casey would just appear on the doorstep twenty minutes after Violet arrived?"

"You didn't have to let Violet come here. You didn't have to say yes and be so *helpful* like you always are. You know things have been . . . weird . . . with us lately. Just that was going to be awkward even if Casey wasn't here, too. You could've asked me first," Nicole whined.

"I couldn't very well say no. It's a delicate situation." Bess defended herself.

"It's not delicate, Mom. Her mom's a whore. And she's in jail because of it."

"Nicole!" Bess Strickland exclaimed, and then they were both silent, probably scared that the outburst had woken Violet. Too late, Violet thought. She was shaking, her heart beating hard in her chest as the word *whore* resounded in her head. She took a step backward, intending to sit on the bed and calm down. The floor creaked underneath her feet and she froze again, her heart hammering harder as she waited for Bess to throw open the guest room door or for them to continue the conversation. But the hall was silent, and she was left to decide how to go out there and act normal when life was anything but.

Casey

From her bedroom she could hear her mother and sister talking in what they probably considered hushed tones, the tension in their voices unmistakable as they discussed what to do about her and Violet Ramsey both unexpectedly dropping in on their little, orderly life. From down the hall and behind her closed door, she could hear only about every third word, but she could tell enough to know that her presence was neither well timed, nor welcome.

It was amazing to her how her family had so seamlessly filled the gap she'd left behind when she'd gone to college. She recalled her mother's tears the day they said goodbye, her sister's earnest insistence that it just wouldn't be the same without her. And yet, they'd figured out a way to go on. Now she was a ghost, there to haunt them. And though she knew she couldn't stay at school, she was starting to second-guess her decision to come home.

When the voices quieted and she was sure the coast was clear, she opened the door, uncertain what to do next. Nicole's door was closed and music played on the other side. Something instrumental that sounded like the score to a movie. Her sister had gotten into theater toward the end of last school year, when she had decided to "try something new," on a whim, as she said it, though Casey always suspected a boy was at the heart of it. Now Nicole talked nonstop about auditions and plays and acting schools. When the two sisters were on the phone together, they struggled to find something to talk about once they got past the latest news at home. Casey always had the sense they were both saying what the other expected, that in their own way, they were each playing a role.

The door to the guest room opened, and she blinked at the girl who stepped into the hall. Violet had been asleep when Casey had arrived earlier that day, walked into the kitchen, and interrupted her mother, who was on the phone with her father, venting over the "pickle" she'd been put in, having to take in Violet Ramsey when she knew Nicole "didn't like that one bit." Her father, in his aloof, fatherly way, listened politely for a moment, then told her mother he had to get back to work and they could talk more when he got home. Casey could hear his deep, resonant voice coming through her mother's phone as clearly as if he were on speaker.

When Bess Strickland hung up and saw Casey standing there, she'd yelped in fright, clutching the phone to her chest, her eyes wide as she took in her daughter's presence. She looked at her like she was trying to place her, like she was an intruder and not her own daughter. Casey shifted on her feet and said "Hi, Mom," like it was a year ago and she'd just had early release and Bess had forgotten all about it, so caught up was she in her social activities and volunteer work. Yet it wasn't a year ago. And Casey wasn't that girl anymore. When Bess looked at her, it was like she knew that.

Now, standing in the hall, Casey must have looked at Violet the way her mother had looked at her, because the younger girl mumbled an apology and quickly closed the door again. "Wait," Casey said, but Violet didn't hear.

Casey glanced over at her sister's door to see if she'd come out to investigate the noise in the hall, but it remained closed and Casey heard no movement on the other side. Satisfied that no one would see, she crossed the hall and quietly knocked on the door to the guest room, where Violet was hiding. Violet had to have heard what her mother and Nicole had been saying, and probably heard it crystal clear since she was just across the hall. She had to be lost and scared and lonely. And though they were dealing with two completely different things, Casey felt more drawn to Violet than to her own mother or sister. She, too, felt lost and scared and lonely.

After her mom had gotten over the shock of Casey's arrival, Bess had relayed what had happened with Violet's mother, spilling what news she'd gathered and, Casey suspected, embellishing some details in places where the actual truth was thin. Her mother was energetic as she spoke, seeming to draw energy from Norah Ramsey's plight. Though they were no longer close friends, Bess Strickland still pretended to like Norah Ramsey, to care about her.

But Casey suspected her mother was jealous of Norah, though Casey couldn't have guessed why. Norah was a single mom, when Bess had a devoted husband. Norah didn't seem to have friends outside of work (which made more sense, in light of recent developments), while her mom was the queen bee of the mom squad. Casey had always thought of her mother's friends as grown-up Mean Girls. Most of them were the mothers of her own friends, which accounted for many of the activities and decisions she herself had made while in high school. Now she wondered how life could've been different—how she could've been different—if that had not been the case.

In the six weeks she'd been away, she already saw it all differently. In her absence, her mother had pulled Nicole—who had never seemed to care before—into her orbit. But instead of social status and cheerleading like with Casey, now Bess cared about play competitions and lead roles. It didn't really matter, in Casey's opinion, what was at stake, just as long as Bess—and her offspring—won.

Casey knocked lightly on the guest bedroom door for the second time. "Come in," Violet's voice said.

She opened the door to find Violet perched, awkward and uncomfortable, on the edge of the guest room bed that only Casey's grandmother ever slept in. "Just wanted to make sure you're OK," she said. Casey gave Violet a fake smile, becoming for a moment the Casey that Violet expected. So much of Violet's life had been upended, Casey didn't need to add to it. "Would you like to go for a walk?" Casey asked.

Bess

She drove with one hand on the wheel and one hand on the casserole dish to keep it from sliding from the seat onto the floorboard of her massive SUV. How she longed for a tiny car, compact and zippy. Instead she drove the vehicle that was chosen and bought for her by her husband, the sort of car required for hauling kids and their paraphernalia. One day, she told herself. One day she would have a vehicle that matched her and not her lifestyle. But not today. Today she was in this car, and in this lifestyle, even if lately it seemed that neither matched who she was inside.

She eased through a four-way stop, feeling the heat from the fresh-from-the-oven dish radiating through the pot holder she'd placed on top of it. She was taking a meal to a family in need, something she did often for a variety of situations. It was, as she told her girls, the least she could do. She had made her go-to poppy-seed chicken casserole, perfect for the ill, the new parents, the bereaved. The ultimate comfort food, replete with creamy goodness and topped with buttery crackers. She didn't know the calorie count and didn't need to. She wasn't eating it. And, in the face of an unexpected and mysterious loss, she wondered if anyone would.

This particular family was one she didn't actually know. Though the kids went to the same school as Nicole, they were younger, which meant Bess hadn't crossed paths with the mother. Still, when the sign-up notice came through her email, she recognized the name from the news. She'd followed the story like so many others. A healthy, active middle-aged man, who by all appearances was living a normal life, had disappeared. No indication of trouble, no reports of suspicious activity beforehand. He was just . . . gone. And in his absence, a wife and two kids were left to wait and to wonder as the police investigated and the media speculated. The school had arranged meals for them, first prevailing upon those closest to them, then branching out to the parents at large, appealing to the question that haunted everyone: What if it was you?

Bess eased her hulk of a vehicle into their narrow driveway and thought the worst thing she could think: She wished it *was* her. She wished that her husband, Steve, would disappear just like this man had. That one day he just wouldn't come home. That she could play the role of the distraught wife as strangers brought her food. That life as she knew it would end, so that, eventually, she could start a new one.

But this she could count on: she would return home from this errand, and, shortly after, Steve would come through the door, carrying his briefcase and complaining about his day. They would make polite conversation through dinner—tonight with extra plates at the table—and then he would disappear behind his office door to do whatever he did in there, and she would be left to watch whatever she could find on television. The best nights were when there was something good on.

She shifted the car into park, the transmission adjusting with a heavy, weary thunk. She opened the driver's side door just as the phone, resting in its spot in the center console, rang. She cast a longing glance at it. She wanted to answer it but couldn't just then. Instead she had to carry dinner to a family in crisis, then go home and serve dinner to her own family, pretending that her daughter's unexpected arrival home from college hadn't scared her, that her other daughter's anger didn't concern her, that her houseguest was a welcome addition, and that she still loved her husband. Casey's arrival bothered her most of all. She sensed that something was terribly wrong, no matter how much Casey acted like coming home unexpectedly was no big deal. While Bess was determined to get to the bottom of it, she couldn't just yet. There was simply too much going on at the moment.

When she could, she would talk to her daughter, insist she tell her the truth about whatever had transpired back at school that sent her running home. The question was, would Casey be honest? Bess recalled being Casey's age. She was very rarely honest with her own mother. Bess liked to think they had the kind of relationship where Casey could tell her anything. But she also knew that Casey had become more distant since the breakup with Eli, less inclined to share more than cursory details. Bess had thought things would smooth over once Casey got immersed in college life and forgot all about Eli.

But it was hard to immerse yourself in college life if you'd left college behind.

There was no time to think about what it all meant. A man had stepped onto the porch and was watching her warily. She climbed out of the car, retrieved the casserole dish, and balanced the bag of rolls and container of green beans on top of it as she cautiously made her way up the front walk. The smell of home cooking wafted up, and her stomach rumbled in response, a reflex more than real hunger. Bess was an excellent cook. Everyone said so. She wondered how many meals she'd made since she'd stood at the altar beside Steve, pledging to love, honor, and plate up the four food groups in a new and creative way every night.

Under the man's watchful eye, she felt oddly nervous, complicit even, as if she were somehow participating in this family's plight by bringing them food. Wasn't that why people reached out to those facing hard times? To help was to separate yourself from those you helped, the distance across their threshold far wider than it appeared. It was acknowledgment that tragedy had befallen this house, yet insurance that the plague would pass over your own.

"I brought food," she said dumbly, offering up the casserole as proof. "Dinner," she said again, as if that wasn't obvious, seeing as how it was nearly dinnertime.

The man stepped forward with his arms extended, studying her face as he did. She wondered what he saw as he regarded her. A pretty woman, or someone who was once pretty?

"This is for Maria Rinaldi," she said. "I'm from the kids' school."

"Yeah, she told me someone was coming," the man said. He nodded in the direction of the porch behind him. "I'm her brother-in-law," he added. He looked back at the house, his face a mixture of concern and sadness.

For a moment she feared he would invite her in. But he simply took the dishes, mumbled his thanks, and closed the door, leaving her standing empty-handed and alone on the porch. "It was the least I could do," she said to no one, then turned and went back to clamber up into the car that was too big for her and head home to the life that was too small.

Violet

She and Casey fell into step with ease, as if they'd walked together many times. Casey's ponytail swung back and forth in time with their footfalls, and Violet found herself watching it, her eyes drawn to it like one being hypnotized by the rhythmic movement. When the ponytail stopped swinging, Violet realized that Casey had stopped moving and came a breath away from running right into her. She started to apologize, to make an excuse for why she hadn't been looking where she was going, when she noticed Casey pointing to something in front of them.

Violet had been so absorbed in the bouncing ponytail, in this walk with the older, cooler girl, that she'd not thought about where they were going. And now they were mere feet away from what could only be called a media circus that had formed on Violet's front lawn. She felt Casey tug on her arm. "We can't let them see you," she said. "I bet they'll figure out who you are."

Casey pulled her into the edge of the front yard of the house across the street. Micah Berg's house. "Ice Berg" they called him, on account of his talent at hockey. But Violet always thought of the nickname as meaning something else—how cold he was. He had, after all, lived across the street from her for most of their lives yet had never bothered to learn her name. She knew almost all there was to know about him. Things he didn't know that anyone knew. Though she'd never said that aloud to anyone, not even Nicole. Now she was glad of that. She suspected her secrets were not safe with her former best friend.

As Casey sought coverage for them in a small natural area closer to Micah's house, Violet thought about Nicole's ugly words about her mother. She would need to keep in mind that Casey was Nicole's sister, so Violet probably couldn't trust her, either. Casey crouched down behind a bush and gestured for Violet to do the same. Together, from their hidden vantage point in the neighbor's yard, they watched the circus. "Man," Casey whispered as if she might be overheard. "There sure are a lot of them."

"Yeah," Violet breathed. The trucks and people made it hard to see her house. She scanned the exterior, hoping to see something familiar, something that felt like she was looking at her home. A man moved just enough for her to glimpse a swath of orange. She willed him to move so she could see if the pumpkin was still safe and sound on the porch, waiting for her mother to come back and explain why she'd bought it early, waiting for the two of them to carve it together. She closed her eyes and tried to envision what they would create: the triangle eyes, the gap-toothed, open-mouthed permanent grin, the light glowing from within.

"Do you know the guy who lives here?" Casey asked.

Violet opened her eyes at the mention of Micah. "Not really," she lied.

Casey glanced over her shoulder at the Berg house. It had once been a busy place, with Micah and his friends coming and going, playing football in the front yard or basketball in the driveway. But since last spring it had been fairly quiet, except for Micah's nightly sojourns to shoot basket after basket alone, the sound of his dribbling a kind of lullaby in recent months.

"I don't like being here," Casey said.

"Were you here?" Violet asked in a low voice. "That night?" she added, even though she didn't need to. Casey no doubt knew what she was referring to. Before today, what had happened at the Berg house had been the talk of the neighborhood. Now it seemed that the drama had packed up and moved across the street, right into Violet's own house.

"Yeah," Casey said. She was silent for a moment. "We were friends."

"You and Micah? Or you and . . ." Violet didn't say her name. She didn't like to.

"Me and Olivia," Casey said. It felt to Violet like Casey said Olivia's name louder, as if in defiance, hoping Micah would hear her name carried on the wind like the accusation it had become since her death. So many people held him responsible, and it seemed no one could, or would, say differently.

There was still talk of prosecution. Violet had resolved to decide what to do about the part she'd secretly witnessed if it ever came to that. She wasn't sure if what was happening with her mom now would change her mind. She looked back at her house, the street that ran between the two houses jammed with vans and people.

"It's his fault," Casey said.

"You don't know that," Violet said, too quickly and too forcefully. She clamped her mouth shut. A few moments of silence passed by before she added, as if it were merely an afterthought, "I mean I've heard he says differently. Maybe it's true."

Casey regarded her for a moment, as if considering engaging in a full-on debate about whether Micah Berg did or did not aid and abet his girlfriend's death. Violet could see Casey decide not here, not now. Instead she simply said, "Well, I hate him."

"You shouldn't hate anyone," Violet replied, her mother's words coming out of her mouth reflexively.

Casey gave a small, bitter laugh in response. "Yeah?" she asked. "We'll see if you still feel that way after all this is over." She gestured at Violet's house with an angry jab, and Violet could tell there were things she was not saying. Not about Micah or Violet's mom. Things about Casey. But Violet didn't ask, and Casey didn't offer. The two of them shifted at the same moment, their muscles cramping from crouching so long, then looked at each other and smiled.

"What should we do?" Violet asked.

Casey shook her head and rolled her eyes. "I honestly didn't think much past hiding when I saw all the people. I was just afraid they'd bombard you like you see on TV."

Violet shuddered at the thought of reporters asking questions she couldn't answer, with cameras recording it all. "Thanks," she said.

Casey shrugged. "Don't mention it."

Behind them came the sounds of footsteps, and they both turned to see who was approaching. But instead of finding a person, Casey was met with a wet nose and a big tongue licking her face. Her pensive mood forgotten, she laughed, her hands sinking into the dog's coat as she reached out to pet him.

"Chipper," Violet said. Chipper was the Bergs' Irish setter, most often at Micah's side, especially lately. Violet often wondered if Micah felt like Chipper was the only friend he had left.

Instinctively, she looked up to find the boy she'd loved from afar for as long as she could remember standing just an arm's length away. She stood, suddenly not caring if the reporters found her. She would not crouch on her haunches as Micah Berg stood over her.

It took her a second to find her voice. "Sorry," she said. "For being in your yard." She hitched her thumb backward, indicating the crowd of people in her yard as explanation. She wasn't sure whether he would recognize her, whether he would realize she was the girl who belonged in that house. She wondered if he was just glad a crisis was occurring somewhere else. Maybe take the heat off him.

He nodded but didn't smile. Micah was wearing his Yankees cap, but with the brim facing front like normal. He used to always wear it backward, before everything happened. It was kind of his trademark. But he didn't anymore. Violet thought it was because he was trying to say he wasn't the same person.

He was holding a basketball, which he now spun nervously as his gaze traveled from Violet to Casey. "Hey, Casey," he said.

"Micah," Casey responded, but she kept her eyes on the dog. She gestured to Violet. "You know Violet? Your neighbor?" There was a tone of sarcasm in her voice, and Violet wished she'd shut up. She didn't want Micah to associate her with Casey's hard feelings about him. She didn't want him to think she shared them.

"Sure," he said, and nodded at Violet again. This was the most interaction they'd had since one time last year when he had a whole conversation with Sean Withers at the locker next to hers, and she pretended she couldn't find her book just so she could smell his cologne for a few moments longer. When he'd walked away, their eyes had met. He'd looked into her eyes and said "Hey," and she swore her heart had literally skipped a beat.

"Y'all wanna go out through my backyard?" he asked now. He dipped his chin in the direction of Violet's house and gave them a cryptic grin. "Not like you can go back that way."

"Yeah," Casey said. "We kinda got trapped." Her voice sounded like she'd forgotten she was mad at him.

Micah rolled his eyes. "I know how that feels," he said, and Violet saw Casey's eyes flash as she remembered that Micah Berg was her enemy.

"Is there, like, a fence back there we have to climb over?" Violet hurried to ask before Casey could say something mean.

"There is," Micah answered. "But I can show you how you can walk around it, cut through the next-door neighbor's yard. They don't mind."

"OK, that would be great," Violet said, sounding childish and stupid to her own ears. But if she kept talking, then hopefully Casey wouldn't.

Chipper had flopped down at Micah's feet, and he roused the dog with the same low whistle she often heard through her open window at night. "Come on, Chip, let's show these ladies out."

The boy and the dog started walking, and the girls fell into step as they followed them toward the backyard. But this time Violet didn't watch Casey's ponytail as they walked. She watched the back of Micah Berg's head, committing this moment to memory so she could relive it again and again in the days to come. It was a comfort to be this close to Micah Berg, to have exchanged words with him and be properly introduced. In a desert, she thought, you're grateful for every drop of water you can find.

Casey

They walked into the house to find Nicole sitting in the front room waiting for them. She hopped up like a jack-in-the-box as soon as the door opened. "Where were you?" she asked, a note of betrayal in her voice.

Casey answered calmly. "We went for a walk." What she wanted to say was, *None of your damn business.* But that would only stir up the old sibling rivalry. Casey was older now, a college student, above such trivial things. Even if she was still angry at Nicole for what she had said about Violet's mother; Nicole was supposed to be Violet's best friend. Talk about insensitive. About as insensitive as Micah Berg—the asshole—comparing his situation to Violet's. Violet had done nothing wrong. But Micah had done plenty. Why was it that lately all Casey did was run across asshole guys who didn't accept responsibility for their actions?

Violet said, "There's a bunch of reporters in front of my house, so we hid in Micah Berg's yard. And he found us there. It was so embarrassing." Casey looked over at Violet, wondering why she was being nice to Nicole after what she had said. She needed to help this girl out, teach her the ways of the world before it trounced her good.

"Micah Berg? Really?" Nicole said.

Violet nodded, biting back a smile.

Nicole looked from Casey to Violet, and Casey could see her sister's wheels turning. "You're *still* obsessed with him?" She delivered the line with the practiced cut of a samurai. She looked to Casey, her eyes flashing with pleasure as if she expected her big sister's praise for being unnecessarily mean to her best friend.

"I was never *obsessed* with him," Violet said, but her voice was shaking as she said it.

Nicole rolled her eyes dramatically. "You're practically his stalker. Or did you stop stalking him after he killed someone?"

"Nicole Eileen Strickland!" Casey yelled. "What the hell has gotten into you? Violet is our guest." She knew she sounded just like their mother, but she couldn't help herself. She clenched her hands into fists to keep from going after her sister, slapping and scratching and pulling hair like she would've done a few years ago.

On cue, their mother came into the room, drying her hands on a dish towel and looking perplexed. "Girls!" she said. "What is going on in here? You haven't been around each other in weeks. How can you already be fighting?"

"Mom," Casey said, "Nicole was just so rude to Violet. You would've been appalled."

Nicole turned to their mother and crossed her arms in front of herself as she tossed her hair dramatically. It occurred to Casey that her sister had turned pretty while she was away at school. She had also turned into a prima donna.

Choking back tears, Nicole said, "I know you said to be nice to her because of everything she has going on but I just . . . I can't, Mommy. I'm sorry." She began to cry in earnest, then ran from the room, leaving Casey to wonder which *her* Nicole was referring to and also puzzling over her sister referring to their mother as *Mommy*.

She glanced over at Violet, who looked completely shell-shocked. "I'm sorry," she whispered. "My sister is apparently crazy now."

Their mother hurried to defend her younger child. "She's just having a bit of a hard time with the . . . nature of what's happening here. It's a lot of change in one afternoon. I'll go talk to her, and I'm sure we can smooth this over. Plus, I've got something for you, Violet. Something from your mom."

"My mom?" Violet asked, and the tone of hope in her voice hurt Casey's heart.

"A note," Bess said. "Her attorney dropped it by. I'll go get it." She turned to leave the room, but Violet's voice stopped her.

"Mrs. Strickland, I appreciate the place to stay, but I think it might be best if I called my stepmom to come get me."

Casey waited for her mother to put her foot down, to tell her, *Nonsense, you can't leave. We'll fix this.* Instead she watched as her mother's shoulders dropped in the defeated stance of one who had given up without a fight. "If that's what you think is best," she said, and then scurried out of the room like the mouse that she was.

"You don't have to go," Casey said, and she could hear the desperation in her voice, the need to fix what had just occurred right in front of her.

Violet turned to look at her. "Of course I do." Their eyes met, and Casey was struck with the sudden awareness that Violet was the wisest person there.

Norah

Dear Violet,

I'm waiting to be arraigned and then I will know more about how soon I can come home. I asked for this piece of paper and a pen so I could write to you, to let you know I'm OK and to tell you not to worry. (Even though I know you will anyway.) I am thinking of you constantly, thinking of all I need to tell you, and worried about how confused and scared you must be.

There is an explanation for all of this, and I'm sure you'll want to hear it. I've asked Mr. Sheridan not to tell you too much, as I want you to hear everything from me. I'm sorry for all of this. I thought I could keep you from it, but I failed. I will come home to you as soon as I can. But in the meantime, be good for the Stricklands; they were so kind to take you in. And know you're in my heart every, every minute.

I love you,
Mom

Polly

She was in the middle of the animal rescue banquet, manning the station she was assigned, ladling steaming sauce over undercooked pasta while trying not to splatter it on the clothing of the attendees, when her phone sounded from her purse, tucked just underneath the table over which she was standing. She resisted the urge to put down the ladle and fish out the phone. She knew it would bug her till she found out who it was that had called. Across the room she spotted Calvin making his rounds, glad-handing the men and charming the women, talking them out of their money just as sure as he had gotten hers out of her. At least tonight his efforts were going toward a good cause.

It was a full fifteen minutes until there was a lull in the hungry crowd and she could look to see who had called. But all she saw was an unfamiliar number. Probably a sales call, she thought. Nothing she needed to worry about. But then she saw the notification that whoever called had left a message. She wondered if it was someone from the bank, responding to her concerned inquiry about Calvin that afternoon. Dwight, her personal banker (as he called himself), was out, but the girl who took the call promised he'd get back to her as soon as he possibly could.

Maybe the unfamiliar number, she thought, was Dwight's. She pressed the right buttons to play the voicemail.

The male voice on the recording was vaguely familiar, a voice from the past, as they say. But not Dwight's. "Hi, Polly," the caller said. "Not sure you remember me since we haven't seen each other in probably, what, fourteen years? Anyway, a long time ago, I was your son-in-law."

Here, he cleared his throat. Polly's heart began to pound. Allen? she thought. Why would he be calling her?

"Anyway, I realize you're not in touch with Norah much more than I am, so you probably haven't heard that she was, well, uh . . . she was arrested this morning. You can, uh, well, you probably should just google it to learn more about why. Anyway, I might need some, um, help with Violet while Norah's away. You see, I travel and I—"

The recording cut off, leaving Polly to stand there holding the phone in disbelief, scanning the room for a familiar face, someone she could beg to take over her station so she could call her ex-son-in-law—that loser—back. Sometimes the extent of her estrangement from her daughter and granddaughter hit Polly with full impact, and this was one of those times. She worried about what was happening to poor Violet if Norah had been arrested.

She recalled the sight of Norah walking back and forth in that ugly striped terry-cloth robe of Allen's, her hair in matted hunks, her eyes bleary, holding a mewling newborn Violet to her chest and lamenting her choice to become a mother. "I'm not going to be any better at this than you were," she'd said. Polly regretted not doing whatever she could to stay in Violet's life, even if it meant going against Norah's wishes. It wasn't that child's fault that things were so broken between her and Norah. She should've fought harder to know her granddaughter.

Calvin appeared at her arm. "You look upset, darlin'," he said, laying on that country-boy drawl that some found charming but she knew was fake. The truth was, Calvin had been born and raised in Pennsylvania and ended up in the South by way of Fort Bragg just before he was discharged. He'd been pretending to be Southern ever since, forgetting he wasn't and hoping everyone else did, too. Calvin was a chameleon—he changed according to whatever his habitat required. She had learned this in the three years since she had married him.

Sometimes, in quiet moments, Polly debated which of her five husbands was the biggest mistake she'd made. It was always a close call as to whom, but lately it had been Calvin because he had lied to her (though they'd all done that in one way or another) and stolen from her. And because he was the one she was currently saddled with. If she wasn't careful, he was going to make off with every bit of her nest egg, as she called it, the proceeds of the only good investment she'd ever made. Thankfully her financial decisions had been better than her marital ones.

"I'm fine," she said. Calvin wasn't the only one who could lie in their relationship. But she only lied when she really had to, and this was one of those times. She'd never told him about Norah or Violet—no sense mentioning people he was never going to encounter, she'd figured at the time. She wasn't going to tell him now, all these years later. And certainly not in the middle of the animal rescue fundraiser. "I'm just tired of standing up. I've got a blister on my little toe, and my arm is sore from dishing out all this pasta sauce. Do you think you could take over for just a minute? Maybe let me run to the restroom and freshen up a bit?"

She gave him her sweetest smile, the one that she used to think he loved. It wasn't until after the "I do's" that she had realized what he'd loved about her had nothing to do with her smile, the color of her eyes, or her calf muscles (things he told her back then) and everything to do with her money. Calvin aspired to a certain lifestyle, and Polly was his ticket to ride. He'd never said that, of course, but she'd figured it out pretty quick. She just wished she'd figured it out before he charmed her into marriage and his right to half of all her assets. Her biggest concern now was the money he didn't know about.

That was another thing she pondered in her quiet moments: How can I get away from this one? The others, thankfully, had left before she ever had to run them off. Calvin, it was clear, had no intentions of going anywhere. As he turned his attention toward a woman there to say hello, she saw an opportunity. She thrust the ladle into his hand, whispered a syrupy "Thank you, honey," and scurried away, still gripping the phone in her clenched fist. Polly stepped outside into the darkness and took big gulps of air as she waited for her heart rate to slow.

She glanced around to make sure she was alone before pulling up Google and entering her daughter's name: Norah Ramsey. She'd kept Allen's name so she and Violet would have the same. "I won't be like you and marry someone else and take his name so my daughter always feels left out," she'd said. Norah had always known how to hit her where it hurt, laying bare Polly's mistakes and weaknesses in that undeniable way of hers. That was why when Norah wanted to stop speaking, Polly had agreed it was a good idea. She'd allowed the distance, telling herself Violet would never miss what she never knew.

Polly watched as the hits came back: *Suburban Madam Arrested*, said headline after headline. So this is what has become of my daughter, she thought. She scanned a few articles, enough to get the gist of what Norah had been charged with, before calling Allen back. The phone rang twice before he picked it up, the tension and anxiety in his voice apparent with the simple word, "Hello?"

How did you get my number? Polly wanted to ask him, but she didn't. She wondered if perhaps he had kept tabs on her all these years just in case he needed parenting backup, a grandmother, like a fairy godmother, dropping in to rescue him from his plight. She pictured herself like Mary Poppins coming out of the clouds holding that umbrella, a beatific smile on her face as her feet met the ground, and she saw her granddaughter waiting there for her. She could be a hero now, she thought.

"What's going on?" she asked Allen.

"Norah was arrested this morning. Did you look up the charges?" he asked.

"Yes," she said. How like Allen to be unable to utter them.

"Well. So. She's in jail now."

"Right," Polly said, already losing patience with him. She'd liked Allen when Norah had introduced them. But Allen had changed, Norah had told her, when she was pregnant with Violet. "They all change," she'd told her daughter. "That's what happens."

"And she sent Violet to stay with neighbors. Violet's best friend, from what I understand. But I guess the girls had some sort of falling out, and now Violet is asking to come stay here, which I don't understand, because she's basically refused to see me lately. I'm, um, remarried and my wife and I have two children—babies, I mean. You know, toddlers. So it's kind of, you know, not her scene with all the crying and toys everywhere . . ." He trailed off, as if waiting for Polly to fill in the blanks.

Unable to let him off the hook, Polly said, "From what I recall, it wasn't really your scene, either."

"Yeah," Allen laughed as if she'd made a joke. "Well, my wife, Tish, that's her name, wanted to be a mom and I, uh, well, I went along with it."

Wasn't that just like Allen, to go along with something he didn't really want and hope it all worked out. She refrained from saying so out loud. "So what do you need from me, Allen?"

"Well, I mean, Violet's fine to be here until they clear the house—I guess right now it's being considered a crime scene or something—but I assume eventually she can go back there. Once that happens, I was just wondering if maybe you'd mind coming here and staying with her for . . . well . . . for as long as it takes?"

The thought occurred to Polly: What if Norah goes to jail for a long time? What kind of commitment is he asking for here? She wondered if Norah had any idea he was contacting her. She would hate this idea. Polly thought of the last time she had seen Violet. The child had been toddling around, gnawing on a graham cracker. Polly and Norah had been speculating over what Violet should call her: Gigi, Mimi, Grammy. They'd agreed she wasn't a normal grandmother and would therefore not have a typical grandmother name. Certainly not Grandma or Granny. They'd laughed and it had felt—for a moment—normal.

Polly had been dressed to go out on a date, newly divorced from yet another of Norah's stepfathers. Violet had grabbed the leg of her white pants, leaving a gummy brown handprint. Polly had shrieked in response and drew her leg—which Violet had been using to balance—back, accidentally knocking the baby to the floor. A fight had ensued. Both she and Norah had said things, ugly things, with raised voices. Things they meant but usually refrained from saying aloud. Norah had scooped Violet up, balanced her on her hip, and wiped away her tears. The two of them had looked at Polly accusingly, a unit, with her on the outside.

She'd left the house angry, yes, but assuming one day she'd go back. They'd make things right eventually. This was how they were. But one day had bled into the other, and here they were with so many years gone by. Her daughter was accused of running a prostitution ring, and her granddaughter was a complete stranger. They'd never come up with her grandmother name, because her granddaughter had never had cause to call on her. But she could change that now. She could take the scraps of their lives and try her best to make a quilt that would cover them all somehow.

Allen was rambling in her ear about how hard his life was and how much a disruption his own flesh and blood was going to be, when she interrupted him. "Find out when the house will be released. Tell them you need it back as soon as possible so that the minor involved can continue her routine, go to school, all that. Lay it on thick, Allen. Sounds like you need her back in that house pretty bad."

"So . . . you'll do it?" The relief in his voice made her despise him all the more.

Polly sighed. She wondered what it was she'd seen in him when Norah had brought him to meet her that first time. Why had she considered him a prize? Maybe because he was brave enough to take on her daughter, when she herself had always been slightly afraid of her. Or maybe because he, like Calvin, had just known the right things to say to sway her. Whatever her impression was at the time, it had been the wrong one. Allen Ramsey was no prize. But Polly was betting her granddaughter was.

Violet

She hovered just outside the doorway, trying her best to listen to the discussion between her father and Tish. It was hard to hear over the gurgling baby Tish bounced and patted. The baby's name was Sienna, and she was, as best Violet could tell, the only daughter her dad really needed. There just wasn't room in his life for two of them. Sienna also had an older brother, the son her father had always wanted. His name was Allen Junior, but they called him A. J. Whenever he was around, her father got this big, wide smile. He called him "Son" a lot, like he still couldn't believe he'd gotten one.

Sometimes her father would walk into a room and look startled, and maybe even a little afraid, to see Violet there, like she was an intruder who'd snuck in. That was exactly what she'd felt like these past three days—an intrusion, barging in on their happy home, uninvited and unwelcome. She'd made a mistake in coming here, and they all knew it. Which was why she was trying to hear what the two adults were saying to each other as they decided her fate. No other letters had come from her mother since the one short one Jim Sheridan had delivered. When he'd called to make sure she'd received it, he'd told her not to expect any more. He didn't want her mother to write anything that could be used against her later. Though Violet wanted to hear from her mother more than anything, she didn't want that.

She wondered if she should just announce that she was going back to the Stricklands. But of course, they didn't want her any more than her father and Tish did. At least Nicole didn't. And apparently Nicole, in Casey's absence, had garnered the deciding vote as to what happened in their house. Violet tried not to think about the void in her life where Nicole had once been, how much harder this situation was without someone to talk to about it all. The two people she used to talk to—her mother and her best friend—had both, for reasons she couldn't comprehend, left her.

She stood there, eavesdropping in her father's hallway, and wished not only for her mother to come home, but to have a place where she belonged again. A place where she could walk right in and not feel like she needed to apologize for having done so. A place where she could call out, "I'm home!" and mean it. She'd had that just days ago, but already it felt like years. Tears pricked her eyes, and she swallowed hard against them.

The baby stopped fussing, and Violet leaned in to hear better. "I can't keep taking her to school and picking her up," Tish whined. "It's throwing off our whole routine, Ally." Violet bristled at her stepmother's use of this endearment. Ally was a girl's name, not something you called a grown man. "So unless you plan to start getting to work late and leaving early, we're going to have to come up with some sort of arrangement," Tish continued. Violet wished her dad would tell Tish she was being a bitch, that this was his daughter and this was the least he could do.

Instead her father used his soothing tone when he responded, the one he probably used to talk clients off ledges and negotiate deals for millions of dollars. "I spoke to that detective this morning, and he says it'll be just a few days more. That's *all*. Then they'll release the house and she can go back." But go back with whom? Violet wondered. She couldn't stay in the house all alone. Could she?

The baby began to fuss again, and Violet used the noise distraction as an opportunity to take a quick peek around the door frame, just in time to see Tish thrust the crying infant into her father's arms like a punishment for telling her what she didn't want to hear. Violet ducked back out of sight. Between the protesting baby and her father pacing the den trying to calm it, Violet couldn't hear what was said next. But she was pretty sure she'd heard him use the word *grandmother*. Which didn't make sense considering her father's mother had died before Violet was born, and her mother's mother wasn't around. Never had been.

Her mother had explained that there'd been a falling out long ago and that they were better off without that woman in their life. When Violet had been in elementary school, they used to have Grandparent Day, and all the grandparents would come to school and do fun things. Her mother let her miss school on that day, taking her to the movies or shopping or something so she didn't have to see what she didn't have. They would finish the day with brownie sundaes with lots of whipped cream and loads of hot fudge. Violet had always looked forward to Grandparent Day, but not for the same reason the other kids did.

Her stomach rumbled at the thought of a brownie sundae. There were no sweets in her father's house, because Tish didn't *believe* in sugar. She wanted to tell her mother that; she wanted to hear what her mother would say about someone who doesn't believe in sugar, like God, or Santa Claus. She wanted to tell her mother lots of things. She wanted her mother, period.

Instead her stepmother came storming out of the den, startling Violet as she rounded the corner and caught Violet standing there. Tish opened her mouth to say something, then let out a shriek of frustration that rivaled her infant daughter's and stormed off down the hall. Violet's father came around the corner to see what had happened, watching his wife's retreating back as he continued to bounce the unhappy baby. He looked bewildered and as unhappy as the infant, but Violet made no effort to say something consoling.

In his arms, the baby—her half sister—stopped fussing when she saw Violet, pressing her lips together and blowing air through them loudly, like a greeting. Violet reached up and the baby reached out. Her father's new daughter didn't know that his other daughter was not welcome there. Her father released the baby into her arms, and Violet held her close, inhaling Sienna's baby scent, feeling her soft squishiness.

She'd tried to help Tish with the kids when she was there and not doing homework. She'd tried to make them glad to have her around, but they'd seemed not to notice, choosing instead to be aggravated. Tish visibly bristled whenever Violet entered a room. It was like she wanted to erase Violet's existence entirely. Sometimes she wondered if Tish wanted an apology from her for living at all, for being the one part of her husband's past that Tish could not take away.

"I've called your grandmother," her father said. "She's going to come and stay with you. It'll make things easier. You'll be close to your school again and . . ." His eyes trailed off in the direction his wife had gone. He looked back at Violet. "It'll be better," he added.

She could see the pain and exhaustion in his eyes. It was her fault he looked this way, her fault his happy family life was ruined. Violet resolved to do whatever she could to make him not look that way anymore. Tish couldn't erase Violet's existence, but Violet could—at least as far as this house was concerned.

She had just one question for her father, one thing she needed to clear up first. "Who's my grandmother?"

Bess

After her self-defense class, she got trapped in a bathroom stall, listening to the chatter of the other ladies—mostly from her neighborhood or Nicole's school—milling around, gossiping instead of going home or wherever. Sharon, Bess knew, was going to Weight Watchers; Laura was to meet with her therapist; Brenda had a dentist appointment. Everyone had a schedule to keep, but Norah's arrest had thrown off all sense of normalcy.

Bess crouched in the stall, willing them to just leave already, her knees pulled to her chin, the last beads of sweat from the class snaking their way down her chest and back. She understood the irony of hiding after a self-defense class, shrinking back when she should be empowered. But the class taught her to defend herself from physical attackers. There was no defense against a group of women hungry for gossip.

Even as her muscles began to cramp and protest her unnatural position, the ladies lingered, wanting to talk, to dish, to discuss their theories about Norah and what had happened. They blamed, they judged, they condemned. They spoke about Norah like she was a piece of refuse, when once they'd all admired her. Norah had been, there was no doubt, the coolest woman in the neighborhood, aloof and successful and gorgeous, mysteriously content with her daughter and her home, never seeming to need a man. Of course, they snickered outside the stall where Bess hid, now they all knew why.

If the women discovered Bess, they'd corner her, ask questions, probe for what she knew. Though she knew more than most, Bess didn't want to divulge anything. It wasn't her place. She was uncomfortable talking about Norah, a woman who was once her best friend, a coveted position Bess sensed they all still envied even though the friendship had ended years ago.

This was the thing people did not tell you about when you got married and had kids: how important your female friends would become. You thought your friendships in grade school or college were important, but they paled in comparison to the friendships you would form with other mothers. No one told you how you would need them to talk to, to process with, to understand what your husband and kids could not. No one understood the release that would come from laughing till you cried with another person who knew you, understood you, accepted you. No one would tell you how hard that person would be to find.

For a long time, Norah had been that person. And then she wasn't.

When the women's voices faded, Bess uncurled herself and exited the stall, looking left to right first to make sure the coast was really clear. She walked across the tile and stopped in front of the mirror, studying her reflection as the scent of sweat and deodorant and perfume swirled around her head, vapor trails of the departed women. She took in the image that met her in the mirror and thought about what Norah had been accused of, the way that success they'd all envied had come to her. Bess inhaled deeply, exhaled deeply, and looked straight into her own eyes. She looked, and did not blink.

At dinner, her husband, Steve, was downright chatty. Bess could feel the tension in the air, but he seemed oblivious, or just in denial about what had happened, what was happening still. Bess studied Casey's profile as she robotically speared and chewed her food. She seemed to be eating normally, so it probably wasn't an eating disorder. Bess tried to take comfort in that as Steve held court. He asked the girls about their days, told a mildly interesting story about a coworker, and was, for a moment, a glimpse of his charming self. He even listened to Bess explain what she did in self-defense class and did a good job feigning interest. She did not mention hiding in the stall after class to avoid talking about Norah. But Norah came up anyway. Steve did, at least, wait until after the girls had disappeared back into their rooms.

Once upon a time, it had been punishment to send them to their rooms, now it was punishment to ask them to come out of them. Bess would go crazy being trapped in such a small space for hours at a time. She needed to be outdoors, her hands in the dirt, her nose filled with the smell of growing green things. She needed to look up and see the clouds, feel the breeze kiss her cheeks. She glanced out the back window at her garden shed, the one Steve had let her purchase and design for Mother's Day last year. She'd long since stopped hoping he'd know what to do for her. She'd just started doing it for herself, then thanking the girls for getting her just what she had wanted as they accepted her gratitude while trying to pretend they knew what she was talking about.

She kept her eyes on the shed as Steve inquired about "her friend." That was how he referred to Norah, as though she had become a stranger when they'd spent holidays together, gone on vacation together, drunk countless glasses of wine in this very kitchen. Norah didn't have much family, so she and Violet had become part of theirs, for a time.

"I don't know anything new," she answered him, her voice so mechanical she sounded like a robot even to herself. For some unexplainable—not to mention inconvenient—reason, she felt her throat tighten, the warning prick of tears behind her eyes. She steeled herself, thought of what her instructor called *fight mode*. You could've chosen flight, but you've chosen fight. Now it's time to dig in. How many times had she heard that phrase?

She dug in.

"Huh," he said. "That surprises me, with the way you women talk." He chuckled, sounding like the stuffed shirt he had become. "It's all anyone can talk about in my office." He picked up his plate and carried it to the sink without being asked. She watched in stunned surprise as he turned on the spigot and began to rinse it. "It's got people speculating," he said. She watched his back, his shoulder blades moving underneath his white shirt, gone wrinkled and dank from a day of meetings and stress, as he rinsed the plate off and placed it in the dishwasher.

"I'm sure there're men in this town who should be worried," she said. It was just an observation, but she knew he would take it as a veiled threat.

He turned to face her. "Not me," he said, looking like a man caught red-handed. "I swear."

She looked at him coolly, narrowed her eyes as if she were deciding whether to believe him or not. She let him squirm for a moment because she could and this is what their marriage had become, weird moments of delighting in each other's torment. She let him squirm, but she knew that though Steve Strickland was a lot of things, a patron of escorts was not one of them. She did their finances, ran checks and double checks, had tricks beyond what Steve probably thought her capable of to know what he was up to. She knew more about his finances than he did. She'd know if he ever paid for sex. She'd know, and she'd have a solid reason to end their marriage. He hadn't given her a good reason in a few years, but she was waiting. The next time would be the last one. She would be done.

"I know," she said.

"OK, good." He laughed nervously. "Wouldn't want you thinking the wrong thing," he said.

But that wasn't the problem, she thought as she took the spot he had vacated behind the sink to finish cleaning up. It wasn't that she was thinking the wrong thing. It was that she was thinking the right one.

She knew her husband very well, knew more than he was aware of. But he didn't know her at all. She wasn't sure that he ever had.

He'd been the Ferris Bueller of their high school, the charismatic, popular guy who could start a whole trend by accident. Once he'd worn mismatched socks because the power was out in his house that morning and he'd been unable to see what he was doing. For months afterward, the other guys at school wore mismatched socks, looking to Steve for affirmation that they were doing it right, hanging on the nod they received in response like a kiss on the ring.

And she'd been the Sloane to his Ferris, caught in his orbit, made valid by his arm around her as they sauntered down the hall. Like Sloane, she'd gazed adoringly at him and thought, He's going to marry me. Back then, she'd thought that would be all she'd ever need. That was her endgame, her purpose for living. She would be complete when she took his name, could call herself his wife. But of course, that hadn't been true. How many girls had been just like her, thinking marriage would somehow make their lives—make them—make sense? The change in names had not changed her. And it hadn't changed him. It wasn't until after they were married that she'd realized that all those times he'd walked with his arm around her shoulder, he'd been looking at everything else but her.

Steve Strickland had had numerous flings since then. They were never serious enough to be called affairs; he didn't care about those women any more than he cared about Bess. Steve loved women because he wanted—he needed—to be idolized, to be revered. He'd been faithful to her in high school because he'd gotten that need met by his popularity. But when he entered the wider world and was no longer the big fish in the small pond, the guy who could get the prom date changed because of his sister's wedding, he'd started seeking out other means to get it, to feel that rush of adoration again.

She knew this about him without him ever offering it as explanation. Spend a lifetime studying someone, and you absorb their emotions, their reactions, their thoughts—no words needed. She knew about his conquests, and he knew she knew. She'd caught him more than once. But she'd forgiven him every time because she'd felt she had no choice but to. They had children, and she could not bear to harm them by taking their father from them. She'd seen the statistics, heard the stories. One of their old friends had gotten divorced, and the next year their teenage daughter had gotten pregnant.

And then there was the matter of money, of supporting herself. She'd quit college in order to work full-time and put him through school. But after the girls had come along, they'd agreed she'd stay home and put all her focus into them. When she had time, the only work she did was in her own garden; she'd had no opportunity for a job that would draw a decent paycheck, no visible means of supporting herself long-term. And Steve, with the help of all his golf buddies (half of which seemed to be lawyers), would've found a way to play dirty, to cut her off as close as he could, to make sure she paid for divorcing the likes of him. If she ruined his reputation, he would ruin her.

She could not risk being a poor single mother, selling this beautiful home they'd built together. So each time she caught him, she accepted his tearful apology, his guilty gifts, his few days of doing more around the house and being more attentive. She got herself a massage, took a few days off from cooking, planned a fancy vacation he'd never have said yes to otherwise. And called it enough. For now. And when the other women told her how lucky she was to be taking fancy vacations and getting massages and having a husband who would watch the kids, she would just smile and agree with them. Then she would keep on doing what she'd always done. Not because it was right, but because it was simpler.

She'd admired Norah's resilience, her bravery, her ability to make single parenting look easy. "I don't have whatever it is you have," she'd said to her more than once.

"You do. You just don't know it," Norah would say. "But I hope I'm there when you figure it out," she'd always add, then wink. But Norah wasn't there anymore, and Bess hadn't figured it out. Not yet. Finished with the dishes, she dried her hands on a towel and stared at her garden shed a moment longer before going to see if the girls needed anything, to tell them she was there if they did.

Nico

The man placed the coffee in front of him, his face open, friendly, as he did so. That would change soon. Nico looked down at the mug that said "World's Greatest Husband" and tried not to feel exposed. He might've been just a dumb jock who had barely gotten through high school English, but his adult self knew what irony was. He had to refrain from sliding the mug back in the man's direction, telling him there must be some mistake. Instead he took a sip.

The man sat down across from him and pushed the sugar bowl toward Nico, his eyebrows raised in question. Nico shook his head. He took it black; he'd had to learn to. There were too many times on a case when you just needed caffeine, no time to fool with adding things to it. You learned to accept whatever was in the Styrofoam cups they passed out.

The man across from him, though, had not learned this. Nico watched as he liberally spooned sugar into his mug, then doused it with cream, too. Nico had come to think of this as effeminate, even though it wasn't, of course. But it said things about a man, about his choices.

"So, Mr. Jones," he said, addressing the man. Nico looked around the house they sat in, just a few streets away from where Norah Ramsey lived. It was a lovely home, decorated in grays and neutrals, the furniture new and tasteful, with clean lines and minimal frills. The overall effect was one of a very high-end doctor's waiting room. You felt comfortable here, but not comfortable enough that you'd want to stay. "I'm sure you've heard about the arrest of your neighbor Norah Ramsey," he continued.

The man set down his coffee and grimaced. "I don't have anything to do with prostitutes," he said. "I'm a family man. You can ask anyone."

You might have more to do with prostitutes than you think. Nico kept his expression neutral. "I appreciate that, Mr. Jones. But I'm not here to ask about you."

Mr. Jones, whose first name was Dave, laughed nervously. "OK, good." Nico waited a moment, not wanting to say what came next. Before he could speak, Mr. Jones spoke up. "Is this about my boss?"

"Your boss?" Dave Jones's boss wasn't why he was here, but if someone had suspicions or information, he'd entertain it. You never knew where a lead could come from.

"Yeah, Richard Mann. He's my boss. I'm a VP, but he owns the company. He's . . . well, I just thought maybe some of the stuff he's into . . . maybe he was one of the men you're looking for."

"We don't know who we're looking for," Nico said, feeling the sting of failure all over again as he said it. He couldn't figure this case out without knowing who Norah's clients were. The truth was, it wasn't the prostitution he really cared about. If some poor Joe wanted to pay for it, let him. But if that same poor Joe had links to the men his brother had been talking about on the day he disappeared, then, yeah, Nico wanted to know who he was. Because that person—that one magical lead—could help him find Matteo. He wrote down the name *Richard Mann* and thanked Mr. Jones for the tip.

Dave Jones's eyes widened. "Don't tell him I said it."

Nico suppressed a smile. "Don't worry, I won't."

Dave Jones scrunched up his face, his eyes becoming slits as he did. "So if you're not here about me, or about Rich, then why are you here?"

Nico took a sip of coffee as he collected himself. He heard his wife's voice in his head urging him to be gentle. To be kind. This man was about to have the rug pulled out from under him; no sense making it harder with his gruffness, his tendency to be a little too "to the point."

"Does your wife have any . . . hobbies . . . that take her out of the house a lot?"

Mr. Jones didn't catch on. "Hobbies? Like golf?"

"Well, sure. Like golf."

Dave Jones scrunched up his face again as he thought this over. "She takes this self-defense class once a week with some of the other ladies from the neighborhood. They all started taking it after that woman was attacked in that home invasion." His eyes widened. "Hey—did you investigate that one? Heard she got beat up pretty bad." His expression softened into concern. "I told Laura. I said, if anyone comes into this house, I want you to run, not try to fight 'em. You'd be better off going to a shooting range than a self-defense class. But you know women. They get a bee in their bonnet and there's no talking 'em out of it."

Nico agreed, smiled, waited a moment. "Does Laura do any other sort of group activities?"

Dave Jones smacked his hand down on the kitchen table. Nico half expected him to holler *Eureka!* "I forgot. You said group activities, and it jogged my memory. Laura goes to these parties a lot. Sells kitchen gadgets and whatnots." He gestured behind them, in the direction of the kitchen cabinets. "She's got a shit ton of that crap from selling it."

"So, she's . . . successful at her business?"

Dave nodded. "I mean, I guess. I don't really know, to be honest. It's her mad money, she says. She needed a fund for the spa. Likes to get massages and facials and crap. I don't know."

"And does she have a favorite spa she goes to?" Nico asked, working hard to sound nonchalant, knowing what came next.

"Yeah. She pretty much goes to the same one all the time. Over on Crossroads Boulevard?"

Nico nodded encouragingly. Keep talking, he thought.

"She says you wouldn't believe how often you have to go to keep it all up." Dave Jones shook his head. "You couldn't pay me to be a woman."

"Me either," Nico said. He did not say, *In your wife's case, it actually pays to be a woman.* He cleared his throat, the universal signal that the conversation was about to change direction. "Actually, Mr. Jones, the spa your wife frequents has been linked to Norah Ramsey's, um, business." He sat, quiet for a moment, and watched Dave Jones's face as he worked to remain impassive even as his eyes revealed the wheels turning inside his head.

"What's that got to do with Laura?" the other man said. He didn't bother to keep the defensiveness out of his voice.

"Well, that's what we've brought her into the station to talk about. She's with a female detective right now."

"Laura's . . . in custody?" The man looked like he was growing short of breath. "On what grounds?"

"I'm not at liberty to go into details about that, Mr. Jones. And she's not in custody as of yet. We're just . . . information-gathering at this point. But please know we don't go around hauling housewives into interviews without grounds to do so."

He wondered if the female officer he'd left Laura with would bear down on her the way he wanted her to. He wanted to use any means possible to get one of these women to crack. He needed that client list so he could find out more about what Matteo had been talking about the last day Nico saw him. On that client list was the name of the man Matteo had seen. If he had the list, he could start narrowing it down. And then he could find his brother.

He looked at Jones, who nodded his understanding, looking meek as he absorbed the gravity of what was happening. Nico continued, "I came here just to inform you of what was happening and thought maybe we could chat about any, um, questions or concerns you may have been having."

"Questions or concerns about what?"

"Well, just maybe you've seen some things, heard some things, wondered about whether your wife has been, well, honest with you about her activities."

Dave Jones didn't hesitate. "Never. Not once. Laura is—well, she's not the kind of person who would do what you're insinuating. I can't—" The man looked down at the floor, clasping the edge of the table like he was on a cliff and the table was a branch, the only thing between him and the abyss. Nico listened as he breathed in and out, in and out, loudly. He sounded like a bull about to charge.

Dave Jones looked up again. "I think you should leave."

Nico nodded and stood. "Of course," he said.

The other man rose as well. He did not extend his hand for Nico to shake, and Nico didn't blame him. He felt for the guy. He turned as if to go. As much as this case was tied to his own heartbreak, he wasn't going to allow it into this room at this moment. He had a job to do. He took a few steps toward the door, then stopped short, pretending he'd forgotten something. This was how he always did this part, using the element of surprise, borrowing a page from Columbo's book. And it always worked, like it did for Columbo.

Nico might not've been smart enough to come up with this stuff on his own, but he was smart enough to borrow the things other smart people had come up with. His years in front of the TV as a kid had served him well. His dad had always liked watching *Columbo* reruns. He was glad his dad had passed away before Matteo's disappearance. The worry would've killed him.

Nico dug in his interior coat pocket as he turned back to Dave Jones, who was watching him warily. "Almost forgot," Nico said, making his voice sound apologetic.

He handed the man the search warrant he'd really come there to serve. He'd never expected the guy to give up his wife. After talking to him, Nico believed the poor schmuck truly didn't know a thing. Of course Nico had to probe a bit, get a feel for the situation. And the guy *had* put his wife at the very spa where they suspected she was servicing men. So, there was that. Once Dave Jones accepted that his wife had been prostituting herself under his nose—and doing God knows what with the profits—he'd divorce her, and they could call him as a witness if it came to a trial.

Sometimes he hated how jaded his job had made him. But sometimes he appreciated the hard shell it had afforded him. He'd learned to feel less with each injustice he'd witnessed, each violation he'd investigated, each cold case that had no hope of ever being solved. Growing numb made it harder to be human—to interact with his kids, to feel his wife's embrace, to accept happiness in the moments when it lighted on him—but it also made it easier when happiness did what it always did: flitted away again.

He watched as the guy opened the folded paper and gave it the cursory read that everyone did. Reading the words didn't change what they said; you had to get out of your house so strangers could turn it upside down, rifle through your personal things, look for incriminating items that would later be used against you or a loved one. He wondered what Laura Jones had hidden, what they would find.

"Do you have anywhere you can go?" Nico asked. This part wasn't his responsibility, but he asked anyway.

"My kids—they'll be home from school soon." Dave Jones started to argue, as if this were something that could be rescheduled. Nico wanted to reach out and give the man a sympathetic pat, but his arms stayed by his side. Dave Jones didn't want his sympathy.

"You'll need to make arrangements for your children," was all Nico said. He stood, motionless for a moment, thinking Dave Jones might say more. But instead he just turned and walked away, leaving Nico to open the door for the officers waiting to come inside the Jones house and do their job.

Casey

Casey got ready to leave, rationalizing as she did. She hadn't gone looking for him. He had found her. And besides, this was just lunch. Not a date. Not even close. She wasn't so weak that she had reached out to the one constant in her life since she had been a sophomore in high school. She hadn't caved and done that. Since she had come home she'd been a strong, independent woman, handling her problems by herself. Until there he was, behind her in line to pick up a pizza, calling her name.

He'd pointed at the pizza as they handed it to her over the counter, closed his eyes, and said, "Black olives and mushrooms, extra sauce." But he might as well have said *I know the way you like your pizza. I know everything there is to know about your family. I know your worst fears and private dreams. I know you.* Only he didn't know her, not anymore. Things had happened to her, things that had changed her that he didn't know about.

They stepped off to the side. He took the pizza from her hands, set it on a table nearby so they could chat. "Don't you need to get your pizza?" she asked, and pointed back at the line.

He waved away her suggestion. "I'll get it after you leave." He gestured at the pizza. "Bess doing some volunteer thing, too busy to cook?" He always thought it was ironic how her mother would cook a meal for another family, then order a pizza for her own.

Casey shrugged. "She's all freaked out about this woman who got arrested in our neighborhood. We had her kid staying with us, but then the kid left because Nicole has turned into a little *beyotch*. Anyway, she sent me out for pizza because she hadn't 'had time to even *think* about dinner.'" This was said in her best Bess imitation. Foolishly she'd thought that upon her arrival, her mother would cook all her favorite meals, welcome her home with maternal love and care. Instead Bess hadn't seemed to notice she was there.

He crossed his arms. "You home for a break already?"

She looked down at the tile floor made to look like red bricks lined up in a pattern, two up, two down. "Kind of just . . . taking a break," she mumbled.

"You're not dropping out?" he asked. She heard the concern in his voice. But also, just under it, hope.

"No," she said, and as she said it, she meant it. She was down, but she wasn't out. Not yet. But she couldn't keep missing classes. The dean had said she could take some time, that the profs would be notified, and she could stay abreast of her classwork from home. But that her absence couldn't drag on. She would have to take a withdrawal or come back. Soon. Meanwhile, the great love of her life—the boy she'd broken up with before leaving for school—stood right in front of her. And all she could think was, Maybe this changes everything.

Thankfully he didn't push her for more details on her homecoming. Instead he said, "Got time for lunch before you go back?" He'd made it sound so nonchalant that she almost believed he didn't care whether she said yes.

The first few weeks after they'd broken up had been grueling—the texts, the calls, the tearful "Whys?" that she could not answer except to say "It's for the best." He'd stopped calling eventually, and she'd thrown herself into the parties, the new friends, the late nights in the dorm. She'd worked to find her niche at school, forced herself to enter fully into this new life, one that hadn't involved him. When he crept into her

74

mind, she would focus on something else. But now, here he was. That had to mean something, didn't it?

"I could do lunch," she said, and made her voice sound as cavalier as his did.

They'd agreed on a date and time. She'd told him she'd meet him—not to pick her up—her mom would freak if she saw him picking her up, but she didn't say so. He'd seize on that if she did. He'd known that her mother was behind their breakup, that it wasn't really what she, Casey, had wanted. Being independent was doing what you wanted, not what your parents told you. But her mother had been so insistent that she break it off, so certain in a way that Casey had not been. So she'd listened, never putting much thought as to why her mother had been so adamant that they cut ties before Casey went off to school.

Now she wondered if breaking up had been truly what was best for her, if her mother was capable of even knowing what that was. If she hadn't broken up with him, none of what had happened would've happened. This she knows for sure. Standing there, she regretted having listened to her mother. She'd placed a lot of confidence in someone who didn't seem to be happy with her own life decisions.

"So I'll see you Wednesday?" he'd asked, and smiled at her. She thought of what had happened back at the university the night she fled, the faces leering at her. Those faces hadn't looked anything like his did. She told herself that what she saw on his face was love, plain and simple. That he was something to grab on to in the midst of her freefall. She felt her hand reach out as if she might literally take hold of him, the impulse overcoming her rational mind. She hoped he thought that she was just reaching out to shake his hand, to behave with the formality of someone who was now just an acquaintance.

Instead his smile widened. He reached out his own hand and took hers, then pulled her to him, erasing the space between them. In his arms she felt a flicker of peace she hadn't felt since everything had happened, a sense of being home in the way that she hadn't felt upon actually arriving home. She inhaled and exhaled, smelling the familiar scent of him, feeling the warmth of his body. He'd been her everything until he'd become her nothing. And, just like that, here he was being something again. She made herself let go, step out of the embrace, creating a distance between them again.

"See you Wednesday," she said.

And then Wednesday was there. It would be a fresh start, a new thing. But what kind of thing, she could not say. She wasn't sure she wanted to think that far ahead. She wasn't sure she was capable of thinking beyond this moment, here, putting on the shoes she would wear to walk out the door, climb into her car, and go meet Eli, who was waiting for her on the other side of town.

Bess

She did not hide after class that week. She did not have to. One of their own was conspicuously absent, causing a somber silence to fall over the gossipers. Laura Jones's arrest, it seemed, had caused everyone to retreat to a place inside themselves, a guarded place, a place no one wanted anyone else to see. In that place were the kinds of questions one would never give voice to, the ones that unearthed and unsettled. How well do we know each other? How well do we know ourselves? Could I? Would I?

In the bathroom, Bess noticed that no one lingered at the mirror. After everyone was gone, she stood in front of it, the only one who dared to take in her own image. She left the studio feeling unburdened, a lightness in her step. Steve had left for a business trip that morning, his absence a gift, freedom stretching out in front of her. No stilted conversation. No tension in the air. No wondering where things stood or where things would end up. He was out of sight, out of mind for a few blessed days.

She got out of the car and rounded the corner to her back door, keys in hand, to let herself into the house, which was, thankfully, empty. Casey was gone, off to have lunch with a friend, she had said. But Bess suspected it was her ex-boyfriend. Casey had never been a very good liar, and Bess could always tell when she was outright lying or just omitting a key truth. She needed to pin Casey down about it, but she didn't want to. She wanted to remain blissfully ignorant. About whether Casey was seeing her ex, and about why she was home. The Strickland household specialized in unasked questions and unrocked boats. Bess didn't know when it had become that way, and she didn't like that it had. She resolved that today was the day she would insist on knowing what was going on. Bess would ask Casey nicely, tell her she was concerned about her missing so many classes, offer to help sort out whatever it was that had brought her home.

Movement in her peripheral vision interrupted her rapid-fire thoughts, stopping her short. Her eyes darted in the direction of the movement, her heart rate picking up speed as her mind shifted into alert mode. Fresh from self-defense class, she was aware of danger lurking in every corner.

A figure moved out of her shed, and she felt the relief of recognition as their eyes met from across the yard. She smiled and lifted her hand in greeting. He smiled back and, like a pantomime, lifted his own hand the same way she had. They stood still for a moment, both grinning like idiots, and she wondered if he felt as happy at the sight of her as she did at the sight of him. She crossed the yard.

"Thanks," he said when she reached him, lifting the sandwich and bottled water she'd left for him that morning as she always did. His face was dirty, his usual days-old stubble grown into a full-fledged beard since she had last seen him. She wondered how he shaved, where he shaved. She pictured him crouching over a mountain stream, using his reflection in the water as a guide, even though there was no mountain stream anywhere nearby, just a lake tucked back in the woods that kids around here went to fish in or park at.

She gestured to her house. "Want to come in?"

He shifted, considering it. Sometimes he said yes, sometimes no. But whether he came inside or not, they always stood and chatted. That was why she had first offered to let him in her house, because she didn't want her neighbors to see them standing in full view, chatting. She didn't want them mentioning the strange man to Steve.

"There might be a cookie in it for you," she teased. The first time she had caught him sneaking out of her shed last spring, she'd attacked without thinking, her newfound self-defense skills wielded impulsively, and badly. He'd laughed at her in spite of himself, and she'd frozen in mid-strike, which had made him laugh harder. That had been the beginning.

"I did kind of want to talk to you about something," he said.

With practiced nonchalance—no sudden or overeager movements, or he shied away—she gestured for him to follow her inside, feeling the corners of her mouth turn up reflexively as he fell into step behind her. It was crazy, she knew this. Casey could be home at any moment, and what would she think if she happened to find her mother entertaining a homeless man in their kitchen, feeding him at their table?

"Mind if I wash up first?" he asked, as he always did.

She nodded and watched as he moved to the kitchen sink, soaping his hands, then his arms up to his elbows, like a surgeon scrubbing in. Soon, the scent of soap replaced the scent she'd come to associate with him. He smelled of outdoors and dirty clothes. It filled up their house as soon as he entered. Once Nicole had come home moments after he'd left and asked about the smell. She'd told her a worker had needed to check the thermostat, the lie coming to her effortlessly.

He took a seat at the table, the same one he always did. The one usually occupied by Steve, which always gave her a sadistic little thrill. Steve would die a thousand deaths if he knew a homeless man sat in his chair, ate at his table with his wife. If he knew the things Bess had shared with this stranger, how natural it had become to talk to him, how she'd come to need the unburdening he offered her. He had, as he always said, nowhere else to be. She was the one with the schedule, the obligations. He had all the time in the world.

He unwrapped the sandwich she'd made and left for him after Nicole and Steve had left that morning. The shed had become his shelter. No one had thought a thing of her installing the dorm-size fridge in the shed. She got thirsty when she gardened. No one knew she'd hidden a bedroll out there, for nights when he needed a place to get out of the cold or rain. At night she'd look down from her bedroom window, the moon shining on the shed, and wonder if he was inside. He came and went at will, so she never knew.

At first it was just good deeds done in kindness, her civic-mindedness in action, something she did as much for herself as for him, like making a meal for a family or volunteering at a shelter. It was her service to humanity, she reasoned; she would do it for anyone. But as their polite exchanges stretched into actual conversations, he had become not just anyone. He'd become Jason, a former resident of this neighborhood who'd abused drugs and thoroughly trashed his relationships.

Though he was clean now, Jason's family didn't trust him and wouldn't allow him to come back home. One cold, dark night, as he had feared freezing to death on the city streets, he'd resolved that if he lived through the night, he'd return to the suburban enclave he'd fled as a young man. It was safer there, he'd reasoned, with more resources. He'd mapped out an existence, stealing food and drinks from garages and outbuildings like hers, sleeping in the same forts he'd once camped out in as a kid. It wasn't ideal, he knew that, but it also wasn't forever. He'd made some decisions recently. He was going to make his way back to real life, or at least some semblance of one, he'd quipped.

Of course she'd promised to help make it happen. What else could she do?

He took his last bite of sandwich, chewed thoughtfully, swallowed. She didn't look at him as he ate, gazing instead at a hummingbird at the feeder just outside the kitchen window. Soon the tiny birds would disappear and she'd have to wait till spring to see them again. Soon it would be winter, and what would he do then? She didn't like to think about the cold nights ahead.

He took a sip of his water, set down the bottle. At the sound, she looked back at him. Sometimes when she looked at him, she saw the man he could be. The man he would be, with her help. She'd told him he could take a shower there, but he never took her up on it. She resolved not to offer this time.

"You said you had something you wanted to talk to me about?" she asked, prompting him. Sometimes he lost track of his thoughts, he had told her, as if someone had lowered the volume in his brain. She assumed it was from all the drugs. Bess had never done illegal drugs, even as a teenager or young adult. The idea of putting something in her body that wasn't regulated by the FDA had always made her nervous.

He grinned, and the effect on his face was like a light coming on in a dark room. He had a great smile. But his teeth could use whitening. She wondered if he would take offense to her putting a toothbrush and toothpaste by the bedroll in the shed. She'd just read about a new brand of whitening toothpaste that was supposed to work miracles.

"I applied for some jobs," he said.

This was good news. This was a positive step. "Wow," she said, nodding her affirmation as she spoke. "I . . . wow. I never . . ."

His grin stayed in place. "I know. I can't believe it, either. It feels . . ."

"Good?" she ventured.

He thought it over. "Strange."

"How did you . . ." She didn't know how to tactfully ask the question on her mind. She tried to picture him going into a workplace, asking for an application. They would think he was just any homeless man off the street. They wouldn't want him, because they wouldn't know him.

"I went to the library, applied online. They have computers you can use for free."

Pleased with his resourcefulness, she nodded a little too enthusiastically. "That's so good that they have that," she said, sounding stupid.

He held up the cell phone she'd gotten him, the prepaid kind. She had one, too, one Steve and her girls didn't know about, her own private thing. She'd given him the number. "Now that I have this, I have a way they can contact me." With the beard, she couldn't tell if he was actually blushing, but she thought she saw his cheeks redden. "I have you to thank for that."

She ignored his thanks, changed the subject. "You'll need interview clothes," she said.

She could tell from the look on his face that he hadn't thought about that. He looked down at his worn, unwashed clothing. The shirt was a castoff from Steve. Shortly after she had met Jason, she'd convinced her husband to weed out his closet, going on and on about the KonMari method until he did it just to shut her up. She'd told him she'd take the discarded clothes to Goodwill. But first she'd offered them to Jason. She'd been surprised how Jason had sorted through them with care, as if he were purchasing them instead of taking a handout. She had admired the way he'd somehow retained his dignity.

"Do you know your measurements?" she asked, a plan formulating in her mind. She would buy him an interview outfit. Not a suit, of course, that was too much for the kinds of jobs he would be applying for. But some nice pressed khakis, a button-down shirt, a tie. She'd buy a blue shirt to match his eyes, which were now sparkling with excitement. She tried not to make eye contact for too long, looking instead at her hands resting on the table.

He shrugged. "I used to know all that, but I've, uh, kinda lost weight since then." Before meeting her, he'd gone hungry a lot. "I do remember my sleeve length is thirty-three. I guess that doesn't change." He chuckled, but there was wistfulness in the laughter. "Funny, the things you remember."

"I've got a measuring tape!" she blurted out. "I could measure you!" Too late, she thought better of her offer. Measuring someone required getting close. Touching them. "I mean," she said, "I could let you use it to, you know, measure yourself."

Seemingly unfazed, he nodded in agreement. "I guess I could do that."

She nodded along. "Measure your waist and your neck, I guess?"

He continued nodding.

"And I'll get you some, what, khaki pants? An oxford shirt maybe? For interviews?"

"That's awfully nice of you," he said. He grimaced. "I hate to keep taking your charity."

She waved her hand in the air, dismissing his gratefulness. "I like doing it. It makes me feel good to help other people."

He started to say something but stopped. The look on his face told her it was something she both wanted to hear and didn't.

"What?" she asked, and felt her heart rate increase.

He gave her a rueful grin and shook his head. "Nothing."

She was about to press, to insist he tell her what he was going to say. But something told her to leave it alone. Instead she said, "I'll go find that measuring tape."

She rose from her chair and went off to find it, coming back a few minutes later to hand it to him. She went to drop it into his hand and walk away clean. But when she reached out, he wrapped his fingers around her hand, holding her in place. Alarm bells went off inside her. He'd never gone so far as to make physical contact with her before. Eating in front of her was the most intimate thing he'd ever done. She met his eyes, and her elevated heart rate turned into a full-fledged pound. Had she made a mistake letting this stranger into her house? Was he going to do something to her? She tried, and failed, to remember the move they'd learned in class. What to do to throw off someone who has hold of your hand?

They blinked at each other, her breath gone thready in her throat. She felt the warmth of his hand holding hers, and realized that, though he was still touching her, he had relaxed his grip. He was not holding her in place; she could freely move away. But she stayed.

"You're the only friend I have," he said. "The only friend in the world."

She thought about this. Their encounter in the spring, her resolve to help him, the conversations that resulted, each of them lingering longer and longer just to keep talking. Hers was the only number in his phone, and she'd be lying if she said she didn't like that. Sometimes he called her just to talk. Sometimes she called him for the same reason. There was something about talking to her secret friend on her secret phone that made her feel more alive, her blood pounding in her veins with new fervor.

"Yes," she said back to him. What she meant was, *You are that for me as well.* But she didn't say it. She didn't have to. He nodded his understanding, as if a bridge had been crossed over in that moment, but a bridge taking them to where, she couldn't say. She didn't dare try to guess.

Polly

She pulled into the driveway, noting that the number on the mailbox at the curb matched the house number that the detective had given her. He'd been here earlier to officially release the house so they could return. He'd left the back door open and a key on the kitchen table for her, he'd said so in a voicemail he'd left her when she had somehow missed his call. From the sound of his voice, he could just as well have been ordering a pizza instead of explaining how to get back into her daughter's home after it had been cleared. Polly wasn't sure that leaving the door to a potential crime scene unlocked was very wise. But she wasn't one to question authority. And this cop in particular considered himself an authority. She could tell.

She let Barney out of the car and waited in the backyard as he sniffed around, then peed. She took a moment to orient herself, her eyes scanning the decent-size backyard, looking for a swing set, a playhouse, something that her granddaughter might've played with. But the yard was devoid of evidence that anyone lived there at all, save a half-empty water bottle that likely had fallen out of someone's bag and been forgotten. There was an ornate cement bench that looked better suited to a cemetery than a yard, and several manicured areas, giving it a parklike feel. But a park no one ever came to. Completely encircled by woods, it was peaceful and secluded. Which was, Polly guessed, the draw for Norah. Barney flopped down in front of her, and she reached down and gave his ears a quick scratch. "Come on," she said, and moved to the back door with her dog by her side.

She turned the knob and, sure enough, the door swung open. She let herself into her daughter's kitchen and stood for a moment, looking around. Instead of a home kitchen, the room looked more like a set for a cooking show. Polly searched for something familiar, something that said her daughter lived there. She scanned the large austere kitchen once, then again, but nothing emerged. There was nothing homey or quaint or sentimental. Not a cookbook with a title she recognized, not a framed painting she'd seen in Norah's old house, not even a name-brand food item that was familiar. It was as if her daughter had completely replaced the past with all new things, things that had nothing to do with her.

She resolved not to take any of this personally, not to make this about her. She was here for Violet. Her falling out with Norah long ago had nothing to do with her granddaughter's need for her now. This was a new thing. That was old and best forgotten. And besides, Norah wasn't there, so it didn't matter. She didn't have to think of her at all. Norah could deal with her own poor choices. And Polly would help Violet deal with what those choices had meant for her.

But first she had to hide the money she'd withdrawn on her way out of town. "Wait here," she instructed the dog, then darted back out to her car. She rooted around in the back seat for the bag of cash she'd stowed out of sight, just in case. She couldn't shake the feeling of guilt that nagged at her for taking the money and leaving town, but it was her money. She'd done nothing wrong, though she doubted Calvin would see it that way. Calvin, when he discovered she'd nearly cleaned out their bank account, would be unhappy. He'd be furious. She braced herself for that call and wondered how long it would be until he figured out he was dangerously close to being broke.

She'd considered turning off her phone, putting it into one of Norah's drawers, and forgetting about it entirely. Letting this stay with

Violet be a fresh start, hiding out here at this suspected crime scene. She could leave her old life behind, use the bag of money to start a new one. Hire an attorney to sort out a divorce from Calvin. Once her other money—the account she was pretty sure Calvin didn't know about—was safely moved to a new and even more secure account, she might just do that.

She walked quickly through the house holding the bag, feeling the weight of the cash growing heavier with each room she passed through. In each room, she contemplated hiding places, somewhere nondescript, somewhere Calvin—if he ever found her, God forbid—would not look. In the den, her eyes came to rest on the fireplace, a massive stone-tiled display that took up most of the wall and looked like it belonged in some Tuscan vineyard, not a suburban McMansion. On the mantel were two gigantic urns meant to look like wine casks. Polly set down the bag and walked over to the front windows to make sure that Violet's stepmother had not arrived to drop her off early. She saw no cars in the driveway and none approaching the house.

Satisfied, she scurried back to the mantel and stood on her tiptoes to reach one of the urns, which looked heavy but was surprisingly light. She pulled it down and set it gently on the floor. She attempted to lift the ornately carved lid from it, but it was stuck. She tugged harder, to no avail. She tried turning it, in case it was screwed on, but it didn't move. Curious as to what she was doing, Barney put his nose on the lid. She gave the dog the side-eye. "You're no help," she said, and pushed his wet nose out of the way.

She was wrestling with the urn, her determination overriding her common sense, when she heard a car pull into the drive. She leapt up and put the urn back where it belonged. She frantically searched for somewhere—anywhere—to stow the money before her granddaughter walked into the house and found her holding it. Desperate, she shoved the bag underneath an overstuffed leather recliner in the corner of the room and raced out the front door, coming to a stop just beside a large pumpkin on the front porch. She attempted a pose that looked rested and serene, instead of frenzied and fearful. She held the pose as she waited for her granddaughter to say her goodbyes. She could just make out a little hand waving from the back seat and recalled Allen's comment about Violet's presence disrupting his happy little second family. What a douche.

When Violet turned away from the car, Polly got the first glimpse of her granddaughter's face in fourteen years. The last time Polly had seen her, she'd been a chubby toddler with grubby hands. Now she was a slender wisp of a girl on the cusp of womanhood. Though they shared some features, she did not look like Norah. When Violet was a baby she had looked exactly like Norah's baby pictures. Polly would've bet she'd grow to be the spitting image of her mother.

But instead Violet looked like someone else, someone also familiar to Polly, someone she barely remembered: herself at fifteen years old. She recognized the burgeoning beauty that was not quite there yet and the uncertainty in her eyes that Polly recalled in an instant: the fear that she was never going to get there. That she would always be skinny and gawky, unsure of the right things to say or do around a boy, and overwhelmed by a world that seemed to come at her instead of waiting until she was ready to come to it.

As Violet drew closer, Polly had to resist the urge to rush forward and take the girl into her arms, to tell her all the things she needed to know, to warn her and to encourage her, to promise that though she'd been absent from her life for far too long, now she was here. That she would never leave her again. This was her granddaughter. Her flesh and blood. But she didn't want to overwhelm the girl. So she kept her arms crossed in front of her. It looked like she was hugging herself, when really she was imagining the day when it would be comfortable, natural, to hug this child she did not know, but knew very well just the same.

Violet

She stepped out of her stepmother's car to see the older woman—her grandmother, she supposed—standing on the porch beside that pumpkin, watching her. She blinked at the woman a few times, then turned away. She craned her head back inside the car to look over the headrest at her two half siblings strapped into their car seats in the back. "Bye, you guys," she said, feeling a sadness as she said it, a finality that didn't make sense. It wasn't the last time she was ever going to see them.

The baby waved her chubby fist in the air in a gesture that was half wave, half fist bump. Violet took it as a sign of solidarity, a baby way of saying, "You got this, girl." She thanked her stepmother's profile for the ride, then grabbed her bag and walked away. Behind her she heard the car shift into reverse and speed away. With her stepmother gone, there was no escaping. She wanted to turn around, chase the car down the street hollering, "Wait! Don't go."

She kept walking toward the stranger waiting for her on the porch. The woman crossed her arms and squinted into the sunlight as Violet slowly closed the distance between them with faltering steps. She couldn't believe this was her life now, that this was reality. She glanced over her right shoulder at Micah's house, wondering if by some miracle he was watching this scene unfold, wishing she'd spot him in his driveway. She wanted a witness to this moment, and he was her best bet due to proximity. Not out of real interest. She knew better than that.

She climbed the few steps to where her grandmother stood and dropped her bag at her grandmother's feet, right in front of the pumpkin. The two of them silently blinked at each other a few times. Finally, Violet extended her hand. "I'm Violet," she said.

Her grandmother gripped her hand and, when the smile bloomed on the older woman's face, Violet saw it was her mother's smile, as plain as day, like a magic trick. If it was possible to reach out and grab hold of a smile, Violet would have, just to take hold of something that was familiar. Instead she only smiled back.

The woman let go of her hand and said, "You have her smile."

"Whose?" Violet asked.

"Norah's," she said. She corrected herself. "Your mother's."

Violet rolled her eyes. "Hardly," she said.

She'd grown accustomed to deflecting any comparison to her mother. Her mother was beautiful. Violet was not. She had accepted this long ago. Any comparisons between them were just something people made out of obligation. But Violet did not have whatever beauty her mother, and apparently her grandmother as well, possessed. She was different from her mother and from her grandmother. She hoped Polly would not be too disappointed that her granddaughter hadn't inherited the family beauty gene.

"I'm Polly," her grandmother said. Violet had wondered what to call this woman. One of her friends called her grandmother Nana, and one called hers Mimi, and one called hers Honey. But none of those names would fit the still young, still quite beautiful, not at all grandmotherly-looking woman who stood in front of her. Violet supposed that Polly would do just fine.

"Nice to meet you," Violet said, and wondered if she should hug her grandmother. Didn't grandmothers like hugging? But Polly didn't look like the hugging type. So she gestured to the front door, which stood slightly ajar. Her mother would not like that. She always yelled "Close the door! Flies are going to get in!" whenever Violet left it open.

"Do you want to go inside?" she asked, inviting Polly in, taking owner-ship of her house even if Polly had apparently already been inside. Violet wondered who had let her in. She pictured that detective from the other day, his foot propped up on their pumpkin possessively. It had probably been him, brandishing the keys like he owned the place.

Polly nodded and motioned for Violet to go in ahead of her.

"Those police didn't clean up after themselves very well, even though that detective promised they did. The kitchen and living area are OK, but your mother's room—and yours, I'm afraid—are a mess," Polly said from behind her. "I wanted to tidy up while I waited for you. But I'm not sure where some things go. I figured you could tell me?"

The question hung in the air as Violet took in the scene. She could tell that the police had tried to put things right after the search, but in spite of their efforts, everything felt off-center, as if the whole house had been picked up by a giant and shaken. They hadn't made it the way it was before. Violet supposed no one ever could.

She felt her grandmother's hand rest cautiously on her shoulder. "Want to show me where everything goes?" Polly asked. Her voice shook slightly as she spoke, and as their eyes met, Violet saw fear in her face, fear that matched her own. Neither of them, she could tell, knew what to do next. The realization brought her a strange sort of comfort. If no one knew what to do, she thought, then nothing you did could be wrong.

She forced herself to smile, if for no other reason than to put her grandmother at ease. "I'm not sure if I know where everything goes," she said, shrugging her shoulders as if it didn't matter. But it did. When her mom came home, she wanted everything to be just right for her. She wanted her mother to be happy when she saw how well Violet had managed in her absence.

"I bet you know more than you think you do," Polly said. "You live here, after all." Polly walked farther into the house, calling over her shoulder to Violet. "C'mon, we'll figure it out together." Violet nodded, picked up the bag she'd hastily packed under that cop's big nose, and let her brand-new grandmother lead the way.

She stepped into her room and stopped short. The cops had been thorough in their search, tossing things aside as they dug for evidence. Though downstairs it appeared they'd at least attempted to put things back, they'd left her room in disarray. Her dresser drawers yawned open like so many mouths vomiting cotton, denim, and rayon blends. The items on top of her desk and dresser had been rifled through as well. Someone had even opened the expensive mascara her mom had bought her. Violet jammed the wand in and out of the tube a few times, then examined the brush. Bits of dried mascara flecked from it. She tossed it into her empty trash can that had been full before the police arrived, the contents probably carted off in some evidence bag. As if her mother would carelessly toss whatever they were looking for into her daughter's waste bin.

She cringed as she recalled throwing away a letter she'd written—but never intended to send—to Micah Berg the same night her mom had brought that pumpkin home. It had been a horrible admission that was part letter, part poem, in which, inspired by the pumpkin, she had compared Micah to a jack-o'-lantern, how his carved smile didn't really reveal the light she saw inside him, that if she could carve the right expression on his face, she would. She'd revealed what she knew about that night, what she'd seen from her window, how she understood what no one else did.

She stood over her trash can, now empty save the ruined mascara, feeling sick at the thought of a cop extracting that letter from her wastebasket and reading it. She should've destroyed it, taken a match to it and watched it burn. What if a cop read it and figured out what she was talking about, went to the Berg house, and handed it over to Micah saying, "I think you'd better read this"?

At that moment she heard the sound of Micah's basketball, the familiar rhythm of bounce, bounce, bounce, then the silence as the ball traveled through the air. Then the thunk of it hitting the rim and bouncing down, or the swoosh of it sinking into the net. She'd missed that sound when she was away, missed the nearness of him.

But this time the familiar sound was interrupted by another sound: a man's deep, resounding laugh. The laughter pulled her to the window to investigate who had joined Micah, worried that perhaps her fear had come true and a cop was there with him, her letter in his hand, the laughter about her. Her heart thumping with fear, Violet squinted through the blinds. Ever since that night last spring, he had played basketball alone, except for his dog Chipper watching from a safe distance, out of the path of stray balls. Once a ball had beaned poor Chipper on the head, and the way Micah had reacted, fawning all over the dog, had made her heart swell inside her chest, made her love him all the more. He was not the person people said he was. Violet knew this better than anyone.

Downstairs, Polly rattled and banged dishes in the kitchen as she attempted to make dinner. "I stopped at the grocery store," she'd said in that too-eager way adults use when they're trying to get a kid to be excited over something that's not exciting at all. "I'm making your mom's favorite dinner." Polly had thought about that for a moment. "I mean it used to be her favorite." She'd glanced around the kitchen, looking uncertain and maybe a little frightened. Violet had left her to it and made the excuse that she needed to unpack, before fleeing to her room. Violet had her own fears; she couldn't help her new grandmother with hers.

She cranked open her window and watched as Micah's dad—the source of the laughter—took a turn with the basketball. The fall breeze, slightly cooler since September had surrendered to October, carried their voices to her. "Watch and learn, Son," Micah's father called out, then proceeded to sink a jump shot. He whooped at his accomplishment. Micah clapped and Chipper barked. Violet had to turn away. Despite what Micah had faced in the past year, he still had not one but two parents at home, a dad who played basketball with him, a dog. Violet had none of those things.

As if in protest to her dismissal of him, her grandmother's dog, Barney, like the purple dinosaur, barked. Violet smiled in spite of herself. She sniffed the air and detected the smell of meat frying. Her mother never ate fried foods. She rarely ate meat. Violet was curious to see what used to be her mother's favorite food, because Polly's hunch was correct: it was no longer her favorite. Violet's stomach rumbled in response. Whether it was her mother's favorite or not, whatever was cooking smelled good. Maybe, she thought as she turned away from the window and headed back downstairs to investigate, it could be her favorite now.

Casey

Eli slid into the driver's side of the car, looking grim as he reached over to stow a grocery bag on the floorboard of the back seat. Casey heard the satisfying clink of bottles hitting each other. She could already taste the beer. She hadn't had a drink since she left college two weeks ago, and she missed it. Missed the helpful oblivion of getting drunk. It was funny how drinking had led to what had happened, and it was drinking that helped her forget what had happened. She could not separate the two, so she didn't try. She just went with it, depending on the liquid to slide down her throat, enter her bloodstream, and bring the freedom she craved.

"Thanks," she said to Eli, who started the car and didn't answer her. When he turned to look over his shoulder as he backed out of the parking place, his eyes grazed over her, looking at her but refusing to see her. She could tell he was angry but didn't want to say so, because who knew if this would be the only time they would see each other while she was home. No sense starting a fight, better to go along. She knew him so well she could read his mind.

"Can we go back to your place and drink this?" she asked, trying to reassure him that he was not just the procurer of her alcohol, but her drinking partner as well. She was not just using him. She wasn't. That Eli had a fake ID and she didn't had nothing to do with it. There had been a time he wouldn't have hesitated to get them beer, to drink it with her. But then they had broken up, and it seemed he wasn't anxious to go right back to the way things were. In that moment, Casey wanted nothing more. She wanted to pretend just for an afternoon that she was someone different, someone she used to be. She glanced at his profile, his face serious, his eyes intense, as he watched the road.

"Please?" she asked, making her voice sound playful. She rested her hand on his knee, partly out of habit and partly as a gesture of reassurance. "Your mom's at work, right?" Eli's mom worked a lot, and his parents were divorced, so they had often had his house to themselves. She missed those afternoons from senior year, the cold ones when they had snuggled on his couch and caught a buzz while watching old movies, and the warm ones where they had donned bathing suits and sat on his back patio catching rays and dreaming of their future.

He moved his knee away from her touch. "Not sure that's a good idea," he said.

She pouted even though he wasn't looking at her. Both of them were silent for a few minutes as she debated her options. Push too hard, and she could push him away. A thought dawned on her: What if he'd met someone since they had broken up? She thought about the girls from high school who'd stayed behind to attend community college, still rattling around town doing the same old things while everyone else had gone off to the hallowed halls of higher learning or whatever. Casey wouldn't put it past one of them to make the moves on Eli after their breakup. She wondered who it could be.

Better to play hard to get, to prove that no matter how desperate those other girls were, she wasn't. Suddenly she found herself wanting nothing more than to spend the afternoon with Eli. "Fine, then, I guess just take me back to my car," she said, willing her voice to sound nonchalant, denying what she felt inside. She was getting frightfully good at that.

Eli shrugged and, at the next light, turned in the opposite direction of his house. She felt her heart sink but willed herself to keep her chin up, like her mother often said.

They were silent all the way back to where they'd left her car, in the parking lot of the restaurant where they'd met. The lunch had started off nicely, the conversation flowing naturally, like the old friends they were attempting to be. She'd relaxed completely by the time their food had arrived, and she could tell he had, too. She'd been so relaxed that once they'd eaten and the check had arrived (which he had insisted on paying for despite her protests), she'd blurted out that they should get some beer, keep the party going. The funny thing was, though his face had fallen when she said it, he'd done it.

He pulled into the parking space next to her car but didn't cut the engine. He turned to her and gestured to the bag behind her seat. "You can just take that," he said.

She felt tears prick her eyes. She had done this. She had ended things. What had she expected to happen? "OK," she said. "If you're sure."

She saw his jaw muscle jump under the skin. He nodded once, then turned back to look at her. "It was good to see you. Good luck at school." In his eyes was the weakness he had always had for her, laid bare. She saw kindness and pain surging inside him, the effort he was making to let her go. It was cruel to ask for anything from him if she herself didn't know what she wanted.

Still, she leaned across the seat and kissed his cheek, right in the spot where his jaw muscle had jumped. "Good luck to you, too, Eli," she said against his skin. And it was manipulation, pure and simple. She shouldn't do it, yet she couldn't stop herself. She moved away, slid back to her spot, and moved to lift the beer into her lap from the back seat. Right on cue, she felt his hand shoot out to halt her.

"You're right," he said to her. "My mom's not home." She could smell it on him, the longing. "I mean, we could go back there. If you're serious."

"As a heart attack," she said, and grinned like she was kidding around, like this was all no big deal, when it was a very big deal, for more reasons than she was willing to admit. She exhaled as he put the car in reverse, then shifted into drive and pressed on the gas. She watched as her car grew smaller in the rearview mirror, disappearing as they left it behind.

Violet

She was outside, presumably to watch Barney pee so her grandmother could clean up from dinner. The dog had whined at the door, and when Violet had offered to be the one to take him out, Polly had looked so relieved that Violet felt guilty about her ulterior motive. Really she was just hoping that Micah Berg would take Chipper out at the same time, and the dogs would run over to check each other out, leaving their caretakers no choice but to follow. It would be like a scene from a movie, a meet cute, though technically she had met Micah before. She didn't count the other brief encounters. She was hoping for more, a real conversation instead of merely acknowledging the other's existence.

She kept her eyes on Barney as she tried to imagine what they might talk about. She glanced across the street, hoping Chipper would bolt from the house. But the Berg house remained quiet and still. Violet grew bored with watching Barney walk and sniff, walk and sniff.

"Just pee already," she said to the dog, but he ignored her.

She'd begged her mom for a dog the year she was twelve, saved her allowance and birthday money, scoured Craigslist listings, researched veterinarians. Her campaign had fallen on deaf ears, though. She could still hear her mother's voice saying, "It's a lot of work, Vi." Standing outside when she should be inside studying for a test, she now saw her mother's point.

Barney wandered near the road, and she called for him to come back. The last thing she needed was for her new grandmother's dog to get hit by a car the first time she was entrusted with him. Barney ignored her and kept sniffing the seam where the asphalt met the grass, testing the boundary lines. She walked over to the dog, cussing under her breath as she did. She'd been trying out cursing recently. It seemed time to learn to talk like her peers, even though her mother said it was classless and the sign of a low intellect. "Only limited minds use cheap substitutes," she always said.

Cursing had never come natural to Violet anyway. She was like an impersonator: she could make herself sound like her peers, but she wasn't. With a pang, she thought of Nicole, how effortlessly she spat curse words, peppering her speech with them like any other word. Nicole had started swearing back in the seventh grade, one of the first signs she was leaving Violet behind. But of course Violet hadn't known that then.

As she got close to Barney, she said, "Stupid-ass dog," when really it was Nicole who was the stupid ass. Or maybe Violet was the stupid ass.

Barney stopped his sniffing and looked up, responding to the moniker as though it was his actual name, as though he'd been called it many times before. Violet smiled at the thought of Polly calling the dog a stupid ass. Perhaps she and her grandmother were alike in some ways. Perhaps she would find out how they were alike while Polly was staying with her. She would find out, and she would tell her mom what she'd discovered when she got home. Then, thanks to Violet's insight, her mom and grandmother would make up, and something good would come of this ordeal.

As her mind wandered, a girl seemed to appear on the street out of nowhere. The girl grabbed Barney's collar. Violet started to call out to say, "Hey, let my dog go!" But when the girl looked in her direction, she saw that it was Casey Strickland. Their eyes met, but there was something . . . off-center in Casey's gaze. Warning bells pinged inside Violet.

"Hey, Violet!" Casey called, tugging on Barney's collar. "I found a stray!" She laughed like this was hysterical.

"It's not a stray," Violet called back. She motioned for Casey to bring Barney to her. "It's my grandmother's dog."

Barney, confused as to who had grabbed him, charged toward Violet, and Casey, not ready for the sudden movement, jerked forward. A panicked look crossed her face just before she fell down onto the asphalt. Violet raced over, grabbing Barney's collar as she looked down at Casey crumpled face-first on the asphalt. Her shoulders were quaking, and Violet feared she was injured and crying. She tightened her grip on Barney and glanced back at her house, wondering if her grandmother had noticed what was going on outside.

"Are you OK?" she asked Casey, her eyes still on the house as she waited for Casey to stop crying. But then she realized Casey wasn't snuffling but snickering. "Casey?" she asked. Barney pulled against her grip, and she knew she needed to either let him go or take him inside. The dumb dog still hadn't peed.

Casey used her hands to lift herself up, twisting around so that she could meet Violet's gaze. "I'm fine," she said, laughing. "I can't believe I just busted my ass like that!"

Violet noticed a scrape on Casey's chin. "You're bleeding," she said. With her free hand, she pointed to the scrape.

Casey looked alarmed and swiped at her chin, then winced with pain. Then she laughed again, though Violet didn't think any of this was funny. Casey still had that off-center look in her eyes, and suddenly it made sense.

"Casey," she asked. "Are you . . . drunk?"

Casey laughed harder at this and wagged her finger in the air at Violet. "Nothing gets by you, Violet Ramsey. I always said you were a sharp one."

"But . . . how?" She almost asked why, but stopped herself.

Casey moved closer to her, still grinning. "Beer," she stage-whispered, then laughed again.

Violet looked up the street in the direction of the Strickland house. But Casey had come from the opposite direction. "How'd you end up here?" Violet asked her. Barney grew disinterested with the conversation and flopped down.

"I was trying to walk it off," Casey said. "Before I went home," she added. "I got dropped off, and somehow I'm gonna have to go back for my car." She rolled her eyes. "That'll be fun to explain to Bess." She shook her head. "First I gotta sober up." Violet watched as an idea bloomed on Casey's lovely face, her eyes lighting up against the fog of inebriation. "Maybe you could get me some coffee?" she asked, and pointed at Violet's house. "You know, before I have to go home?"

Casey's phone sounded, and she looked momentarily confused about what the sound was.

"Your phone," Violet said, growing bored with this whole scene.

Casey looked down at her phone, and her face went from amused to panicked. "It's my mom again. She wants to know where I am." She gave Violet a desperate look. "Can I tell her I'm here hanging out with you?"

Since this was the truth, Violet said she didn't see why not. The phone had stopped ringing, but Casey fished it out of her pocket, fumbled around with it for a few seconds, then presented it to Violet. "Will you please text her? You know, pretend you're me? I'm all thumbs."

Not knowing what else to do, Violet accepted the phone. Barney lifted his head and watched the transaction.

"Say I came to check on you," Casey said, then nodded to herself, pleased with her lie.

Violet squinted at the phone screen, saw several missed texts from Bess, most of which said some form of **Where are you?** and used the word *disrespectful*. She wrote a text that she hoped would get Casey out of trouble. She pressed "Send" and handed back the phone.

Casey waved it in the air like a trophy. "You're the best!" she said, too exuberantly.

"Let's go see if we can get you some coffee." Violet started walking toward the house, hoping her grandmother wasn't still in the kitchen. She didn't want to explain this situation to her. But when they got inside, the kitchen was empty. Violet could smell the lingering aroma of the country-style steak her grandmother had made, now mixed with the scent of dish soap. Barney trotted off in search of Polly, and Violet set about popping a pod into the Keurig.

Casey slumped into a chair at the kitchen table and put her head in her hands. "I fucked up," she said, too loudly.

Violet spun around and shushed her. "My grandmother is here," she said, her teeth clenched and her eyes wide. The last thing she needed was for Polly to think that Violet hung out with drunks. Ever since she and Nicole had stopped being best friends, Violet didn't hang out with anyone. And with the news about her mother circulating through the school, it wasn't likely she was going to be finding a new bestie anytime soon. Other than whispers and pointing and the occasional slur against her mother, no one acknowledged her at all.

"Sorry," Casey said, and looked rueful.

Violet set the coffee down in front of her. She didn't offer cream and sugar, as she'd seen people in movies give drunks black coffee. Casey obediently took a sip. From the back of the house, Violet heard her grandmother call her name. She and Casey gave each other panicked looks.

"Yes?" Violet responded, making her voice sound level and measured.

"Did Barney go?"

"No," Violet called back. "It seemed like he just wanted to explore the yard."

"OK," came the reply, then a sigh. "I'll take him out again in a little bit."

Violet wanted to avoid Polly coming in and striking up a conversation that would surely give Casey away or at the very least raise questions. She picked up the coffee and whispered, "Let's go up to my room." Casey stood up and followed the coffee. "I'm going to go study," Violet hollered out in the direction of the downstairs guest room. "Got a big test tomorrow!"

"OK!" her grandmother called back.

"I think the last time I was here I was maybe ten?" Casey said as they climbed the stairs. Her tongue seemed to trip over her *s*'s.

"Mm-hmm," Violet responded, concentrating on keeping the coffee from sloshing over the rim of the mug. They made it up the stairs and safely into Violet's room. She directed Casey to have a seat on her bed, then handed over the coffee and shut her bedroom door. She took a seat at her desk and looked longingly at her psychology book. She hadn't lied to Polly. She really did need to study. She hoped she could get Casey out of there in short order and get cracking, as her mom liked to say.

Casey's phone rang again, and this time she didn't seem surprised. She dug into her pocket and pulled it out. She examined the screen, shrugged, and put it back into her pocket. "I'm not talking to him right now," she said. She looked at Violet as if it was her turn to talk.

"Talking to who?" Violet asked, more out of obligation than real interest. Violet assumed it was some suitor from her college, pining away because Casey wasn't there.

"Eli." Casey gave her a sly grin. "That's who I was with today."

This was news, and Violet could tell that Casey knew it would be. Their breakup at the end of last year had spurred almost as much gossip as Micah's party. Eli and Casey were the couple most likely to last forever. No one—least of all Eli—had seen the breakup coming. People had their theories as to why it had happened. Some said Eli had cheated on Casey. Some said Casey just had never loved Eli, that it had all been an act and with the end of high school came the end of the act. Some speculated that one or the other or both were addicted to drugs. Some said that Casey was gay and was going to come out in college. Violet herself had wondered what had made Casey do it. But of course she'd never imagined she'd be in a position to find out.

"Why were you with Eli?" she asked, feeling her pulse rate elevate slightly as she went there, to that curious, some might say nosy, place. But why not ask? Casey had come to her, asked her for help, used her house as a place to hide from her mother. Casey had sought Violet out, not the other way around, and now it seemed like she wanted to talk about it with someone. Why not be the someone? If nothing else, it would be satisfying to know something about Nicole's very own sister that Nicole herself had no hope of knowing. It would be nice to know a secret.

Drunk, Casey's inhibitions were gone. They had learned about that in psych, how alcohol affected your brain, removing your "gatekeepers." Casey didn't seem to care that she was spilling a secret. Of course, Violet didn't have anyone to tell, so she could do very little damage to Casey. She was, actually, a safe space.

Casey leaned forward and lowered her voice. She tried to focus on Violet but was unable to. Instead she set down the now-empty coffee cup on Violet's nightstand and looked down at Violet's comforter, tracing the floral design with her finger. "We ran into each other," she said to the comforter. "At the pizza place. It wasn't planned." She glanced up at Violet to make sure she was listening, or to make sure she believed her, Violet couldn't tell. So she just nodded.

Casey dropped her eyes back to the comforter and went back to running her finger along the flowers. There were a lot of flowers on Violet's comforter; it would keep Casey busy for a while. Maybe as long as it took for her to tell her story.

"So he said we should maybe get together while I'm home. Have lunch. It was very . . . safe. No big deal, you know?" She glanced up a second time, and for a second time Violet nodded. "But it kinda went wrong," Casey said. Her voice went small. She sounded younger than her years.

"So you got drunk because it went wrong?" Violet guessed.

Casey smiled. "No, the getting drunk went right. He has a fake ID. I asked him to get us some beer. I thought it would be . . . fun. You know, we could relax a bit. At lunch we were like two people who'd just met. I . . . felt bad. I didn't want it to be like that." She stopped talking, her finger stopped moving. But she didn't look up this time. "He was so sad when we broke up. I feel responsible. I thought if we had a nice time, things would be . . . better."

Violet cast about for something to say, but she couldn't think of anything, so she kept quiet. She did not know about being in love, or breaking up, or what it felt like to be drunk. Except for last Christmas Eve when her mom had let her have a whole glass of champagne and she'd gotten what her mom called "tipsy." It had been a not-unpleasant feeling, but it hadn't lasted long.

"So we went back to his house, and his mom wasn't home, and we were drinking too fast, and too much. And the next thing I knew, we were . . ." Violet watched as Casey pulled her knees to her chest and threw her arms over her head, hiding her face between her knees. From underneath the covering of her arms, she let out a frustrated, embarrassed groan. "I'm so stupid!"

Violet tried to make her feel better. "Well, you weren't stupid alone. He was stupid, too."

There was silence for a while, and Violet thought that perhaps she'd made a good point and Casey was taking in the wisdom she had offered, maybe even deciding Violet had been the exactly right, if not unlikely, person to talk to. Finally, she raised her head, eyeing Violet. Violet waited for the thank-you that was surely coming. She waited to hear, *You're so good to talk to. Really wise beyond your years. No wonder my sister liked you so much. She's an idiot for letting you go. Maybe you could be my best friend now.*

Instead Casey just looked at her. This time her eyes were able to focus. The coffee had begun to work. "You don't understand," she said. "I'm not stupid because I had sex with him. I'm stupid because it was a stupid thing to do. I thought I could handle it, and . . . I kind of freaked out."

"Did he . . . force you?" Violet felt righteous indignation rise up in her. No means no. You can stop at any time, and your partner should respect your needs. The truth was, if any boy ever wanted to be with her, she didn't think she would stop it, because she would be so amazed, so flattered. This was not something she was proud of. It was not the kind of thing an empowered woman would do. A voice inside her—a mean, condemning one—said, But it is the kind of thing the daughter of a whore would do. The word *whore* pinballed through her whole body, and she recognized the voice inside her: it was Nicole's. She spoke up, if for no other reason than to drown out Nicole's uninvited opinions. "If he forced you, you had a right to freak out. No matter what."

Casey just shook her head sadly. "It's not like that," she said. "It's . . . a long story. One I shouldn't be telling you. You're just a kid."

Offended and hurt, Violet sat up straighter. "I'm not a kid. I'm a sophomore."

Casey gave her a sympathetic smile. "I thought the same thing when I was your age. Thought I knew so much, was so grown up. I had no idea. And you don't, either."

Angered by the dismissal, Violet spread out her arms to indicate the room they were in. "Excuse me, but am I not sitting here in a house that was recently searched by the police, living with a grandmother I've never met, while my mom's in *jail*? I think I know a few things about life being hard or whatever." She could feel her breath escaping from her mouth in quick, angry puffs. Casey had some nerve. She thought of all the times Nicole had railed on her sister, calling her entitled and spoiled and clueless. In that moment, she agreed with her ex–best friend.

Casey stood up. "I'm sorry. I shouldn't have said that." She picked up her coffee cup from the nightstand. "I'll just go." She lifted the mug like a concession. "I'll put this in the kitchen sink."

Too angry to respond, Violet just nodded but wouldn't look at her.

In the doorway, Casey paused, listing slightly to the side even as she attempted to stand still. "Thank you for being there for me tonight." She held the mug up like someone toasting. "For the coffee."

"You're welcome," Violet mumbled.

"Can I come by tomorrow maybe? Go for a walk again or something? You're right, you do know way more at fifteen than I did. You've been through a lot. I'm sorry if I made it sound otherwise."

Violet lifted her head, grateful for the acknowledgment. She looked over at Casey framed in the doorway. "I guess," she said, like she didn't care. But the truth was, she cared a lot. Casey felt like a friend, which was perhaps why her callous comment had hurt so much.

"I think we're both dealing with a lot right now?" Casey said it like it was a question, but of course it wasn't. Perhaps, Violet thought, if they hung out some, Casey would tell Violet why she had freaked out, why it was her fault and not Eli's that whatever had happened between them went wrong. And maybe, if Violet got the chance, she could tell Casey what she knew about the night of Micah's party that no one else did, get Casey's advice on what to do about it. And maybe she could actually talk to her about her mom's arrest, try to uncover if what people were saying about her mother was true. She could tell Casey how it felt to hear kids in the hall whisper terrible things when she passed by. They whispered and pointed, whispered and pointed. But not one of them ever spoke directly to her.

"So . . . tomorrow?" Casey asked.

Violet couldn't tell if she was asking because she felt bad for what she'd said, or because she really wanted to hang out with her. She didn't care. She did her best to sound nonchalant as she said, "Sure." But she felt like Casey could feel the weight of the word, just as much as she'd felt the weight of whatever Casey hadn't said as she sat on Violet's bed, tracing the flowers with her finger from sepal to petal to stamen to carpel, over and over again.

Nico

October 8

He parked in the driveway of Norah Ramsey's house, feeling like an
interloper, knowing he was not welcome yet compelled to return, if not
to get answers, then to keep the scent that told him he was close to his
brother. Ever since he'd linked Norah to the spa that Matteo had been
talking about on the last day he had seen him, Nico had been convinced
that she was the key, that she would lead him to his brother. In Norah
Ramsey's house, he could smell Matteo as if he had only walked out
the door moments before. He knew that Matteo had likely never been
to Norah Ramsey's house, but the two of them were linked in his mind
now. When he was at her house, he felt closer to Matteo. The longer the
investigation dragged on—the longer his brother stayed missing—the
harder it was to differentiate between the real and the imagined.

When Matteo first disappeared last spring, Nico saw his brother
everywhere. He was a face in every crowd, the driver in the car next to
him at the red light, the busboy at the table across the restaurant. More
than once, he'd called his brother's name aloud, startling his wife, her
back going ramrod straight, her mouth an O of surprise.

At first, Karen was patient, kind about it. But as the months went
on, and he got more, rather than less, obsessed with his brother's
absence, her sympathy dried up, curling and shriveling like a dead

flower. They started to fight about it, snipey, snippy words exchanged with increasing frequency and fervor. She said he needed to face reality, to accept that it was likely that Matteo wasn't coming back. He hated her for saying it, though he knew she was only voicing what everyone else was thinking. But he couldn't forgive her for it, and he responded by staying away more often—always in the name of the case. For her part, Karen seemed to stop noticing he was gone.

It had taken surprisingly little time for his marriage to become a casualty of Matteo's disappearance. By the time Nico had left their home, his leaving had merely been a formality. He'd felt next to nothing as he'd packed his things, only letting himself shed tears that night when he'd said goodnight to his children over the phone and laid his head on a flat pillow in a cheap efficiency hotel that rented by the week. Still, it didn't change the fact that before he drifted off, he gazed at the unfamiliar ceiling and asked aloud the same question he'd been asking for months: Where are you, Brother?

Before he went to Norah Ramsey's door, Nico reached for his phone to check for any texts he'd missed while driving, but all he'd missed was a notification from his family's security system. Though he no longer lived there, he still tracked his family's comings and goings, their average moments on ordinary days. That was, after all, what he missed most. He could watch his son carry a soccer ball outside to kick it around. He could watch as his daughter rushed out the door to school carrying the coffee she insisted on drinking in spite of Nico's protestations. He could watch as his wife retrieved packages from the porch. But there were other moments he'd seen lately, ones that were not average or ordinary, ones that involved his wife and daughter that increasingly concerned him. But how to bring it up when that would mean admitting how he'd come upon the information? He could hear Karen now: You're *spying* on us?

He decided not to click on the notification just yet, no sense seeing something he could do nothing about. He looked through the remnants of dead bugs and bird poop on his windshield, staring at Norah Ramsey's house and thinking instead of the thing he could do something about. Inside that house, he was convinced, were answers about his brother. Answers he'd yet to find. It was clear to him: find Matteo, fix his family.

He tucked the phone into the clip on his belt and got out of the car. He paused for a moment, debating whether to go around back, where he could possibly see something new and revelatory going on in the kitchen. Or maintain a sense of decorum by going to the front door like any other visitor. Though he felt a claim on the house, a right to access it, the people inside knew nothing about that. He had to be careful with Norah Ramsey's mother. Though she claimed to be estranged from her daughter, she could be lying. People lie all the time. He thought again of the notification on his phone. Even the people you thought you could trust. Nico didn't trust Norah Ramsey's mother. Fair or not, by being related to Norah, her scruples were questionable as far as he was concerned.

He knocked on the door, and the sound of a dog barking surprised him. Norah Ramsey didn't have a dog. Other than a daughter, from what he'd learned, Norah Ramsey had no attachments whatsoever. She seemed impervious to connection, maybe incapable of it. Nico guessed that in her line of work, this trait came in handy. He listened to footsteps approaching and thought about the people in Norah Ramsey's life. He made a note to take a stab at Norah's ex-husband, the kid's father. Perhaps he'd talk about her. Perhaps he had guilty knowledge he didn't know was guilty knowledge.

The door opened to reveal a slightly older version of Norah Ramsey. Two words flashed through his mind: *teen pregnancy*. He wondered just how much older than her daughter Polly Cartwright could be. It couldn't have been much. Always inclined to conduct an interview, he had to stop himself from asking. Instead he just said, "You must be Polly."

She nodded, distracted as she pushed the dog, a large muddy-brown mutt of indiscriminate origin, out of the way of the door with her foot and scolded him. "Down, Barney."

He flashed his badge. "I'm Nico Rinaldi. We spoke on the phone a few days ago."

Polly nodded again, this time pushing the insistent dog out of the way with a bit more force. "I know who you are," she said, her tone not friendly.

"I just wanted to come by and make sure the two of you are getting settled in OK." He gave her his kindest smile, the one he reserved for women, children, and the very guilty. "I told my guys to try to tidy up. Hope they didn't leave you with too much of a mess."

Polly furrowed her brow. "If that was cleaned up, I'd hate to see what messy was." She leaned against the door, creating a bigger opening from her weight pushing against it. The dog saw his moment and bolted between them, right out the open door. He bounded down the porch steps and loped across the front yard, his longish ears flying behind him like pigtails. Stunned for a moment, both Nico and Polly just watched him go.

Polly came to her senses and turned toward the stairs behind her. "Violet!" she yelled, already sounding right at home in the role of caretaker. She looked back at Nico and waved her hand in a shooing motion. "Why are you just standing there?" she hollered at him. Violet came to the top of the stairs and Polly hollered again, "Barney got out! You've got to come help us catch him!"

Us? Nico thought. He started to argue, but when he saw the urgency on Polly's face, he didn't think taking the time to debate whether dog chasing fell under his job description was in his own best interest. He just turned and ran in the direction the dog had gone. Perhaps, he thought as he ran, his efforts would ingratiate him with Polly, make Violet see him less as a threat and more as a friend.

"Officer!" he heard Polly call from somewhere behind him.

"Detective," he muttered the correction through gritted teeth and stopped running.

He glanced over his shoulder to see her gesturing to his right. He assumed she meant for him to turn back in that direction so he pivoted right and obeyed. He tried to recall the dog's name as he ran back toward Norah Ramsey's house. In his mind's eye he saw Polly nudging the dog with her foot. She'd said his name. He replayed the scene in his head again, saw her mouth forming the name: Barney, like Fife, the hapless cop from Mayberry—the very thing he didn't want to be, but felt increasingly like, the longer his brother stayed missing.

He continued running until he reached the house directly across the street from Norah Ramsey's. He knew the house, recalled what had happened there back in the spring. It hadn't been his case, but it had been the talk of the town for a while, the nightmare of every parent. He and Karen had shuddered together, thinking that was the worst thing imaginable. Then Matteo had disappeared.

"Barney!" he called. He was out of breath from running, which made it harder to raise his voice loud enough to be heard. Huffing and puffing, he put his hands on either side of his mouth and called again. "Barney!" He looked from left to right, hoping for a glimpse of brown fur flying free. But everything was still. He turned and saw Polly and Violet approaching with matching worried expressions.

"You see him?" Polly asked as they caught up to him. Beside her, Violet made eye contact with him, not bothering to repress her sneer.

"No," he admitted. "He just took off," he added, sounding lame. Norah's kid had a way of making him feel inadequate. She looked at him like she knew something about him that no one else knew. It unnerved him. He pretended to scan the horizon, but really it was just a way to get out from under her gaze.

"I knew I shouldn't have opened the door to you," Polly said, looking at Nico like it was his fault the dog had made a break for it.

Violet spoke up, her voice quavering. "How's he going to know how to get back? He doesn't know his way around here yet."

Polly patted Violet's shoulder. "He's a dog, honey. They've got better smellers than we do. He'll sniff his way home."

A cartoonish vision filled Nico's mind: himself on all fours, sniffing out the path his brother had taken, finding him with his nose. He bit back a sad smile as the image faded, the flash of childish hope fading with it. "Want to split up and search?" he asked.

"Over here!" a voice answered before Polly or Violet could.

Nico looked up to see a teenage kid standing on the driveway, gripping two excited dogs by their collars, one on either side of him. They were taking turns trying to leap onto the other, nearly knocking down the sturdy, stocky kid with the force of their jumps.

"I've got him!" the kid said. But Nico didn't know how long that would be true as both dogs strained against the boy's grip. He wanted to get the dog back inside Norah Ramsey's house, bid them all goodbye, get back in his car, and view the alert from his security camera, checking on his family the only way he still could.

The three of them hurried over to the boy and the dogs. Polly had smartly brought Barney's leash and quickly snapped it onto his collar, chastising him all the while. "Bad dog, Barney," she said. "Bad dog." Once the leash was secure, she tugged him over to her side and commanded him to sit, which he did, looking penitent even as he kept his eyes on the other dog, who followed Barney's lead and sat by his master's feet, too. For a moment there was just the sound of the dogs panting in unison, like a pair of obscene callers. "Sorry about that," Polly said to the kid. "I'll try to make sure he doesn't get out like that again."

The boy, who avoided meeting Nico's eyes, looked at Violet. "I didn't know you had a dog."

"I, um, I mean, I d-don't," Violet stammered a response, looking pained.

Polly wrapped an arm around Violet's shoulder proprietarily. "I'm her grandmother. I'm staying with her for a while. Barney is my dog. He's anxious to learn his way around here, I guess. Make new friends." She laughed, and they all seemed to relax. The situation was contained, the crisis avoided. For now.

The boy leaned forward and patted Barney's contrite head. "Nice to meet you, Barney," he said. He looked at Violet again. "He's welcome to visit Chipper here anytime. Chipper loves to play with other dogs, and there's not many around here."

"That's a nice offer," Polly said. "Isn't that a nice offer, Violet?"

Violet, looking like she'd rather die than speak again, simply nodded and ducked out from under her grandmother's arm.

"I'm Polly Cartwright. And you are?"

"Micah," said the boy, his voice lowering as he added, "Berg," as if he were ashamed to say it. And Nico knew why. Last spring the kid had thrown a party—pretty de rigueur teenage stuff: parents out of town, kids drinking and trashing his house until the neighbors complained and the cops busted up the party in the wee hours. A typical house party until Micah had made a 911 call in the morning to report that he'd discovered his girlfriend, Olivia Ames, unconscious and unresponsive.

When the emergency responders arrived, they found that the girl was dead and had likely been dead since around the time the cops had appeared the night before. The news of the girl's death quickly spread and, along with it, outrage. People said that Micah had waited to call on purpose. They said he'd known she was unconscious when the cops arrived but had been afraid to lead them to her, protecting himself and securing her fate at the same time. Worst of all, before she slipped into unconsciousness, she'd texted a few friends one ominous line: **Micah did this.** Everyone conjectured what her cryptic text had meant. Most agreed with the theory that he'd been complicit in getting her to drink enough to kill herself and that, before she'd lost consciousness, she realized it and texted her friends.

Just last year, this kid had been a high school hero, sporting his handsome good looks with the kind of swagger that comes from being the total package and knowing it. They'd called him Ice Berg in testament to his prowess as a hockey player. He'd eschewed the more traditional sports to pursue hockey with the kind of vigor usually reserved for lobbyists and addicts. He was good at it, built for it, with enough attitude to compensate for any lack he had. But the party and Olivia's death had changed all that.

Now he spent most of his time alone, blamed by both his peers and their parents for Olivia's young life cut short. Though charges had never been filed, rumors circulated that they still could be. The kid's parents had gotten him a lawyer, and the DA was still sniffing around, looking to make an example of Micah Berg. In the meantime, the kid lived in a sort of self-imposed exile, waiting for the hammer to fall. Nico, for his part, didn't know what to believe about the kid. But looking at him in the flesh, he didn't look like a monster. He just looked like a boy who'd taken on more than he could handle. Nico knew the feeling.

"Nice to meet you, Micah," said Polly, oblivious to his history. "This is Violet, but I'm sure you already know that. You two must go to the same school? And you're neighbors, to boot!" Polly seemed to possess an unflappable cheeriness that her daughter, based on his many interviews with the now incarcerated Norah Ramsey, did not. Nico guessed that Polly would be a lot easier to crack than her daughter would be.

"We're in different grades, Polly," Violet said, sounding miserable. "I'm a sophomore. He's a senior." She looked at Micah. "Thanks," she said to him. "For your help."

She mumbled something about having to study and started walking back in the direction of her house. Nico couldn't get a bead on whether she was just uneasy around this older boy, or if perhaps she, like the others, held him responsible for what had happened. Nico looked at the boy and wondered if the story he'd told—and stuck to—was true or not. He'd said that he had had no idea Olivia was there, only discovering her body when, hungover, he went to try to clean up the next morning. She'd been in the guest room, curled on a narrow strip of floor between the bed and the window. A cursory glance of the room would've revealed nothing. She was out of sight except to someone trying to walk every inch of the house and survey the extent of the damage, the amount of work ahead to clean it up.

He'd said that earlier that night, she'd told him she was leaving with someone else, that they'd fought, and she'd left angry. Micah claimed he never saw her again after that, that he'd gotten drunk and passed out, waking late the next morning to find the real nightmare beginning.

"I just wish I could take it all back," he'd said. Some took that statement as an admission of guilt. But Nico, for his own reasons, understood how someone completely innocent of wrongdoing could still wish they could take words and actions back, could undo what had been done.

He stuck out his hand to the kid. "Thanks," he said, and waited for Micah to reciprocate, waited for the moment he could look him squarely in the eye. Maybe if Micah would look him in the eye, he could somehow know whether the kid was guilty or not. Maybe Nico could get back the mojo he seemed to have lost—that sense of knowing the right thing, of trusting his gut. Had he ever had that? If not, he'd certainly thought he had. Nico missed the days when he'd had it all but, of course, hadn't known it. And wasn't that the human condition? Like this kid's, his life had changed profoundly and irreversibly last spring. Like this kid, he was still trying to figure out what the hell had happened.

Micah Berg gripped Nico's hand. Though the kid gave it a good, strong shake, he didn't quite look him in the eye. Instead his gaze took in the expanse of Nico's face with a sweeping glance before releasing his grip and reaching down to scratch his dog's head. "Good boy," the kid said to the dog. "You're a good boy."

Nico decided not to attach too much meaning to the exchange. He bid both Polly and Micah goodbye and trudged back to his car, feeling sadder than before he'd arrived. He wished he hadn't dropped by in the first place, wished he'd never gotten involved with these people, or this place.

Polly

Polly dragged her belligerent dog back into the house, made sure to shut the door securely behind her, and unclipped Barney's leash from his collar. He sank down and rested his chin on his paws in that way he had that he knew would work on her anytime he'd been naughty.

"Typical male," she said to him. "Guilty as sin, but thinking you can weasel your way out of it by looking cute."

She rolled her eyes and walked away. Sometimes walking away was the best thing to do.

She'd walked away from Calvin, but he wasn't letting her go so easy. She wasn't stupid: she knew it was her money and not her he was pursuing. She'd ignored a call from him just as that cop had rung the doorbell. It was the call she'd been expecting since she'd backed out of her driveway with her dog beside her, the back seat loaded with her belongings and a bag full of money. It had taken longer than she had expected, but he had called. She could feel the silence between them breaking like glass shattering.

She'd had to will her heart to calm down enough to open the door to the cop and appear serene and composed. It was almost a godsend that Barney had bolted when he did, effectively ending the cop's attempt at banter. She wondered what he'd been getting at with his concerned act. How dare he stand there and pretend like he cared, when he was the one who had hauled her daughter to jail, took her granddaughter's mother from her?

He may have smiled at her, but behind the smile had been an agenda. If Polly had learned anything in five marriages, and many more relationships besides, she'd learned what a man looked like when he was trying to hide something. She closed her eyes and steeled herself to listen to whatever voicemail her husband had left her. Tomorrow, she thought, tomorrow she would call a lawyer. Tomorrow she would figure out what to do with the cash she'd hidden. It wasn't safe to leave it here, at a possible crime scene. That detective had warned her the first time they had talked that they could search again at any time.

Calvin's voice blared in the quiet room, and she grabbed for her phone to turn him down so Violet wouldn't hear, though the girl was all the way upstairs, in her room, behind closed doors, where she stayed pretty much all the time, always saying she had to study. But no one needed to study that much. Tomorrow she needed to figure out that situation, too.

Polly reached down and touched her toes ten times, something she did whenever she needed to release stress, then rewound the message to start it over. "Sugar," said Calvin, using the pet name he'd employed to charm her when they first began dating. For a moment the term of endearment filled her with hope, but the word was just like that fake smile on that cop's lips.

"It's your husband. I've just been over to the bank and spoken with a Mr. Dwight Richards, who says he has no idea what could've happened to my wife or our money. He suggested that I call you and straighten out our little domestic dispute. So that's what I intend to do." There was a pause, and in that pause she felt the violence that lay inside Calvin, coiled like a snake, so it shouldn't have surprised her when he hissed the next sentence. "I'm going to straighten this out however I have to." Then the line went dead.

She looked around, fear gripping her as she scanned her surroundings, as if she were going to find Calvin there, peering in the window, figuring out a way inside. She took a deep breath and reminded herself that Calvin didn't know where she was. He didn't even know she had a daughter, wouldn't possibly link the news about the suburban madam's arrest to Polly's disappearing act. And she'd turned off the tracking on her phone before she'd even backed out of their driveway. So he'd never find her that way. She stood still and kept on taking deep breaths, telling herself it would all be OK. When Barney came slinking into the room, looking for solace, looking for forgiveness for his escape, she offered it willingly. Not because he deserved it, but because she needed to offer it. She needed to bury her face in his warmth and give absolution, hoping that in giving it, she'd somehow receive it, too.

Violet

When she took Barney outside again, it was on the leash. She gave him the evil eye before they ventured out into the yard, and he cowered appropriately. She took that to mean he'd learned his lesson. He did his usual sniffing and walking, and she let him lead the way, allowing the leash to slacken more and more with each step until he was walking far ahead of her and she was barely holding on.

Instead of watching the dog, she was keeping her eye on Micah's house, thinking of that mortifying exchange earlier, hearing Polly go on and on about how they must know each other. Like they were friends or something. She would never admit to Polly that she'd had more conversations with Micah Berg in the past two weeks than she'd ever had in her life. She wondered if Micah had guessed that the man in his yard that afternoon had been a cop. She'd bet that Micah felt about cops the way she did right now. At the very least, they had that in common.

Movement across the street caught her eye and, though she didn't want to, she felt the little zing of excitement that coursed through her body whenever Micah was near. She'd felt it earlier that afternoon when he'd been standing right in front of her, hoping that it wasn't the kind of thing you could give off, like pheromones or anxiety. Was attraction obvious to other people? Could they feel it in the air? She watched him walk out of his garage, grab the basketball, and dribble it, the sound of ball on asphalt its own kind of siren call. She smiled to herself, let herself imagine walking across the street, stealing the ball, and magically sinking a shot before he even realized what was happening. He would say, *Hey, who taught you how to play like that?*

And she would say, *I learned from watching you.* And then he would look at her; he would finally feel the chemistry she felt, and he would realize after all this time, that the girl from across the street was the one for him. And he would reach for her and . . .

By the time Barney tugged the leash out of her loose grasp, he was already in the road. Thankfully there were no cars coming, so he was able to scoot the rest of the way across and lope into Micah's front yard with the leash dragging uselessly behind. She gave chase, hollering "Barney!" as loud as she could, giving far too little thought to what she looked like as she did so. She would think about that only later, when she was tucked in bed and remembering it all, dying a little inside at the recall.

Chipper, for his part, realized what was happening before Micah did and trotted over to greet his new pal, wearing what could only be described as a doggie grin. The two practically embraced in the same area that Casey and Violet had ducked into two weeks before. Violet couldn't believe that had been so recent. It felt like a whole lifetime ago. That had been before she went to her dad's. That had been before she'd met Polly. Hell, before she'd even considered Polly's existence. At the thought of Polly, she glanced over her shoulder to see if her grandmother had seen what happened. There was no sign of her yet. She hoped she had time to retrieve Barney and get back to the yard like nothing had happened.

She reached down into the pine straw to grab the leash handle. She fussed at Barney like she'd seen her grandmother do, but he didn't seem to hear her. He was having too much fun tussling with Chipper. "Barney, come *on!*" she said in her most authoritative voice. And, though it did nothing to dissuade the dog from playing, it got Micah's attention. He caught the basketball on the rebound and pulled it to his chest as he assessed the situation. When he began walking toward them, she closed her eyes for a moment, willing herself to be cool, to say the right words, to be anyone but her actual self.

"Got yourself a runaway, huh?" he asked, and grinned. He didn't have on a baseball cap at all this time, but she could see the ring around his head where the hat had been.

"I'm so sorry," she said. "I was letting him explore a bit, not paying close enough attention, and he just took off. Yanked the leash right out of my hand." Standing this close to Micah, she recalled what she'd been thinking about when Barney had made his getaway. She felt her cheeks grow warm. She hoped that in the dusk it would be hard for him to tell she was blushing. "It'll never happen again." She tugged on Barney's leash to no avail. The dog was strong in his stubbornness.

"It's no problem," Micah said, looking unconcerned. They stood in silence for a moment, watching the two dogs play. Micah spoke up. "Mind if I take his leash off? He's going to get tangled up in it. I don't think he'll go anywhere if he's got Chipper here."

Violet glanced over her shoulder again, checking to make sure Polly wasn't standing in the front yard looking pissed. But Polly wasn't there at all. She'd seemed preoccupied at dinner, and Violet had wondered if she'd already grown tired of being stuck there with her granddaughter. Violet wouldn't blame her if she left. It wasn't like they'd instantly bonded, with all the lost years falling away the moment they laid eyes on each other. It was more like they were very polite roommates who'd been randomly paired online. Though Polly had every right to leave, and no real obligation to her long-lost grandchild, Violet couldn't help but wonder: Who would stay with her if Polly left?

"I guess that's fine," she said to Micah. He reached down and unhooked Barney's leash from his collar as Barney played on, oblivious to the fact that he was no longer tethered to anything. He was free if he wanted to be. Sometimes you didn't need a leash to keep you in place, Violet thought. Sometimes you just chose to stay.

"So," Micah said to break the silence, "he's your grandmother's dog?"

"Yeah," she said, thinking that this wasn't the way she had imagined someday having an actual conversation with Micah Berg.

"How long have they been here?"

"Coupla days."

"She seems like a pretty nice lady," he said. "Kinda young. For a grandmother."

"I think she was pretty young when she had my mom." She blanched internally at the mention of her mother. She wondered what he'd heard about Norah, wondered what he thought.

"You think she was?" he asked. "You don't know?"

"We haven't really talked about it," she said. How to explain to this boy that she and her grandmother hadn't really talked at all in her whole life?

He nodded. "Yeah, I guess it's not something that would come up." He chuckled. "So, Grandma, how old were you when you had my mother? Twelve?" He started to laugh, then looked at her, alarmed. "Sorry if that was offensive. I didn't mean it to be."

She held up her hand. "Not at all." She chuckled, too. "It's the truth."

His eyes grew wide. "You think she was twelve?"

She laughed. "No! I mean it's the truth that it's not something I would outright ask her."

He nodded, spinning the basketball around in his hands. She wondered whether it was because he was bored or nervous. It had to be boredom. There was no way he could be nervous around her of all people. Of course, after months of exile, he *was* out of practice socially.

"You can go back to basketball," she offered. "I can just let them play for a few more minutes, and then I'll take Barney back home."

He shrugged. "Nah, I'll just hang here if you don't mind. I can play basketball anytime. We don't often have company." He looked away, realizing the admission in what he'd said, then added, "Not lately, that is."

She wanted to say that she was sorry about Olivia, about what had happened that night, and all that had come after. She wanted to say something that would make the awkwardness less awkward, or just lighten the mood. She wanted to tell him what she'd overheard that night, ask him why he'd never told anyone that part. But instead she just stood there, mute, the whole of her knowledge closed up inside her. Her mother wasn't the only one who could hold on to a secret. If Violet hadn't inherited her beauty or her coolness, at least she had inherited that.

"Besides, I like seeing Chipper this happy," he added, and she was grateful that he did what she could not do, steering the conversation away from maudlin and back to upbeat with seven words. So he hadn't lost his social mojo after all.

"I think Barney was lonely," she said.

He glanced over at her as she said it, and she feared he thought she was insinuating something else, something not about the dog. She hadn't been, but how to clarify that without naming the things that sat between them, the things that had rendered them both lonely: his shame, and hers. They had that in common, too.

"I mean maybe he had a dog buddy back at my grandmother's house," she hurried to add. "Maybe he's missing him."

"Or her," Micah said. "It could've been a her." This time it was her turn to glance over at him, to wonder if his words had been some sort of hint. He gave her a playful grin, and for a moment he looked like the old Micah, the one she knew only from afar but loved just the same. Though that Micah had never deigned to speak to her, and this one—the broken version—was choosing to keep the conversation going when he'd had every opportunity to go back to playing basketball. Her brain told her not to take this to mean anything, but her heart took it anyway, seizing upon it and holding it close.

"Yes," she managed to say, feeling momentarily brave. "It could've been a her."

"Lonely no more," Micah said, his voice so low she wasn't sure she'd heard him correctly.

She was about to ask him what he'd said when she heard Polly call her name from across the street. In response, Barney stopped playing with Chipper and turned his head toward his master's voice. Quickly, before he could decide to bolt over to Polly, Violet rushed over, grabbed his collar, and snapped the leash onto it. She stood up and faced Micah. "Guess I better go," she said.

"Wanna bring him back over tomorrow?" Micah asked, and she heard the note of hope in his voice. This was nothing; she understood that. And yet, nothing could become something with time. She understood that, too. Once, that big-ass pumpkin on their porch was just a tiny seed.

"Sure," she said. "I'm sure Barney would like that."

He grinned and held up the basketball. "I'll be here."

She laughed and turned to go back home, to where her grandmother was waiting in the yard. Barney strained against the leash and the sound of the basketball bouncing resumed, and, away from Micah's gaze, Violet let a smile fill her face.

Hours later, loud, angry voices woke her. She swam to the surface of consciousness and, groggy and confused, blinked in the darkness, trying to discern where—and whom—the voices were coming from. She sat up and listened harder. For a moment hope flickered inside her. Had her mother returned home? Disappointment quickly replaced hope when she realized it was only male voices speaking. It wasn't her mother, and it wasn't Polly. The angry tones continued, coming, she determined, through her open window.

She reached for her nightstand to get her glasses, slipped from bed, and moved silently across the room to where the breeze was making her sheer curtains dance. She'd fallen asleep watching them earlier, recalling Micah's invitation to return with Barney the next day, rehearsing things she might say to him. She glanced back over her shoulder to check the time on her bedside clock: 12:37 a.m. It *was* the next day.

She hunched down to get a better view out the window, angling herself so no one could look up and see her face framed there, watching like a creeper. She observed two figures standing in Micah's front yard, close to the street. The nearby streetlight provided enough light that she could clearly see them both. One of the figures was Micah. The other was Olivia Ames's brother, Devin, who was supposed to have graduated with Casey Strickland but didn't because he had stopped going to class after his sister died. Violet realized she hadn't seen him at school this year and wondered if he'd just completely dropped out. That would be a shame, she thought. Another casualty of that night.

Violet watched as Devin attempted to stand still yet swayed like a tree in the wind. Micah reached out to steady him, a reflex. "Don't you fucking touch me!" Devin yelled and, as Violet watched, threw a sloppy punch that, thanks to the element of surprise, managed to connect with Micah's jaw—though Violet could see he'd intended to punch Micah right in the nose.

Micah staggered back, holding his jaw. "You need to go home, Devin," he said, and as he turned to walk away, Devin tackled him from behind, felling him with ease. Violet winced at the hard thud of his body hitting the ground. Before she knew it, she was running out of her room, down the stairs, and jabbing the alarm code into the security system so she could get out her front door, thinking as she ran about déjà vu and how much this night was like the night Olivia died—the temperature, the time, the breeze—one in fall and one in spring, yet so similar. But in the spring, she hadn't run out to Micah's front yard. She hadn't intervened. And she'd always regretted it.

This much she knew for certain: Olivia Ames would be alive if she had intervened. Devin Ames would've graduated as planned and been off at college, not facing off with Micah, drunk and confrontational, there to blame him for what had happened, ready to demand a pound of flesh in restitution. But Devin should blame Violet, too, for being too scared to admit she'd been spying on the party that night, the wallflower never asked to dance, the pitiful Cinderella not invited to the ball. And in her silence, her desire not to be exposed, she'd inadvertently allowed what had happened to happen.

By the time she arrived, Devin and Micah looked like a rolling log of a human, arms flailing and feet kicking cartoonishly. She shrieked, "Stop it!" and scanned the house, expecting lights to go on, for Micah's parents to run out and help. But the house stayed quiet and dark, not even Chipper barked from inside. The boys continued to roll, cussing and spitting. In desperation, she reached out and grabbed someone's shoulder—she didn't care whose—and yanked at it roughly.

Interrupted, the owner of the shoulder looked over with puzzled indignation. Devin Ames blinked at her, and, in the pause, Micah skittered out from under him. Once again two people, they each lay still on the ground like casualties on a battlefield, heaving in unison as they both stared at her like they'd seen a ghost.

"You woke me up," she said, attempting to explain her presence there, but it came out sounding like an accusation. She wondered what she must look like to them: Violet Ramsey, the madam's daughter, wearing an old tennis-camp T-shirt and cutoff sweatpants and her glasses instead of the contact lenses she usually wore. She wished she'd just stayed in bed, because now what? Did she just turn around and leave while they watched her go? Demand an explanation as to what was going on?

She had a pretty good idea what had brought this on, though. Today, she knew, had been Olivia's birthday. They'd mentioned it at school, had a moment of silence in her honor. Devin must've decided getting drunk in her honor was an equally good idea and, liquored up, come to Micah's house to confront him. She looked back at the house and wondered again where Micah's parents were.

"I think you should go home, Devin," she said. "Before my grandmother calls the police. She's in there, waiting for my sign if she needs to." She looked back over her shoulder as if affirming that her grandmother was inside her house, watching with her phone at the ready.

Still, she was surprised when Devin hauled himself to his feet. He had blood on his lip and the beginnings of a swollen eye. Micah must've gotten in some jabs while they were rolling around. Good for him, she thought.

Devin looked from Micah to Violet, then back again. "I'm never coming back here again," he said. "This place is cursed." He waved his arm in the space between Micah's house and Violet's. "Bad people live here." He narrowed his eyes at Violet, and for a moment, she feared he knew her part in what had happened to his sister. She wondered if he could see the guilt on her face. "Buncha whores and murderers are all that lives here," he said. And then he walked away.

Violet almost ran after him. She almost did the same thing he'd done to Micah and tackled him from behind, used her body as a missile intent on taking him down. But what would she have done with him once she had him down? And what would he have done in retaliation? Better to let him go than to continue the cycle of attack and defend, attack and defend. At some point, someone had to be the one to let it go. She decided it might as well be her. Let him speak ill of her, of her mother. It didn't make him much different from anyone else. Hell, even her supposed best friend had. She hadn't punished Nicole for her words, so she might as well let a drunk guy twice her size off the hook, too.

When he was gone, neither she nor Micah moved, both frozen in stunned silence as his footsteps faded into the darkness. Violet wondered vaguely how he'd gotten there. He must've walked. She wondered where the Ames family lived. She'd never thought about it before. She'd never considered where the girl who died had lived. All she'd cared about was that Olivia Ames had been Micah's girlfriend, had held a position she could only dream of.

"Thanks," he said. From behind her she heard the rustle of grass that told her he was getting to his feet. Still dazed and breathless, it took him a while. She waited silently as he stood, took a deep breath, and moved toward her. She tried not to think about what she was wearing, or how she hadn't brushed her teeth, or that they were alone together in the dark.

She turned to look at him. "I didn't really do anything," she said, because it was true. She'd screamed at them to stop. She'd lied about her grandmother waiting to call the police if needed.

"If you hadn't come along," he said. "I'm not sure what would've happened. He was out for . . . I don't know. Blood or something. It's like it wasn't even him. I know—knew—the guy, and I'd never seen him like that before."

"I guess he's a mean drunk," she said.

He chuckled. "You speaking from experience?"

He was standing close enough to touch, close enough that she could smell the adrenaline still clinging to him though the fight was over. "What if I was?" She tried to make herself look tough, experienced, like maybe he didn't know all there was to know about her. She tried to look like an accused madam's daughter would look, thinking of Devin's parting words and feeling shame stir in her belly and begin crawling up to her heart. She had no idea what the daughter of a madam should look like. She had no idea what a madam herself looked like, unless it was her mother.

Like he was reading her thoughts, he said, "I'm sorry for what he said about you. About your mom."

She nodded, then shrugged. "Doesn't matter," she said, ignoring the stupid tears that pricked behind her eyes as a response to his kindness. No one had said "I'm sorry" to her about her mother since Jim Sheridan on that first day.

"You didn't deserve to get lumped in with me," he said. He pointed across the street at her house, and she marveled at the fact that neither her grandmother, nor his parents, had woken up through this whole thing. "You should probably keep your distance," he said, "so that doesn't keep happening."

She spun around and gave him a smirk. "You think that's because of you?" she asked, and laughed. "I guess you haven't heard what they've been saying about me at school."

He shook his head. "I mostly keep my earbuds in all the time now. Had to drown out their voices."

"Well, you can probably take them out, because most of the talk is about me now. How I must be like my mom. How I probably work for her after school. It's . . ." She thought of what some guy—someone who'd never spoken to her before—had said just that day. He'd thrown a dollar at her and said, "Is that the going rate?" as his friends laughed loudly, pushing and shoving each other as they moved en masse down the hall, pleased with themselves. She'd left the dollar on the ground for someone else to find. "It's pretty bad," she said.

"Want me to be your bodyguard?" he asked, and pretended to flex his muscles. He held his hands up. "I mean, I would, but I'm honestly just trying to steer clear of everyone, keep my nose clean so I don't get in any more trouble than I'm already in."

She nodded. "It's fine," she said. "I'm fine."

He gave her a look. "Now that's not really true, is it?"

She rolled her eyes, feeling the tears threatening again and doing everything she could to keep them at bay. "What difference does it make?" she said, and her voice was thick in her throat. "There's not a damn thing I can do about it."

She felt his arm go around her shoulder and tighten as he gave her a side hug, the kind you'd give a friend. The kind she'd seen him give countless girls through the years. The kind she herself had never imagined being the recipient of. She let him pull her closer, until her head was touching his shoulder. For a second—just one—she let her head rest on his shoulder, then pulled away and gave him her bravest smile.

He looked at her, held her gaze, and for a long moment it was just the two of them breathing. "Why is it that people have the power to make decisions that fuck up other people's lives?" he asked.

She thought about it, about Olivia and Norah, how their decisions had brought them here, to this yard in the middle of a school night. "I don't know," she answered.

"It doesn't seem fair," he said.

There were so many things she wanted to say. But something told her not now, not here. So she just said, "It's not." She smiled at him, and he smiled back. "What's not gonna be fair," she continued, "is when that alarm goes off in the morning."

His smile widened. "True," he said. "See you at school?" he asked.

She saw him at school all the time, but he never seemed to see her. She cocked her head, raised her eyebrows. "If you'll take your earbuds out, I'll even speak to you."

He grinned. "Deal." She started to walk away, knowing enough to take her leave at the right moment, surprised at the instinct kicking in. But his voice stopped her feet from moving. "Hey, Violet?" he called.

She turned and looked back at him. "Yeah?"

He crossed the yard to close the distance between them, coming to stand in front of her. For a moment he didn't speak, and she wondered what he was up to. His face was impassive as he looked into her eyes. For a panicky moment she feared he was going to kiss her. She thought of her sleep breath. This was not what she wanted for her first kiss. She took a step back to make sure he got the message. Not now, bucko.

"I need your help," he said. Her face must've registered her shock, because he quickly added, "I mean, you don't have to or anything. I just . . . thought . . ." Then whatever courage he'd mustered up evaporated.

"No, it's fine. What is it?" She couldn't stand to see him looking deflated any more than she could stand to see Devin Ames knock him to the ground. She wondered why he hadn't fought back harder, then remembered what he'd said about staying out of trouble. He'd been willing to let Devin beat the crap out of him if it meant no more cops at his house, no more drama associated with him. That, she realized, is why he'd thanked her. By coming over at all, she'd come to his rescue.

"I, um, wanted to, um . . ."

She guessed at what he was getting at. The nerves, the words that were hard to get out. Was he going to ask her out? It seemed impossible, yet what else could it be? It was just like on TV when a guy is nervous to ask a girl out. She asked a demure "Yes?" She couldn't believe this was happening, here, now, with Micah Berg, in his front yard, while she was wearing her *pajamas*, or at least what passed for them. This, she told herself, would be a moment she would always remember. How special that it was so out of the ordinary. It would be so much more memorable. She smiled at him to encourage him to keep talking, to ask his important question.

"I w-wanted to ask about your m-mom." He finally stammered out the words, but they were so different from what she'd thought she'd hear that she just blinked a few times, trying to figure out how to process what he'd said. What was he asking? At once she felt both offended and very, very foolish. Of course Micah Berg wasn't asking her out. Of course he was just like every other guy, turning the news about her mom into something perverted. Because she didn't know what else to do, she just turned and started walking away fast.

She heard his footsteps behind her and picked up her pace until she was nearly running. She heard his speed pick up, too, his feet hitting the grass, and then the pavement, as he crossed the street, catching up to her with ease as they both reached her front yard at the same time. The grass tickled her bare feet, the dew leaving drops of wetness like rain on her skin as she slowed her pace, admitting defeat. Though the air had taken on the chill of fall, her cheeks were flushed hot with anger. She hoped her grandmother really would, by some miracle, call the cops this time. Micah Berg deserved whatever he got. She hated him for this. Hated herself for running outside in the middle of the night to help him, to save him.

He grabbed her arm, but she twisted away. "Violet, please," he said, and the desperation in his voice was unmistakable. She couldn't help it; she turned back to look at him. He was huffing, and his face was red and swollen where Devin had hit him. He would be bruised in the morning.

"What?" she asked, the indignation in her voice as unmistakable as the desperation in his. She set her jaw, willed herself not to cry. She'd been so stupid, thinking he could be interested in her. He was just a stupid jock, riddled with teenage-boy hormones, thinking he could cash in on his proximity to the so-called prostitute's daughter. "What do you want with my mother?" she asked through gritted teeth.

He glanced at the front of her house, as if he was worried about her grandmother coming outside. "Can we go back to my house? Please? It's really important." He hitched his jaw in the direction of his house. "We can go inside and talk there, where it's private."

She crossed her arms and glared at him. "You can ask me whatever it is right here. I don't exactly want your parents to wake up and find me in your house in the middle of the night," she said.

He shook his head. "They're out of town," he said. "Gone to help my sister move into a new apartment. Hers flooded or something."

"They left you here alone?" she asked, astounded. After everything that had happened, it was hard to believe they'd do that again.

He rolled his eyes at this. "It's not like I'm gonna do anything again," he grumbled.

She widened her eyes at him. "You were just brawling with a guy in the middle of the night, on a *school night*, in your front yard. That's doing something, Micah."

He put his hands up and gave her a wounded look. "Hey, I didn't start that. He texted me, asked to speak to me. Stupid me, I thought maybe he'd had a change of heart, was gonna say he believed me or something. I didn't know he was gonna start a fight."

"Whatever," she said. "I'm not going inside your empty house with you at this time of night."

He squared his shoulders and glared at her. "What is it you think I'm gonna do? Kill you?" His shoulders dropped and he sighed deeply. "Man, I thought maybe you were different from everyone else. Just forget it," he said, and began to walk away. He took a few steps.

"Wait," she said.

He froze and turned back to look at her. She saw the hope there, and she couldn't bear to dash it. It was a funny thing, she thought, to hold someone else's hope when lately so many other people had been holding hers in their hard, calloused hands.

"No monkey business," she said, then instantly regretted her choice of words. She intended to sound tough but came out sounding like a grandma.

He just laughed in response. "You're a funny girl, Violet," he said.

He started to walk and motioned for her to follow him. So she did, catching up to him so that they walked side by side. They crossed the street, then his yard, and, this time, went inside the house. Chipper, asleep on the couch, thumped his tail as they walked in but didn't bother to rise.

"Some guard dog you are," Micah said to him. "I'm out there getting my ass kicked, and you don't even bother to bark." He gestured to the kitchen table for her to sit and opened the fridge. He looked over at her, the light from the fridge illuminating scratches on his face. He was going to look bad tomorrow. "Water?" he asked, holding up a bottle.

She accepted the bottle and twisted the top off, taking a long, grateful gulp and thinking as she did how funny life was; she was inside Micah Berg's house at 1:12 a.m., drinking water with him at his kitchen table, the two of them completely alone. If she still had a best friend, this would be quite a story to tell her. Nicole probably wouldn't believe it. Violet herself hardly did. She had a fleeting, panicky thought: It was the middle of the night; maybe she was dreaming. She waited till Micah looked away, reached down, and pinched herself on the arm. It hurt. Nope. This was real.

She took another sip of the water and held up the bottle. "The water was a good idea," she said. The water was a good idea? Just add that to the monkey business comment, why don't you? She wished she could reach into the air and retrieve her stupid words. He'd already said she was funny, and she was pretty sure he didn't mean funny ha ha, but funny odd. Way to reinforce it, she thought. "What was it you wanted to ask me?" Maybe he'd forget she'd said it if she turned his thoughts back to why he'd invited her in.

He looked dubious, or maybe embarrassed. He took a sip of water. "OK, I'm just gonna say it."

She looked at him, trying to make her face impassive while at the same time desperate to know what it was that he was so nervous to ask her. She nodded once, as if to say it was OK, whatever it was. Inside she wanted to scream, *Just say it already!*

"Well, you know about your mom, right?"

She refrained from saying duh and just nodded her head.

He shook his head and closed his eyes. "Of course you know about your mom. What I meant is do you know that part of the reason they won't let her out of jail is because they want her client list and she won't tell them where it is?"

Though the adults in her life had told her nothing, she'd read whatever she could online. She nodded once, feeling the shame of being Norah Ramsey's daughter like a scarf around her neck. Sometimes the scarf tightened, and this was one of those times. She could barely breathe as she waited for him to speak.

He took another long pull of the water, a different kind of liquid courage from whatever Devin Ames had been drinking. "I think my dad's name might be on that list," he blurted out.

She looked at him, waited for him to meet her eyes. As he did, the scarf loosened and she could breathe again. Shame, it seemed, was best when shared. It didn't even have to be the same kind of shame.

"Why?" she asked, her voice barely a whisper. She took another sip of water. "I mean why would you think that?"

"I overheard him on the phone. He was talking about it. It sounded like he might . . . know something." He shook his head. "I could be wrong. I might be. But"—he put the water bottle on the table and studied it—"this family can't go through one more thing," he said. "If he were exposed . . ." He looked back at her. "It'll be the end of us."

She felt the prickle of awareness dawning. He was getting at something. Something that involved her. "I don't—"

He held up his hand before she could say, "Know anything."

"I don't expect you to have any magic answers. But I just wanted to say that if you know anything, if you have the faintest clue where she could've hidden that client list, well . . ." He shrugged, looked down at the table, inhaled and exhaled loudly before looking up again. "You owe me nothing. I know that. But just, please, tell me. If he is on it, then I want to destroy it."

"But—"

"I know what you're going to say: He deserves it. If he did that, he's a bad guy, my mom should know. Believe me, I've thought about all of that. But the truth is, I don't care about that. If he made a mistake, he made a mistake." He pressed his palms on the table. "So have I."

She nodded once, an acknowledgment. She wanted to tell him what she knew about his mistake. She almost did, right then, but decided now was not the time. Later. She would tell him; she would offer to tell others. She would help him fix that if she couldn't help him fix this. The police had searched their house and found nothing. Violet hadn't even known what her mother was up to. She'd believed she owned a marketing company. She'd just never known exactly what her mother was marketing.

"My dad stood by me," Micah continued. "He never doubted my story. He's a good man, and his name on some list from the past doesn't change that."

She nodded again, thinking as she did. Spinning back through times with her mother, wondering if there could be something she had missed, something that seemed innocuous at the time.

"He's my best friend," Micah said. "Really, my only friend anymore. I just thought if I could help him out, however possible, I should at least try. After everything he's done for me." He drank the last of the water and crushed the bottle, twisting it as the loud crackling noise reverberated through the room, waking Chipper, who sat up and glared in their direction. "Besides, I honestly don't think my mother could handle it. I think it would be the end of her. Or at the very least, the end of them."

Violet did not say that maybe it should be the end of them. That if his father had done something like that, maybe he wasn't the man Micah thought he was. She did not say any of that, because she suspected that was the last thing Micah wanted to hear. All he wanted to hear right now was that Violet had some secret knowledge she'd never told anyone. So she spoke up.

"There is a storage unit," she said, the words spilling out of her, even as she wondered if she should be saying what she was saying. She recalled the times her mother had taken her there to put something in or take something out. She knew some of her father's things were there but hadn't bothered to consider the rest of it, till now. "I don't think anyone knows about it. I've not seen it mentioned in any of the reports I've read. I'm pretty sure they didn't search it."

He looked eager. "But maybe we could?"

"I don't see why not," she said, feeling slightly sick as she said it, hoping she was doing the right thing. Right or not, she'd said it now. There was no taking it back.

Polly

She sat in the front room, in a dining table chair she'd pulled over to the window, and watched for her granddaughter to come out of the house across the street. There'd been a moment when Violet had walked back to the house like she was going to come inside, and Polly had breathed a sigh of relief. Crisis avoided. But then the boy had run after her, had caught up to her and said something. Whatever it was had worked, and Violet walked back over to his house and went inside with him, leaving her to wait, to watch, and to wonder what exactly was going on with those two.

That afternoon in the yard, they'd seemed to barely know each other. Now they were chummy. It didn't make sense. But, of course, they were teenagers. They didn't always make sense. They ran hot. They ran cold. They were rarely lukewarm. Polly thought about the handsome boy across the street with his disarming grin and sculpted arms. She doubted Violet ran cold when she was around him.

She wondered if she should march across the street and demand that Violet come out of that house, make a scene if she had to, for Violet's own good. She wondered if that boy was calculating enough to use what was happening with Norah as some sort of emotional bait for her poor, unsuspecting granddaughter. Polly got the sense that Violet wasn't exactly experienced with boys. She wasn't aware yet of what she had, of what awaited her. Polly had been the same way at that age.

Polly stared hard at the dark shape of the house across the street, debating what to do. This boy could lure Violet in and take advantage of her. And if that happened on her watch, Norah would never forgive her. Not that Norah had a position to judge anyone right now. But if Polly knew her daughter, Norah would still find a way. She tried to choose which of them to alienate: Violet now or Norah later. She thought about Norah at fifteen, with her anger and her rebellion and her quiet seething regard for Polly. She didn't want Violet to feel that way about Polly. But she also didn't want Violet to be taken advantage of, forever changed by some boy who didn't know what he held in his hands. Polly stood up and went to the bedroom to put on a sweater and shoes. Better to cause a scene more properly attired.

She was slipping her feet into flip-flops when she heard the front door open and close. She tiptoed down the hall and around the corner just in time to see Violet's skinny ankles disappearing up the stairs, returning to her room. Polly checked the lock on the front door, made sure the alarm code was reset, and went to her own room, climbing back into bed with relief. Barney, thankfully, stayed asleep on the bed and didn't bark at Violet's entry as he'd done on her exit, waking Polly to the fact that her granddaughter was up to something, that this sweet, innocent child had secrets and agendas of her own. She supposed that everyone did.

Bess

She saw the news at the garden center on a TV playing behind the register. It was not one of the big chain garden centers but a small family-owned place. She preferred it, always went there first, resorting to the larger, more impersonal places only when she had to. At this store, they took the time to know her, to remember her.

"Isn't that near your house?" the clerk asked. He knew where she lived, knew all about her soil and where the sun rose and set on her property.

She watched the words scroll across the screen: "Body Found in Remote Lake." The footage was of the water's edge and the standard-issue shoes of officers walking back and forth. She thought of the home invasion that had occurred last year in a nearby neighborhood, the self-defense classes she took, not because she really thought the classes would make a difference, but because she needed to feel like she was doing something to fight back. She tasted the familiar metallic fear, told herself not to panic. But it was a body, a dead person discarded in a lake. Wasn't that cause for panic? And the clerk was right: the lake was within walking distance of her house.

She forced herself to smile at him as she took her bag of plant food in one arm and her new Monstera plant in the other. "That is near my neighborhood. But it's not actually in it. Thank goodness!" she heard herself say brightly, as if it were some other person talking, a person who believed that as long as danger was a certain distance away, it could be kept at bay.

She put her purchases in the car and slunk behind the steering wheel, staring at the front of the garden center as she collected herself. She reached for her phone, her secret phone, and pressed Jason's number into the keypad, hoping he would answer, hoping he was OK. She listened as it rang and rang, with no answer. She huffed and dropped the phone back into her purse. She sat quietly for a moment longer, then headed home, driving the longer way that would take her by the turnoff to the lake where the body was found, as if she might spot something from the road, something that would put her mind at ease.

She spun terrible scenarios about Jason as she drove: He had decided to do drugs again and, high, fell into the lake and drowned. He had been caught stealing out of someone's shed, and the home-owner accidentally killed him, then put his body in the lake to hide what had happened. Her route home took her right by the rutted-out dirt road people took to get down to the lake, a place used mostly for fishing and by teenagers looking to hide from their parents, the kind of place you had to know about to access.

She tried to slow down, but a cop stationed on the road waved her on, his expression impassive. She continued on to her own neighborhood, turning into the entrance with a sense of fear. When she passed Norah's house, she saw a woman standing in the driveway getting something out of a small car. Norah's mother, it must be. She should go by, introduce herself, see if she could assist in some way. After what had happened with Violet and Nicole, it was the least she could do.

She pulled into her own driveway to find a familiar car parked there blocking her entrance to the garage. She put her car into park, turned off the engine, and closed her eyes for a moment. When she opened them again, Eli's car was still there. She gripped the steering wheel tighter, then tighter still, barely suppressing the scream that lurked in her throat. This was the last thing she needed right now. She got out, slammed the car door a little too hard, then marched up the front walk, using her key to unlock the door.

She expected to find Casey and Eli sitting in the den, music playing, her legs resting on his lap like she used to do. But when she walked in, there was no one there. She almost called out, "Casey?" but something stopped her. Maybe they'd left in Casey's car. She checked the garage, but Casey's car was sitting in its usual spot. Maybe they'd gone on a walk. Casey had been taking lots of walks lately. And then she heard it, coming from upstairs, a giggle, then a lower voice. They had a "no boys in your room" policy, and Casey knew that. But maybe, since being away at college, she'd forgotten the rules or thought they'd changed. Bess marched up the stairs to remind her daughter just what the rules were.

She threw open the door and saw skin. So much skin. Male skin and female skin tangled up in one flesh-colored tableau. Bess saw Eli's short dark hair and Casey's long blonde hair, and then Casey's round O of a mouth as Casey realized that she and Eli weren't alone. Bess heard her name being called, but not her real name, her other name, a name she used to think summed up her sole purpose on earth in just three letters. But lately, between Nicole's bitchiness and demands and Casey's moodiness and secrets, she wasn't so sure she wanted that to be the case anymore. Regardless, she heard it echoing off the lavender walls of her daughter's room, "Mom!"

She turned and ran back down the hall, trying to process what had just happened, struggling to make sense of it. Her daughter had invited her ex-boyfriend over and slept with him? For what? Nostalgia? Rebellion? Loneliness? Bess went to the Keurig, slammed a pod into the holder, then slammed it shut. Just please, she thought, don't let it be for love.

She listened to the spitting, hissing noise as the coffee filled her cup. She breathed in the smell, tried to think about that and not her daughter, upstairs right now, getting dressed with the boy she'd been having sex with in Bess's own home while she was out running errands. Casey used to be so smart; there was no way college had turned her this dumb. She needed to press her daughter again to tell her what was really going on; she would have to demand the truth. She took her mug, dosed it with more sugar and cream than usual. She didn't know if she was ready for whatever Casey had to tell her.

She took the mug and went and sat at the kitchen table. She looked at the chair Jason usually sat in, wondering if it was hypocritical of her to expect her daughter to confess her secrets when she had no intention of doing the same. Jason was this secret thing, her secret thing. And besides, it wasn't hurting anything. She was helping him; that was all. Sure, she'd come to care about him, but it was inevitable to care about someone who depended on you the way he did, someone who listened to you the way he did, someone who allowed you to say anything you wanted for as long as you needed to talk.

She wanted to call him again, to make sure he was OK. But with Casey coming downstairs at any moment, she didn't dare. Instead she took a sip of coffee, and she waited, listening to the little thumps and low murmured bits of conversation. She tried to imagine how Casey was going to get him out of the house. Almost any exit would involve Eli having to walk right by her. She could picture him walking quickly past her, head ducked, eyes downcast. The walk of shame, indeed.

She took another sip and thought of the day she'd told Casey she had to break up with Eli. She'd used reason and logic, appealing to her daughter's rational side. It made sense, she'd said. She would be a day's drive away at a university; he would still be home, working and attending community college. Their lives were going in two different directions. Why not go ahead and save themselves from the heartache and drama of maintaining a long-distance relationship? Why not give herself license to fully embrace college life without worrying about Eli back at home? It was a high school relationship, and they would no longer be in high school anymore. High school relationships, she had said, were not likely to last into adulthood.

"But you and Dad worked out," Casey had countered. Exactly my point, Bess had thought but of course not said. She did not want her daughter to know that the main reason she was discouraging her high school relationship from lasting was because her own had. She was trying to save her from the same fate.

It had taken some lobbying, a lot of tears, a short spate of depression, and a good bit of arguing until, eventually, Casey had come around to her way of thinking. It had been, Bess firmly believed, for the best. That was the last thing she'd said to Casey when they left her on the steps of her dorm and drove the eight hours home: "It's for the best, you'll see."

But, clearly, it had not been for the best. None of this—not Casey's mysterious and unexplained reappearance, not her long walks and at times questionable sobriety, not her sneakily reuniting with Eli, and certainly not this latest situation—felt like "the best" that Bess had had in mind. Bess had wanted a clean slate for her daughter, a fresh start. Not a re-creation of Bess's own life, reproduced like a photocopy. Casey deserved more. And wasn't that noble? To want more for your child?

She heard footsteps on the stairs, Eli's heavier clomping, Casey's tiptoe step. She was surprised Casey was walking him out and not hiding in her room. Bess sat perfectly still, waiting for what would happen next. She expected Casey to take him out the front door and then scamper back upstairs. Would Bess go confront her after he was gone? She knew she should, but the impending conversation was a weight sitting on her chest. When she tried to form the words to say to her daughter, they remained shapeless and foreign inside her head, like speaking another language entirely. She wished Casey was at college where she belonged, away from here, doing whatever she pleased while

Bess remained blissfully ignorant. That was the deal, but Casey had broken it.

She heard the footsteps coming closer and looked up to find Eli standing in the opening that led into the kitchen. Though it had been only a few months since she'd last seen him, he looked bigger, more filled out, more mature. As he opened his mouth to speak, his face looked as if an invisible someone were pointing an invisible gun at his head. But he spoke anyway. "I wanted to apologize," he said. "For what happened. For being in your home like that. I disrespected you and I'm sorry."

She circled the mug with both her hands and blinked at him. She admired his bravery. When he could've slunk away, he'd faced things head-on. She had a thought: Maybe he was a good guy. Maybe she'd done the wrong thing in encouraging Casey to break up with him. "Thank you for saying so," she said. "If you don't mind, I'd like to speak to my daughter alone now."

He nodded and turned back to Casey, who stood just behind him looking mortified. "Call you later?"

Casey nodded just once, and he walked out, leaving the two of them alone. Bess had an image of him stepping out the front door, then breaking into a sprint to his car. She wouldn't blame him. She wished she could sprint out of there, too.

Instead she turned to her daughter and opened her mouth to speak. She sat there for a moment, frozen, with her mouth agape, as she searched for the right words to say. But no words came out. "I . . . ," she said. She closed her mouth.

"I'm sorry," Casey said, filling the silence. "I shouldn't have had him here."

Bess opened her mouth again, but this time in shock. This time the words came tumbling off her tongue. "You think having him here is what you did wrong?"

"Of course that's not all. It was just the first thing." Bess watched two spots of color appear on Casey's cheeks. She thought of when

Casey was three and had gotten into her makeup. She'd put lipstick on her cheeks, thinking it was blush. It had looked similar to what Casey looked like now, the defined red circles in the same spots. Bess had been angry at her then, too. Back then it was just for ruining makeup, which could be replaced. Now it was for potentially ruining her life, which couldn't.

"You've been seeing him since you've been home, haven't you?"

"A few times is all. I ran into him getting pizzas. I didn't plan it." She said this like it mattered, like intent was the big issue.

"You planned today. He didn't just happen by when I was gone."

Casey reached over and picked up a candle off the counter, inspected it like it was the most interesting thing in the room. "I guess," she said to the candle.

Bess stood up and carried her empty mug to the sink, ran the water to rinse it, thinking as she did of what to say next, where to take the stalled conversation. Should she just tell her never to do it again and let her go? Should she have the safe-sex talk with her again, just as a refresher? Or should she dig deeper, finally probe as to why her daughter was even in her kitchen now and not back at the University of Alabama, where she was supposed to be? Bess wished she had a guide for this type of thing, a script to go by. So much of parenting was ad-libbing, an improv act that wasn't the slightest bit funny.

She shut off the water and loaded the mug into the dishwasher. "I need to know why you came home," she said. She turned to look at Casey. "Is it because of Eli?"

Casey looked down at the floor. "No," she said.

Bess waited Casey out, let the uncomfortable silence stretch out between them.

"Are you struggling in your classes?" she tried again. It was like being the first to blink in a staring contest.

"No," Casey said again.

Bess felt her heart pick up speed. So it wasn't because she missed the love of her life too much, and it wasn't because she was having a hard time academically. Those were the two easy ones. She swallowed. "Did something happen?" she asked.

Casey's eyes darted over to her, then away. Bess watched her look out the window, as if she'd suddenly taken an interest in birds. She knew her daughter was deciding what to say, weighing and measuring her words. *Tread lightly,* a voice inside her warned. *Don't push her.*

Casey looked back at her, her eyes wide. "Can I talk about it when I'm ready?" she asked.

Bess exhaled, ashamed at the relief she felt. "As long as you promise that you will. If nothing else, we need to talk about your plans for school this semester. This can't be good, you missing so many classes," she said.

"I've been talking to the dean. I'm good on that end."

Bess nodded, sensing that they'd just made progress and she shouldn't push any further. Right now, she assured herself, she was right to relent. They both needed a reprieve. This wasn't cowardice, it was striking a delicate balance with her daughter. "Just promise me we'll talk soon."

Casey gave her a small, sad smile. "I promise," she said.

As soon as Casey disappeared up the stairs, Bess grabbed for her other phone, hidden in the deep recesses of her purse, down where the stray pennies and random pieces of gum hung out. She brought it to life and hoped for a missed call. There was none. She thought about dialing his number again but didn't want to seem needy, or desperate, even though she was. She needed to know he was not the person they found in the lake; she needed to hear his voice.

She hid the phone back in her purse, but that didn't mean she stopped thinking about Jason. She thought about him as she worked in the yard, giving her plants borders in a way she couldn't with her own children. She thought about him as she cleaned her already clean house, scrubbing away the things she didn't want to see. She thought about him as she used the elliptical upstairs, sweating and pumping her legs up and down in an effort to get it all out—all the stress, all the worry, all the nagging doubt. Of course none of it worked.

The more she worried about Jason, the less she worried about her daughter and what had happened to her. She felt the tug of guilt over that. She knew she should be thinking about Casey—about what she'd walked in on with Eli, about what had brought her home from college and why she wasn't ready to talk about it yet. But those things seemed so huge, so insurmountable.

It was better, and easier, to worry about someone who mattered, but not that much. Someone who'd become important to her only recently, instead of nearly two decades ago. If she focused on Jason, she didn't have to focus on Casey. If she could get ahold of him, if she could talk to him, maybe she'd tell him about Casey, about how worried and scared she was, how out of control she felt.

Jason would understand. He would say, in that way he had, "Oh, darlin', I'm sorry." Steve never said things like that to her. And that was why she needed Jason now, more than ever. She went back to her purse, fished the phone out again, and dialed. She listened to it ring and ring and, when he didn't answer, she finally, after a long and valiant effort to keep the tears at bay, ended the call and went to the shed to cry alone.

Nico

He stood at the outer edge, banished from the action because of his potential connection to whoever was in that body bag. They'd told him to go home and wait for a call, but he knew they didn't really expect him to. More like they had to say it for the sake of protocol. He saw them cast sympathetic glances his way from time to time. And he tried to respond with what he hoped looked like a brave smile.

He kept a safe distance, watching the investigators in an effort to keep his eyes from straying to that body bag, to resist the temptation to run over to it, unzip it, and see who was inside. The captain told him he didn't want to see that. Matteo or not, whoever was in that bag no longer looked human after spending time underneath the water.

When they were kids, Matteo used to put algae on his head and chase Nico around the pond near their house, moaning, his arms outstretched in a zombie-walk parody. "I want to eat your brains," he would say. Now it felt like Matteo had eaten his heart, devoured it all for himself, leaving nothing for Nico or his wife and kids. Now it was Nico who was the zombie. He glanced over at the bag, half expecting Matteo to sit up out of it, eye sockets empty, his open mouth a permanent yawn. Nico shook his head and pulled his phone from his pocket to distract himself.

Sure enough, he had a notification. Right on schedule, his daughter had come home from school. He clicked on the camera to watch her arrival, turning to walk a bit farther away so that he could listen. She usually sang as she ambled up the driveway and let herself into the house. Since the separation, Karen had been working part-time, gone when Lauren got home from school. He felt bad about another change for the kids, worse about the fact that his daughter was home without supervision, which made his monitoring of the family's security cameras more important, he rationalized. And that wasn't going to change.

Karen had emailed him last night to tell him she'd been offered more hours and perhaps with "things the way they are," it'd be best if she took the work. They were reduced to emails now. It was the safest, least emotional way to communicate. Phone calls could escalate; texts were easy to ignore. He couldn't believe it had come to this, but he was powerless to stop it. In order to stop it, he'd have to know if it was Matteo in that bag, and if it was, he'd have to know who put him there. And then he'd have to see that person brought to justice. He knew himself, and he would not be satisfied if the mystery of Matteo's disappearance had just been solved. One answer would inevitably lead to a whole host of new questions.

He forced himself to focus on the camera, watching as a random bird flitted across its unblinking field of vision once or twice. He glanced up, scanned the scene in front of him again, and contemplated just leaving. But what if he missed something—some piece of evidence, a tip kindly passed on discreetly by a fellow brother-in-arms, a diver finding something significant in the submerged car. Anything could happen.

He looked back down at the camera, hearing the sound of voices—not just one, and not his daughter's. He watched as two boys appeared. They laughed low and mumbled things to each other as they approached the door, their heads ducked low and away from the camera's eye like they knew it was there. He wondered where they'd come from. Were they from her school bus? But these two boys looked older than her. The week before, he'd seen her get dropped off by an unfamiliar car, but the windows had been tinted black, and he couldn't see the face of the driver. He'd called Karen, tried to work it into conversation as to whether Lauren still rode the school bus to and from school. Her voice had gone up an octave when she asked why, in that way that told him he had better tread lightly lest she get suspicious.

"Oh nothing," he'd said. "I just thought she'd said something about getting a ride because of her piano practice."

"Lauren isn't playing piano anymore. It isn't in the budget," Karen had said, using that tone that told him this was something he should've known, another failure on his part. But instead of getting angry in response, he'd expertly steered the conversation toward finances and away from why he was asking about how Lauren was getting to and from school. He couldn't afford for his wife to figure out he was monitoring their comings and goings and take away his only means of keeping tabs on the family.

Even if he didn't live at home anymore, it was his job to look out for them, to protect them at all costs. He looked up at the body bag, now with a stretcher beside it. Then back down at Lauren, standing outside the door, talking to the two thugs. He would bet money that Karen never checked the security camera unless she was home and was looking out for herself, her safety. Though she loved and cared for the children, safeguarding them had always been his jurisdiction.

"Tell them to leave," he said aloud, as if Lauren could hear him. "Don't you dare let them into my house." From the angle they were standing, with their chins dipped low, he still couldn't see their faces, and he wondered if they were boys from the neighborhood or if she'd met them somewhere else. Strangers. They were strangers, and they were with his little girl while she was home alone. Alone and unprotected.

It was all he could do not to run to his car and speed back to his house. But he kept his cool; took deep, even breaths; and willed his daughter to be as smart as he'd raised her to be. He exhaled loudly when the boys finally said their goodbyes and ambled off down the drive. As Lauren safely entered the house and he heard the click of the lock turning behind her, he exited out of the security app in time to see the body bag hefted onto the stretcher. The attendants began pushing it over rocks and uneven ground up to the ambulance parked several hundred yards away, waiting to take the person—whomever he was—to be identified. Now Nico would wait to see if his questions would be answered, and whether those answers would spark a great many more questions.

Polly

She listened to the message a second time, making sure she had a handle on the situation, keeping the panic at bay a moment longer. This time it wasn't Calvin calling, but Dwight, her personal banker, letting her know that her husband had been to the bank and would she please call him back because he had "some concerns." She clutched the phone to her chest, rolled her eyes to the ceiling as if seeking heavenly aid, though she and the Lord had stopped speaking years ago. It was never too late to ask, she thought. She recalled her second husband, Paul Ferry, who had loved God far more than he'd loved her. In the end, it had come between them.

During that marriage, she'd carted Norah to church, well, religiously. Maybe that had done damage to the child, brought them all to this point in time. Norah had known Polly was no church lady, eyeing her with a knowing that made Polly so uncomfortable she had scolded the child. Polly had pretended to be someone she was not so that Paul Ferry would love her. Had this been a message she'd transferred to her daughter? That it's OK to be duplicitous for the sake of a man?

She'd been a bad mother. That was why she was here; that was why Norah was in jail. In that moment, guilt joined anxiety, a dynamic duo that could take her out completely if given the time. But she couldn't give in to them. Not today, with Violet coming home from school and dinner to make. You worry about one thing at a time, she told herself.

Now, you call Dwight. Later, you figure out where you went wrong with your only child. She hit the button to return the call.

"Dwight?" she asked when he answered. "What's going on?" She had intended to keep the panic out of her voice, but she failed from the get-go.

"Well, Calvin was here. And we just about didn't get him out. I thought he was maybe gonna pull some kind of siege until we got you here. Like a hostage situation?"

"Uh-huh," she agreed, picturing Calvin stalking back and forth in front of a cowering Dwight. In her mind he held some sort of automatic weapon, though Calvin possessed no such thing. He did own a shotgun, though. And a little pistol. She'd never bothered to consider what kind.

"After he left, I had a talk with our manager about getting one of those scanners for weapons installed. I'll be honest, Polly, he seems unhinged."

Dwight was also not able to keep the panic out of his voice.

"Yeah, he keeps leaving me messages when I don't answer his calls," she said. "He's getting angrier."

"And you're sure he doesn't know where you are?"

She looked over her shoulder, as if Calvin might be lurking. "Pretty sure," she said.

"You better make certain sure. He's looking hard for you. And hell-bent on finding you." She shivered a little at his choice of the words *hell-bent*. Calvin had more than a little of the devil in him.

She thought about calling the police, but to tell them what? The last thing she needed was questions about her money. And if she called the police, they might start digging deeper because of her connection to a suspected criminal. No. She was on her own with this one. "I'm somewhere he would never know to track me down at, and I've got the GPS turned off on my phone so he can't see where I am. I think I'm safe."

"OK," Dwight said, though he didn't sound convinced. "Just one thought—I know it was your money that you brought into the marriage, and I certainly understand your desire to keep it. But in a court of law, he might be able to get half of it. You sure you shouldn't just hand it over, issue him divorce papers, and turn him loose?"

"Maybe," she said to appease Dwight, to make him think she was being reasonable. The truth was, this *was* her money, brought into the marriage by her, and certainly *not* earned together. Calvin had already spent more than his share, helping himself with the entitlement that only a good-looking man could possess. She didn't intend to hand any more over just because Calvin was potentially violent. She'd dealt with violent men before and lived to tell the tale. She'd take her chances with this one.

"Well, you think on it, and contact me if you'd like to make some arrangements. I'd be happy to meet you somewhere, get the money to give him, and then you could be free to go on about your business, whatever it is."

"That's kind of you, Dwight, and above and beyond the call of duty."

Dwight laughed nervously. "I'm just protecting my own neck, truth be told. I'd like to know that joker isn't going to be a problem. I really don't want to see him ever again."

"Me neither," said Polly.

She promised to call Dwight once she'd made her decision, even though her decision was already made. She would hunker down and hope that Calvin would eventually give up and move on to some other sugar mama. She tried not to think about how relentless he'd been in his pursuit of her, how determined he'd been, wearing her down like water wears down a rock. Eventually she'd just given in. But she was done giving in to men, letting go of things she valued—her money, her pride, her daughter—to keep them happy. She thought about Norah, staying in jail instead of giving in and producing her client list. She would take a page from her daughter's book and stand her ground, despite her fear.

What was that quote someone had posted on Facebook? "Courage is being afraid and doing it anyway." Something like that.

"One more thing," Dwight said as she was about to hang up. "You never told me you had a daughter. All this time I thought you never had children."

Her blood went from hot to cold in an instant. "What makes you say that?" she asked, even though she knew the answer.

"Calvin mentioned it. He said you were probably hiding out with your daughter. Is that where you are?"

She swallowed, her heart flopping wildly inside her chest. She wondered how in the world Calvin could've found out about Norah. And if he knew she had a daughter, then he might also know her name, or where she lived. She'd underestimated Calvin.

Polly chose her words in response to Dwight carefully, hoping she sounded far calmer than she was. "I prefer not to say where I am," she said. "You understand." A feeling came over her: the feeling that Dwight might not be entirely on her side. Never trust a man, her gut told her. Even one as benign as Dwight Richards. "I better go, Dwight," she said. "Thanks for your concern."

"I'll wait for your call," he said.

"OK," she trilled, forcing herself to sound unconcerned as she hung up the phone. "Don't hold your breath," she said aloud as silence on the other end told her Dwight was no longer there.

She jumped at the sound of the doorbell ringing, her body jolting like she'd been shocked. She crept out of her room and tiptoed down the hall, ignoring Barney's wild barking. She peered around the corner to where she could see the door. She couldn't see anyone looking through the glass panels on either side, so she tiptoed to the peephole, working to stay out of sight.

Just as she put her eye to the peephole, the doorbell rang again, as if the person on the other side knew the exact moment to depress it for maximum effect. The call from Dwight had gotten to her, made her paranoid. She needed to calm down. Just because Calvin knew that Polly had a daughter didn't mean he knew Norah's name. It was different from hers, after all. And Norah, for her own reasons, had stayed off the radar and wasn't easy to find herself. Overreacting would only make things worse. Just because Calvin knew she had a daughter didn't mean he was at her door.

And he wasn't. It was a lovely thin blonde woman with one of those sassy short haircuts—a pixie, Polly believed it was called—and the kind of wide, certain smile featured prominently in toothpaste commercials. Polly deemed she was safe, unless Calvin had employed this person as a decoy. "You're being ridiculous," she breathed as she opened the front door.

"Yes?" she asked the woman, who immediately thrust out her hand. Beside her, Barney checked out the guest, sniffed the air, and walked away. So different from his response to that detective. Barney was a good judge of character.

"You must be Violet's grandmother," the woman said.

Polly nodded and shook the woman's hand and gave her *her* most winning smile. It was a veritable smiling contest. But Polly couldn't shake the feeling that neither smile was genuine.

"I'm Polly Cartwright," she said, then instantly regretted using her last name. If Calvin came sniffing around—if he got this far—the name might tip someone off. She would not make that mistake again.

"I'm Bess Strickland," the woman said.

Ah, Polly thought, you're the one who kicked out my granddaughter in her time of need. You're part of the reason I'm here. I should thank you.

"We're neighbors of Norah and Violet." The woman hitched her thumb to the left. "We live up the street."

Polly nodded and said, "That's nice," because she didn't know what to say.

The woman stooped down and lifted a large vase of flowers that Polly hadn't noticed till then. She'd been too busy scanning the street for a glimpse of Calvin's truck. Bess thrust the vase into the space between the two of them. "I brought these for you."

"Did you carry these all the way down here?" Polly asked, the shock obvious on her face. "That vase is about as big as you are."

The woman grimaced. "Stupid, I know. It was an impulse. A foolish one, I guess."

"Well, they're lovely," Polly said, and reached to take the vase out of the woman's—she'd already forgotten what she had said her name was—hands. She held the vase awkwardly, flower petals tickling her chin and the earthy scent of gardenias filling her nose. "Thank you so much," she said, a cue for the woman to leave. But she stayed right where she was.

"I wanted to check on Violet," the woman said, an earnest look on her face. Her name came to mind just then: Bess, an old-fashioned-sounding name, but it suited her. "How's she doing?"

An honest reply formed in Polly's mind: Your guess is as good as mine. She stays in her room most of the time and doesn't talk much. Last night she snuck out with a boy in the middle of the night, and I have no idea if that kind of behavior is normal for her. I mean, I wasn't comfortable with it, but what can I say about it? I barely know the child.

Instead she just said, "She seems fine. Considering."

Bess nodded vigorously, agreeing, it seemed, with the word *considering*. "She's been through so much." She made a wretched face. "I felt so bad about what happened at my house." She looked to Polly, as if expecting her to comment on whatever awfulness had transpired in her home. Polly stared back at her blankly.

"She didn't tell you about it?" Bess prompted. Polly shook her head and shifted the heavy vase in her arms. Bess noticed and gestured toward the doorway. "Why don't you go put that down? It's heavy, I should know."

Polly nodded and turned to carry the vase deeper into the house, thinking Bess would wait for her on the porch. Instead, behind her, she heard her footsteps following. With Bess behind her, she was safe to roll her eyes. Now she had company, and who knew when the woman would leave? She carried the vase on into the kitchen and set it down in the middle of the table. She stepped back to admire it. She always did like fresh flowers on a table.

"Must've cost you a pretty penny," she said, gesturing at the arrangement.

Bess waved her arm dismissively. "Oh, it didn't cost a thing. I collect vases from Goodwill, and the flowers are from my garden."

"You grew these?" Polly took in the variety of flowers—zinnias and gardenias and asters and geraniums and, right in the center, a large sunflower. She couldn't imagine having the kind of garden where all of these grew, this lovely, even into October. Her yard must be gorgeous. She glanced over at her guest. Lovely like she was. Polly wondered if Bess knew she was lovely, or had forgotten, as some women do.

"It's the end of the season," Bess said. "I was lucky to still have these to offer. When I can, I like to take them to people. Try to brighten their day." She shrugged it off as if it were nothing.

Polly looked from the flowers to the woman. "It worked," she said.

A smile bloomed on Bess's face, then quickly died again. "I mainly wanted to apologize. For not keeping Violet like Norah intended. If I had, you wouldn't have had to come here. You'd be off living your life, oblivious."

Polly gave her a polite smile in response, not saying anything about the life she had left behind. How, while Allen's phone call had entangled her in her daughter's mess, it had also freed her, in a way. If not for this place to come to, she would still be back in Hickory, debating leaving thieving Calvin and wondering how to pull it off. But she could say none of this to a stranger. For a moment Polly wished she had a friend to confide in, though her trust of other women had dried up years ago when her best friend had run off with a man she'd believed would be her third husband. She'd not really let anyone in after that, deciding she was better off telling her troubles to a dog.

"It was no trouble," she said. "I was happy to help." This was as close to the truth as she could get.

Bess shook her head. "Well, I still feel like I failed Violet, and Norah."

"You two are friends?" Polly asked. In school Norah had been popular, well liked, a circle of girls always around her, eager to do her bidding. The way Polly saw it, it wouldn't have been a far jump for her to successfully run a ring of escorts.

"Well, we're neighbors," Bess said with a light tone, but her face looked sad. Polly could tell there was more to the story that Bess didn't want to get into. And she respected that. "She knew she could call on me when she was in a bind," Bess added. "And I would call her if I needed something."

Polly could tell that Bess was the type of person who rarely, if ever, needed something. But she didn't share her observation. She just said, "Well, that's nice. Good neighbors are so valuable."

"They certainly are," Bess said. "Of course, I didn't feel like I was much of a good neighbor in this case." She pointed at the flowers. "I guess that's why I brought these. An atonement of sorts."

"A beautiful one at that." Polly cocked her head at Bess. "But you know you don't have to atone for anything, right?"

Bess's eyes widened. She blinked. "Well, sure. Of course. I know. I was kind of making a joke. Being dramatic."

"I just want you to know that Violet and I are fine." She amended herself. "We'll be fine." Polly didn't want this woman feeling responsible for them. She was just a neighbor, after all.

"I know you will. I know Violet's in capable hands." As if summoned, the sound of the front door opening and closing signaled Violet's arrival from school.

"Violet?" Polly called.

"I'm home," Violet said, followed by the sound of her feet clomping up the steps. So much for a proper greeting. So much for Violet's arrival signaling to Bess it would be a good time to leave.

When the sound of the footsteps faded, Bess kept talking, this time in a lowered voice. "Are you hearing anything about when Norah might get out? I mean, do you know how long you'll have to stay here?"

This was a good question, one without an answer. Polly shook her head. "Norah is refusing to cooperate with their investigation. They want her to turn over her client list, possibly testify against some of the, um, gentlemen. If she keeps refusing, they're saying she'll have to do time."

Bess leaned forward, her eyes wide. "And you'll stay here if that happens?"

Polly shrugged. "Not sure. I guess I'll cross that bridge when I get to it. Right now I'm just taking it one day at a time." She sounded like she was in Alcoholics Anonymous. But alcohol was not her addiction; men who turned out to be worthless were.

Bess nodded her agreement, but then a concerned look filled her face. "And you're not worried or afraid being here?"

Polly cocked her head. "Afraid?" For a moment she thought that Bess was referring to Calvin. But how could she possibly know about him? Calvin was Polly's secret, one she would carry alone.

Bess gave her a stalwart smile. "Oh, don't listen to me. I'm a worrywart."

"No," Polly pressed. "What made you ask that? I'd like to know." If there was some danger—something she needed to protect Violet from—she wanted to know. As if Calvin wasn't enough.

"Oh, I was just thinking about that body they found." She hitched her thumb behind them, referring to where, Polly couldn't have guessed. "In a lake down the road. Everyone's talking about it, speculating. I mean the two things being so close together and all, and the timing.

People like to talk, you know. Make connections where probably there aren't any."

Polly made herself say, "Uh-huh," in her most blasé tone, when inside her wheels were turning. A body? In a lake? Near here? She'd read that a man had gone missing around here—and now she wondered if that was him that they'd found. "Have they said who it is yet?" she asked.

When Bess answered no, her voice quavered and she looked stricken.

"Are *you* worried?" Polly asked her.

"N-no," Bess said.

Polly raised her eyebrows to indicate that she knew Bess was thinking something she wasn't saying.

"I mean there's this homeless man I've been . . . helping, and I haven't seen him around in a while. So, I've been concerned. You know, that it could be him." Bess gave her a smile that didn't quite reach her eyes. "That's all." She said it as if that really was all. But Polly knew a bullshitter when she met one. The fact that Bess wasn't telling her something made her all the more interesting, all the more relatable.

"Yes," Polly said. "I can see how that would be concerning."

"Well," Bess said, "I guess I better be going. Gotta see about dinner."

Polly nodded and smiled. "Yes, I better do the same." This time the smile was genuine; the thought of making a meal for her granddaughter, a comfort. She enjoyed seeing about Violet's dinner each evening, making meals she once had made for Norah, deciding how much the child was like her mother based on her reactions. She considered it a little experiment, one more way to learn more about her granddaughter. Tonight she was making Slap Your Mama pork chops, a recipe she'd gleaned long ago from a coworker. Norah had always loved those. Norah could say whatever she wanted about Polly's mothering skills, but she'd always eaten well.

Bess turned to go, then turned back. "Would you like for me to let you know if I hear anything? You know, about the body?"

"Well, sure," Polly said. It would be nice to gain any information Bess could share. Polly had the feeling she was the hub of the gossip wheel, always the first to know. Polly had known many like her through the years. Usually she steered clear of them, but something about Bess's demeanor told her that there was more to Bess than met the eye. It wasn't what she said; it was what she worked to withhold. Polly guessed that most of the people who knew Bess took her at face value. And that that was a mistake. She guessed that if you bothered to dig deeper, you'd find not just one secret, but a whole cache of them. It made Polly like Bess Strickland.

She grabbed a piece of paper from Norah's desk, scribbled down her number, and handed it over to Bess, who waved the paper. "I'll be sure to call," Bess promised, and tucked the paper in the pocket of her jeans.

"Thank you," Polly said. "Call anytime." And as she said it, she realized she meant it. It would be nice to get a call from someone else besides her personal banker and her angry, thieving husband. "And thanks for the flowers," she called after Bess as she headed for the door.

Bess turned back for the second time. "Don't mention it," she said. And then she was gone.

Violet

At lunch that day, she hadn't eaten alone—a nice change. A new girl had come up and asked, "Is this seat taken?" When Violet said no, she'd sat down. The girl chatted about herself. It was her third day at school. She'd moved from Cleveland, Ohio, and was super nervous about making friends. She hadn't asked why Violet didn't appear to have any, for which Violet was grateful. Violet filled her in on things about the school, told her some tales and legends, all the while keeping an eye on Micah across the cafeteria. Though he still sat near the people he once called friends, he didn't interact with them, and they didn't interact with him. He kept his head down, focused on his tray full of food and his phone, though Violet doubted it was because anyone was texting him.

She chatted with the new girl through lunch, and, for a moment, it had felt like perfectly normal people having a perfectly normal lunch. Then the girl leaned forward, putting her elbows on the table, which was not proper etiquette, but a high school cafeteria was not the place to point that out. She hadn't whispered, because it was too loud in there for that, but she'd ducked her head before she spoke, as if someone might read her lips from across the room.

"I actually sat here on purpose," the girl said, her tone confessional.

Violet nodded, intrigued as to why anyone would want to sit by her. Ever since she and Nicole had stopped hanging out, she'd found a few acquaintances—she wouldn't call them friends—to eat and chat with, but they avoided her after the news had broken. Now she sat in the back corner of the cafeteria, scarfing down her lunch as fast as she could so she could go to class early and get a head start on homework. Her grades had never been better.

The new girl continued, "I wanted you to know that my mom died, kind of recently actually, and I thought maybe we'd have something in common. Since we both lost our moms."

Violet looked at the girl, blinking as she tried to process what she'd said. Lost her mom? She hadn't lost her mother; she knew exactly where she was. Sure, she wasn't physically with her right now, but she'd be back soon. Wouldn't she? Violet looked around the cafeteria. Did everyone here know something she didn't?

She'd scoured news articles to find out all she could—the things the adults wouldn't tell her—and she'd seen nothing that said that Norah's fate was determined as of yet. Based on what Violet had read, if her mother would just give up that stupid client list, she'd already be home. She hoped her mother could explain why she wouldn't just do the one thing that would reunite them. Violet hoped that when Norah did explain it, it would somehow make sense, so Violet could forgive her for what she'd put her through.

She thought of last night and Micah's request. She'd told him she'd help him. But she hadn't considered that finding the client list might help her, too. Maybe her mom wasn't willing to give up the information, but *an anonymous informant* could. And then the police would have no choice but to let Norah Ramsey go, because they would have what they wanted. Violet envisioned the headline just above a photo of Norah reuniting with her daughter after being released. Violet could make this happen.

She glanced over at Micah again, watched him as he looked down at his phone, surrounded by a cafeteria full of people but utterly alone. What if they found his dad's name on her mom's client list? Would she have to betray Micah to free her mom? She didn't want to think about that, about what could come. She would pretend to help Micah, and she would decide later what to do if the time came. It might not come at all, she consoled herself.

She turned back to the girl and started gathering up her things. "If you'll excuse me, I see someone I need to talk to. It's kind of urgent." She pointed in Micah's direction and stood up.

"Sure," the girl said. A worried look crossed her face. "I'll see you here tomorrow?"

"You bet," Violet said. She gave the girl her best, warmest smile, the one she'd used countless times to reassure her mother that nothing was wrong when really she'd failed a pop quiz or not been invited to a party or her best friend had inexplicably dropped her. Violet marveled that those things had ever seemed like problems. She made to leave, then remembered her manners. She turned back. "I'm sorry for your loss," she said. Then she walked quickly away, thinking as she did: But your loss isn't mine.

Bess Strickland was in her house when Violet got home, back in the kitchen buttering up her grandmother. Violet heard her voice and grimaced. Polly called her name and she replied, then walked upstairs, letting them hear her loud footsteps, before she tiptoed back downstairs so she could listen in on whatever those two were talking about. Thinking she was safely tucked away in her room, they would talk freely, and she wanted to know what they were saying.

Mostly they talked about nothing. She could hear a wariness in her grandmother's voice and an overeagerness in Bess's. Bess, Violet could tell, wanted Polly to like her. She liked that Polly wasn't falling under Bess's spell so easily. When the conversation turned to Norah's release, Violet's ears pricked. Though it sounded like they didn't know any more than she did. Actually, Violet knew more.

She knew about the storage unit her mom kept, had gone there with her several times over the years to stow things away or retrieve things. They'd had it since Norah and Violet's father had split up. She knew there was a filing cabinet and some old computer supplies in there. It was the place their old junk went to die. She hadn't considered that there was anything of importance in there, but that was back before she knew her mom had been hiding secrets. She had rented it in Violet's name, something she'd said she did so her dad couldn't find it. At the time, Violet had accepted the explanation at face value. But now everything her mom had done looked fishy.

Bess was now talking about a body. Violet tilted her head to try to hear better because the two of them had lowered their voices, perhaps out of reverence for the dead or perhaps because they really wanted to make sure she didn't hear, which made her want to hear all the more. A dead body had been found in the lake down the road.

It seemed, from what she could make out from the conversation, that the cops had said it could somehow relate to her mother? Was that possible? She now realized her mom was capable of things she'd not considered, but her mother wasn't capable of murder. Violet knew that, but she also knew that if there was a dead body possibly linked to her mother's case, things had just gotten even more serious. She needed to take action fast.

With the stealth of a cat burglar, she pivoted on her toes and tiptoed back upstairs to the safety of her room. She pulled her phone from her backpack and found the new contact she'd added in the wee hours of the morning. She held the phone and looked at Micah Berg's name there among the others. For a moment she let herself appreciate the miracle that she now had his number, and he had hers. Once upon a time, she would not have believed this possible. Then she pressed the call button, because there were things more important at hand than a silly crush. There were possibly lives on the line, and one in particular Violet wanted to save.

Casey

After the utter humiliation of her mom walking in on her and Eli, she had to escape the house and her mother's brooding silence. The discovery of the body in the lake was all anyone on social media was talking about, so she decided to go check it out. She cut through the woods, something she'd done more than once. One of her good friends in high school had lived near there, and they'd often walk to the lake to get out of earshot of their parents so they could talk freely. They'd walk laps around the lake, discussing boys and school gossip and anticipating a future that shimmered in front of them. Casey couldn't have fathomed that her future would be anything but #blessed. She'd never considered she'd end up back home not even halfway through her first semester at school.

She exited the woods and made the short walk over to the lake just in time to see the stretcher bearing a black body bag pushed by several men up the hill to a cluster of emergency vehicles. Cops milled everywhere. Trying not to be too obvious, she stood at the edge of the small crowd that had gathered to watch the techs collecting evidence, the officials walking around looking concerned and important.

She eavesdropped as she watched, piecing together what had happened by the bits of conversation she overheard from her fellow nosy neighbors. The body had been inside the submerged car for a good while, though they didn't know how long yet. The car had been discovered when, after the recent summer of drought, the lower lake level yielded its secret. A fisherman had spotted the top of the car just under the water. The officials would transport the car to some special cop garage and search for evidence. The death could've been an accident, but foul play hadn't been ruled out. Anyone knew that foul play meant murder.

The ambulance carrying the body drove away with no siren, no lights. There was no hurry, no urgency to do anything for whoever was in that bag. Without the ambulance around, Casey didn't have much to see, but the alternative was going home. So she stood and watched. She had thought that perhaps she'd take a photo to share on social media, but standing there it seemed like the wrong thing to do. A person's life had ended tragically, and they deserved respect. So she kept her phone in her pocket, not even pulling it out to check the texts coming in on the regular from Eli, who was still freaking out about what had happened.

"Your mom hates me now," he'd said in her room before he left.

"She wasn't a huge fan before," Casey had quipped, making Eli look more mournful.

A cop approached the group, looking tentative and apologetic. He held his hands up. "We're gonna have to ask you guys to move along," he said, his voice shaking from nerves. He was a rookie; he looked to be around her age.

Casey studied him, recognition niggling at her. He looked back at her, recognition dawning in his eyes, too. She knew him from somewhere, but where? He hadn't gone to her high school. He wasn't a neighbor. She could see that he was trying to place her as well. They smiled at each other, and she felt something else, too. Something surprising. Attraction. A stirring inside of her in a place she thought that Russell Aldridge had snuffed out. It was one thing to want Eli. To want him was to want to get back to herself, before, back to the comfort of someone who knew her then. But to want someone strange and new? She found it unexpected, and welcome. She was not dead inside as she had feared. She'd felt it partially with Eli, but that had felt like going backward, regressing. This felt like going forward, daring to hope.

She stepped closer to him, waited for him to finish addressing the crowd. "You look familiar," she said.

He nodded and motioned for her to move over to the side of the crowd. Together they took a few steps, creating enough distance that no one could eavesdrop. Satisfied that they were out of earshot, he spoke. "You do, too." He looked at her like she was the only person there. The crowd made no move to obey his dictate, but he didn't turn back to them. He'd forgotten his duty. "Have you been here all afternoon?" he asked.

She shook her head. "No, I just walked over." She hoped that would make her seem less nosy. "From my neighborhood." She hitched her thumb in the direction from which she'd come. "I like to walk," she said, the word *walk* triggering a memory. "Wait. I know where I've seen you before. You were at my neighbor's."

He squinted, thinking. "Who's your neighbor?"

"Norah Ramsey. She got arrested?" She didn't say what she had been arrested for; it was too embarrassing.

"Oh yeah," he said, smiling widely. He had dimples. "You walked by. You were concerned someone had been murdered."

"And now someone has," she said, her eyes straying to the lake.

"Now, we don't know that," he said, caution in his voice. He'd been instructed to do damage control, keep the peace as much as possible. "Could easily have been an accident."

She crossed her arms. "You don't really believe that, do you?"

"I believe that the medical examiner—and the evidence—will determine the truth. In the meantime we shouldn't try to guess. It can only lead to rumors and fear."

She laughed. "They told you to say that."

He laughed in spite of himself. "Maybe."

"Dixon," a warning voice intoned from several yards away. In response, his eyes strayed to the crowd, still gathered. He was falling down on the job.

"I gotta go," he said apologetically and walked back to the front of the crowd.

She watched him go, feeling interrupted, as though, if given more time, something would've happened, something significant. She wondered if this was what adult life was going to be: a string of moments that leave you wondering what might've been. He repeated his admonishment to the crowd, this time more forcefully, making up for his screwup in front of his superior. She stood for a moment longer to look at him, then turned and walked away.

She had almost reached the woods when she heard the swift footfalls of someone running up behind her. It scared her and she froze, which was the worst thing she could do. She should've broken into a run, but her instincts seemed to be working against her lately. She couldn't trust herself to do the right thing. She turned around, ready to scream as loudly as possible in hopes that someone back at the scene would hear her.

But it wasn't a criminal chasing her into the woods; it was the opposite. The cop stood there, breathing heavily from his sprint to catch her. He held his hands up, indicating he meant her no harm.

"You left." He panted out the words.

"You told us to," she teased. She felt that flicker of attraction again, the thrill of wondering if this person could be something more.

He made a face. "I kinda had to."

She shrugged. "I need to get home anyway."

"Yeah, I need to get back there," he said. "We're packing it in soon. It's gonna get too dark to do much more." He shrugged. "And there's not really any more to do anyway."

She nodded, studying him as he talked. If he had already graduated from the police academy, that meant he had to be older than her, though by how much she couldn't guess. He had a baby face, the kind of handsomeness that bordered on pretty. She thought about Eli's wider masculine features compared to this guy's aquiline nose and prominent cheekbones. He also had a thinner frame, but toned from police training, she guessed. Eli had been a football player and was broader, bulkier. Not fat, but not exactly built.

When she pictured a future with Eli, she could already envision the beer gut he would likely develop as some men do. She'd told herself his broadness made her feel safe, comforted and comfortable at the same time. But this guy made her feel something else, something daring and new. She felt instantly guilty for comparing the two of them like that, for this small, private betrayal of Eli, who loved her so much. But did she want to be loved like that, or did she want to have fun? She had a thought: What if she didn't have to choose? What if, just while she was here figuring things out, she could have both?

"Maybe we could hang out sometime?" She blurted it out before she lost her nerve. "I mean when you're not working?"

She saw him visibly relax. He smiled again, and she could tell he knew that that smile opened doors. He'd used it before and he would use it again. And she didn't care. She didn't need love. She needed something else. She wasn't sure what yet, but she wanted to find out. "Say when," he said.

She smiled back at him. For a moment they were just two good-looking people smiling at each other at the edge of the woods. She could see that he recognized the same thing about her smile, that she knew how to use it. Or she did once. She'd forgotten about it, or given up on it. She'd become someone else for a while. But perhaps now she was coming back to herself. It felt good to flirt without fear, to feel in control of a situation for the first time in a long time. Because, at least for now, for this moment, she was in control. She could see it in his eyes. She could steer him any way she wanted, and he would allow it. He would follow wherever she led. She felt the power just as sure as if she were holding it in her hands. It felt like taking in oxygen, pure and sweet, for the first time in a long time.

"When," she said.

Bess

She was closing down the house for the night, turning out the lights in the kitchen, when a flash of movement in the backyard caught her eye. She reached to turn out the last remaining light, the one over the sink, so she could see out better. She leaned closer to the glass, squinting to make sure her eyes weren't playing tricks on her. She watched as Jason slipped into the shed and closed the door behind him. She stood stock-still for a moment as relief filled her. His wasn't the body from the lake. He was alive and in her shed.

"Bess?" Steve, back from his short trip, called from the den. "You going up?" This, she knew, was his indication that he was retiring for the evening and that she should join him.

When she tried to speak, her voice came out in a croak. "Y-yes."

But she made no move to go. She stood in front of the sliding glass door that led into the backyard and took in her reflection. She wore her white nightgown, the one Steve called her "Ma Ingalls gown," but she loved it. It made her feel feminine and unconventionally sexual. Long white nightgowns weren't exactly featured in the display windows of Victoria's Secret, but it made her think of gothic romances, long sweeping lawns behind dark gabled mansions, the white nightgown standing out against the black night. She wondered if Jason would think so, or if he would tease her, too. Then she shook her head at her fanciful imagination and went to join her husband in their bed, where she belonged.

She woke up from a nightmare, sitting bolt upright with her heart in her throat and the blackness swirling all around her, as if it were alive. She sat there for a moment, waiting for her heart rate to slow down, her breathing to return to normal, the blackness to start to recede. She looked at the clock on her bedside table. It was 3:27 a.m. . . . her birthday was March 27, but she tried not to attach too much to the numbers.

The dream had been, of course, about the body in the lake. And why not? She'd thought of little else all that day. It made sense that her subconscious would keep processing it even in sleep. That's all the dream was: a manifestation of her obsessive thoughts. She told herself this to reorient, bringing her mind back to reality. It was just a dream, albeit a disturbing one. She recalled bits and pieces. In it, she'd been at the lake. An officer had told her she could open the body bag and so she had, finding Casey's face just underneath the wide black teeth of the zipper. She'd screamed and zipped the body bag closed again. Then she'd opened it again, this time finding Nicole's face. She'd done this again and again, seeing the faces of those she loved each time. Not one of the faces had been Jason's.

She looked over at Steve, but he slept on. She slipped from the bed, needing to go and look at her girls sleeping safely in their beds to reassure herself. She padded across the room, barefooted, and opened the door without a sound. She looked over her shoulder before she left the room to see if perhaps Steve had felt her leave their bed. He snored in response. She rolled her eyes and closed the door behind her.

Nicole's room was closest, but Bess went past it to check on Casey first. She had seen Casey's face first in the dream, so she felt more compelled to check on her. She wondered if she would've had this same dream if Casey had stayed at school like she was supposed to, if she hadn't found her and Eli in bed, if she knew what was really going on with her older child. She opened the door quietly, the door moving across the carpet the only sound. For a split second she wondered if she'd find Eli again, the two of them spooned together in the bed Casey had gotten for her fourteenth birthday, covered with the quilt Bess's grandmother had made that Casey had decided was "retro" and therefore cool to have on her bed. Bess thought it was ugly, but she never said so.

But Casey was alone, sleeping on her stomach just like when she was a baby. The doctors had strongly admonished Bess to put her baby on her back to sleep, but Casey knew what she wanted. She would fuss until Bess put her on her stomach, going against her better judgment in order to make Casey happy, not knowing it would become a metaphor for parenting. She stood and listened to Casey breathe, not daring to move any closer lest Casey wake up and find her there, watching her. In high school Casey had dubbed her "Stalker Mom," a play on the term *soccer mom*. Eventually even Steve had started calling her that. Bess didn't appreciate the negative connotation for what she felt was just involved parenting. She didn't know why her family couldn't see her concern for what it was: love.

She backed out of the room and quietly closed the door behind her, moving next to Nicole's room. Nicole slept curled up on her side in the fetal position in her daybed. As a baby Nicole had slept in whatever position Bess had put her in, an easy baby. She'd been an easy kid, too. So her recent transformation into a demanding, sneaky, rude teenager had come as a shock to Bess. It felt like a betrayal. Her darling baby had turned into a stranger recently, talking and acting like someone she didn't know. She stood in the doorway and recalled Nicole's unacceptably harsh words to poor Violet Ramsey. She should've punished her, taken something away or grounded her. But the truth was, after Violet had left, she'd been too distracted and exhausted to deal with it. Nicole's recriminations were always epic. To punish Nicole was to punish herself.

She closed Nicole's door, but instead of returning to her bed, she decided to go downstairs to get a glass of water. As she took the stairs, her white nightgown flowed behind her, and she wondered if she looked like a ghost haunting her own house. If she was gone, she wondered, would they miss her? Sure, they'd miss the meals and the house management and the endless chauffeuring, but would they miss *her*? She thought of Norah telling her all those years ago that she should leave Steve. "I can't do that to my children," she'd replied. But since then, she'd often wondered if staying had even mattered to them the way she'd thought it would. She often wondered if she should've been more selfish. The more time went by, the more she had to admit that Norah had been on to something. And she had just been too scared to upend her careful existence.

In the kitchen she filled a water glass and thirstily drank it down. Then refilled it and drank a second glass. She put the glass down and looked out the window over the kitchen sink at the moon in a starless sky. He was out there right now, just feet away. She'd worried he was dead, but he wasn't. If she was brave, she would go to him right now. She would wake him and ask him why he had never called her back. She'd tell him how worried she'd been.

And in telling him that, she would be admitting that this was more than her helping him get back on his feet; this was more than a simple good deed. It didn't make sense: that she'd developed real, actual feelings for him of all people. Why not a father at the school? Why not a neighbor? Why not her self-defense instructor? These were likely suspects. Jason wasn't. Why—and how—had she come to care about this man who may or may not be telling her the truth about who he was, this man who she knew next to nothing about save what he'd told her? He could be anyone. But he wasn't anyone. Not anymore. Not to her.

Quietly, she unlatched the sliding glass door and slipped out of the house, telling herself she was just going to breathe in the cool night air for a moment. And she did. Then the moment stretched long, and longer, until she couldn't deny the pull inside her. It drew her to the shed, and she let it. She'd been unselfish for so long. For one night, for one suspended period of time, she could be selfish; she could do something that was just for her and not think about the people inside her house sleeping unaware.

She opened the shed door, thinking that the noise would awaken him. But he slept on. The moonlight illuminated the room so that she could see him well enough. She stood watching his motionless form lying there on the pallet on the floor, flat on his back, his chin pointed to the ceiling, his breathing even and deep. Without thinking much about it, she moved closer to him, dropped to her hands and knees, and crawled up beside him, forming her body to his, smelling the earthy, outdoor smell of him. He reminded her of her garden—of dirt and weeds and roots. Perhaps that was why she had come to care about him. He reminded her of the thing that was most familiar, most natural, to her.

He stirred, then startled, pulling away from her with panic on his face. "What the hell?" he yelled.

"Shhh," she said, scooting backward, away from him. "It's just me. It's just me." She looked to make sure she'd closed the door, fearing his outburst had somehow woken her family.

He lowered his voice and pulled the blanket closer to his chest, like a modest woman, exposed. "What are you doing in here?" he asked.

It was a fair question. One she didn't have an answer to. "I don't know," she admitted. She thought about it. "I had a bad dream," she said, which sounded silly and childish.

He gave her a bemused grin and settled back down on the bedroll she'd made for him. He held out his arm, indicating she should move back where she'd been before she'd woken him. She did, lying flat on her back beside him, her chin pointed at the ceiling like his, his arm as her pillow. For a moment they both lay there in silence, breathing in unison in the darkness.

"I was worried all day, about you," she said. "They found a body in the lake down the street, back in the woods. I was afraid it was you. I called you a few times, but you didn't answer the phone."

He remained quiet for a few minutes. "My phone was stolen," he said. "I was in town to get some food. I was in line, and I wasn't paying close attention and, when I looked back down, my bag was gone."

"Oh, Jason, I'm sorry. That sucks."

He twisted slightly toward her as he reached under the quilt. He brought his hand back out, revealing a switchblade in his palm. He flicked his wrist, doing the complicated maneuver to open it up, like an actor in *West Side Story*. "I wish I'd seen the guy who stole it. I'd have used this on him."

"Jason, you shouldn't have that. It's d-dangerous." She ignored the thought that accompanied those words: He's dangerous.

"I got it when I lived on the streets in the city. You have to have something there, just to flash around, you know, so people will know not to mess with you. I've just always kept it on me. You never know." He shrugged, did the fancy maneuver again, and repocketed the knife. "I promise I've never used it. Not once." He looked at her, made a sheepish face. "Sorry if it scared you."

"I just don't like knives. Or guns."

"This from the woman whose hands are basically lethal weapons."

They both laughed at that, each recalling how they had met, grateful for the release of shared laughter.

He changed the subject. "The biggest bummer is that I used that number on the applications I submitted, so if anyone calls, I'll never know. But hey, some other bum might get a job now." He tried to laugh at his joke. "It's not like anyone's gonna call anyway. No one wants a homeless druggie working for them."

"Ex-druggie," she said. She paused. "Right?"

He gave her the same bemused grin. "Yes, ex."

"I was worried today that that's what happened. That you'd had a weak moment and maybe done some drugs and OD'd—I saw on *Dr. Phil* once how it's easy for people who get clean to OD because they go back and do the same amount they used to—or whatever—and it's too much because they've lost their tolerance and so it kills them and . . ." The worries of the day rushed back in a whoosh of emotion. The tears came, and she knew she was powerless to hold them in. "I was afraid that's what had happened and maybe you'd fallen in that lake and it was you they found." She didn't know if he could even understand her through her tears.

He pulled her to him. "Shhh," he said. "I'm here. I'm OK. I'm sorry I scared you."

She nodded into his shoulder. Again, they were silent. As each minute passed, they relaxed into each other more and more.

She was starting to think he'd fallen back asleep, when he spoke. "I have to admit: it's nice to have someone worried about me. Someone who's waiting to see if I come home." He chuckled. "Though I guess this isn't really a home."

"It's a start," she said.

"You really think that?" This time he sounded like a child, small and scared.

"I do," she said.

"Thank you. For believing in me. I can't tell you—I mean I honestly can't put into words—just how much that means to me. How much you've helped me. I don't know what I'd have done if you hadn't found me that day sneaking out of here."

"I'll get you another phone. Tomorrow," she said.

He raised up on his elbow and looked down at her. "It is tomorrow," he said.

She smiled up at him, thinking what they must look like, huddled together in a garden shed, on a bedroll, her in a white old-lady nightgown, him in the clothes he'd worn that day, both of them grinning like idiots. "I guess it is," she said. And then he kissed her, just a chaste touch of his lips on hers, there and gone. But the touch memory, and the feeling that came with it, would stay with her for hours.

"I should get back inside," she said.

"Yes," he agreed. "And I'm sorry if that was wrong of me to do."

"It wasn't wrong," she said. And as she said it, she knew that that wasn't true, but it was true, all at the same time.

Nico

He'd made John Hobgood, the medical examiner, promise to call him as soon as an ID was made on the body, no matter how late it was. He'd slept with his phone on, resting on his chest so it would wake him. He was a notoriously deep sleeper, thanks to spending his youth sharing a room with Matteo, who had been a night owl, playing music, talking on the phone, leaving the lights on till the wee hours. Nico had had to get his sleep somehow, burrowing into unconsciousness with the same determination and tenacity he applied to the rest of his life. He didn't know whether to blame Matteo or thank him for that.

When the phone rang in the wee hours, he woke up, immediately alert and aware, none of the usual confusion and fog clinging to him. He knew exactly who would be calling and why.

He answered the phone. "It's him, isn't it?" was all he said.

There was a pause. "Yeah," Hobgood said. There was another pause. "I'm so sorry, man," he added.

Nico found that he couldn't form words to answer his friend, a man who'd bent some rules and outright broken others for him on investigations in the past. A man he owed many favors to. A man who would understand that he simply couldn't speak at that moment. A man who would expect that the only response he'd receive from Nico was the dial tone buzzing in his ear.

Violet

She texted Casey first thing that morning but got no response. It was Sunday, the day she and Micah had planned to go to the storage unit. But now that it was happening, she didn't think she had the balls to go through with it alone. She needed Casey to go with her but hesitated as she wondered whether Casey could be nice to Micah for a whole afternoon. Still, Violet didn't know how to be alone with him for that long. And she had no one else to ask. Feeling desperate, she tried Casey again an hour later. She put 911 in the text this time, hoping that would get Casey's attention. Sure enough, her phone rang almost immediately.

"Violet?" Casey's voice sounded anxious. "What's wrong?"

Violet paused, feeling bad that she'd worried Casey. "Well, um, nothing big."

"Nothing big? You don't use 911 for nothing big! That means emergency." The tone of Casey's voice sounded familiar. Violet had heard it a number of times, but always directed at Nicole, not her.

"I'm sorry," Violet said. "I texted you earlier and didn't hear back, and I was starting to get worried I wouldn't hear back in time."

"I was asleep," Casey grumbled.

"Oh," Violet said. She hadn't considered that. She'd barely slept the night before and had been up since light first streaked the sky, trying to figure out what to wear and what to say. She would be with Micah Berg for hours. A few minutes of conversation was fine; she'd managed that already. But hours? She couldn't be funny and smart for hours. It was impossible.

"So what was your nothing-big 911?" Casey asked. Violet could hear her covers rustling. Casey truly had just woken up, wasn't even out of bed yet. Violet felt heartened that she hadn't blown her off.

"Well, I'm going with Micah Berg today for this, um, well, it's kind of a secret mission, and I wondered if maybe you'd like to go with us?" She wondered as she said it if Micah Berg would want Casey to know his suspicions about his father. Probably not, she decided. She hadn't thought this through, thinking more of her own nerves than Micah's needs. "I'm doing some investigation into my mother's case. You know, on my own. And Micah said he'd go with me."

Casey sniffed. "Well, he doesn't have much else to do, so he might as well." Violet could picture her pursing her lips in that way she did when she didn't like something.

"Well, I just thought maybe you'd like to come with us? Help us out?"

There was silence, and for a moment Violet was conflicted. If Casey said yes, Micah might be mad that she was there. But if she said yes, then there would be someone else to take the pressure off being alone with him for that long. "I'd normally say yes, but I can't today. I've got a lunch date."

Violet felt relieved and disappointed at the same time. "Oh, with Eli?" she asked, even though she no longer cared. She needed to get off the phone with Casey and get back to figuring out what to wear and what to say. Maybe she could make a list of topics to discuss, questions to ask, and amusing anecdotes that she could share to keep the conversation going.

"Actually, no," Casey said, surprising Violet. "Not with Eli. With someone I met. Someone new." Casey was being coy.

"What about Eli?" Violet asked, feeling strangely defensive of Casey's ex-boyfriend. Maybe because she knew what it felt like to be dumped by a Strickland sister.

"He's around, too," Casey said, and giggled.

"Casey!" Violet said. "You"—she realized she was talking loudly and lowered her voice lest her grandmother overhear—"you had *sex* with Eli."

Casey's tone changed. "I'm well aware of that, Violet."

"Well, isn't that supposed to mean something?" Violet didn't know what it meant exactly, only what she'd seen on TV and heard whispered about in school.

Casey was quiet for a long time. When she spoke again, her voice was flat. "It doesn't mean nearly what they tell you," she said. "It doesn't have to mean a thing." There was another long pause, and Violet was just about to speak up when Casey spoke again. "Just ask your mother," she said.

Violet sputtered as she tried to come up with something to say in response, but Casey interrupted her.

"No, Violet, I don't mean that as a dig against her. I mean it as a compliment. I think maybe your mom had it figured out. She took control of sex. She used it to help herself. And I think maybe that's the best thing any of us can do. I think she was onto something."

"My mom's in jail," Violet said, hearing how small her voice sounded, how weak.

"She won't stay there," Casey said. "You watch and see." Violet could sense her smiling as she spoke.

"You don't know anything," Violet said, angry at Casey for saying what she'd said, for smiling as she'd said it.

Casey started to justify her comment, but Violet hung up the phone. She didn't have time to waste on Casey Strickland and whatever was going on with her. She needed to get to that storage unit and see what might be hidden there that could help Micah Berg and, more importantly, could help her mother.

Hours later, hot, tired, and dirty, Violet couldn't believe she'd worried about what to wear. She'd chosen jeans and a solid-color T-shirt, which seemed understated and suited for combing through a storage unit for something they hoped they would know when they saw it. But after digging through the stacks of boxes, all they'd found of note were some rather embarrassing photos of Violet, age three, and some old letters from a guy Norah had dated right after her divorce. Micah had started to read them out loud, but Violet had silenced him with a look. She didn't want to hear whatever that loser had had to say to her mother.

"Look for papers, notebooks, legal pads, flash drives, floppy disks—anything that could contain a list," she'd instructed Micah when they arrived. "And look for anything with the name Lois on it."

"Lois?" Micah asked. "Is that, like, your mom's code name or something?"

"No. It's her silent partner. No one can figure out who she is. I read about it online. Someone who—if we could find out who she is—could probably tell us anything we want to know about that list."

But they'd found none of those things so far.

She stood in front of the warped mirror on top of an old vanity that her mother had shoved into the corner and stared at her grubby reflection. She wiped away a smear of dust that had blended with the sweat on her face and decided she should've foregone the makeup she had so carefully applied and worn athletic shorts and an old T-shirt. She glanced over at Micah, flipping through a box of things that belonged to her father, oblivious to her presence. She shouldn't have cared at all what she looked like for him. He'd hardly noticed.

"We've got just those boxes left," she said, pointing at a stack of boxes behind him. "And then we're done."

He looked over at the last boxes and nodded. "I've basically lost hope that there's anything in here."

"I'm sorry," she said. "I'd hoped we'd find the list."

He shrugged. "At least we tried." He held up a magazine, an old *Sports Illustrated*. "You mind if I keep this?" he asked.

She didn't know why he would want some old magazine, but she didn't figure anyone would miss it, so she nodded. "You can keep anything you want from that box," she said.

"Whose stuff is it?" he asked.

She shrugged. "My dad's."

"How long have they been divorced?" He closed up the box, taking nothing else from it.

"Since I was two. I don't remember them ever being together."

"That's kinda sad," he said. "I can't imagine my parents not being together."

She wanted to ask: But you can imagine your father with a prostitute? But she didn't. Mostly because she didn't want to say the word *prostitute* to Micah Berg.

As if he were reading her mind, he said, "You're probably wondering why I'd be looking for what I'm looking for if that was the case?"

She gave him a smile without showing any teeth. "Little bit, yeah."

"I wouldn't have thought him capable of something like that, but with everything that's happened, he's just been—I don't know—different. Toward me, toward my mom. He seems like he doesn't really want to be at home, like he's sad all the time. And when I overheard him talking about . . ." He paused, then continued. "Well, about your mom's arrest." He glanced over at her apologetically. "He seemed like he was talking about it as more than just neighborhood news, as if he—I don't know—had some involvement, or knowledge. Maybe." He looked around the small room crammed with stuff. "I could've been wrong." He sighed. "I hope I am."

"I hope you are, too."

The silence between them stretched uncomfortably, so she turned to the last stack of boxes and opened the top one. The sight of a whole stack of papers renewed her hope. She picked up the stack, thinking that underneath there could be a drive or disk or anything that could contain the file. But she found nothing under the papers, so she dropped to the ground and began going through them, discovering legal papers from her parents' divorce, a whole pile of them traded between their attorneys for years.

Some of the papers mentioned her. Her father, unsurprisingly, had not fought her mother for custody. But that was the only thing, from the looks of it, that he hadn't fought her on. Violet sorted through them, trying to make sense of the legal jargon, to understand just what had transpired between her parents. It had been, from the looks of things, a bitter divorce. Her father had had the better attorney. If there was a winner in the divorce, he had won, conceding to give her mother the home they'd shared but leaving her with little support to afford it. She found pages of back-and-forth between the attorneys over this issue. How could her father have done that to them, to her? Her mother had never told her any of this, and of course, she did not remember. As far back as her memory went, they'd always been OK, better than OK, really. They'd always had the money to do whatever they wanted. Something must have changed. And then it dawned on her what had.

Micah came over and sat down beside her, his eyebrows raised hopefully. "Is there something in that box?"

She shook her head, feeling ashamed, though she didn't know why exactly. It wasn't her divorce. But in a way, it was. And the decisions that had come after, as her mother had built her business with a relentless drive Violet never understood, as she somehow got involved with this prostitution ring, all of it had started here, in these papers, as her mother had fought to keep her daughter in her home, to provide for her child. No wonder Norah had taken this storage room out in Violet's name. She hadn't wanted her ex anywhere near her things, because he seemed intent on taking whatever he could from her. The client list wasn't in this storage unit, Violet understood. But their past was—a past her mother wanted to lock up and walk away from. Violet pulled the stack of papers to her chest.

"Seriously. If it's bad, just tell me," Micah said. "Don't hide it. I need to know."

She shook her head again. "It has nothing to do with your dad. I promise."

He tried to tug the papers from her, but she held on tight, her eyes hard as she looked at him. "Seriously. It's old stuff. Legal stuff. It's nothing."

He crossed his arms and cocked his head. "So prove it. Let me see."

She shook her head more forcefully. "I swear to you on my mother's life that this has nothing to do with the list," she said.

He blinked at the intensity of her words, then nodded, satisfied that she wasn't keeping something from him, and stood up. He reached out his hand, offering to pull her up. She shifted the papers into the crook of her left arm and reached out. He pulled her up, and the weight of the papers pulled her forward, into him. For a moment their bodies touched and their hands stayed clasped. Neither of them blinked as they studied each other. The only sound she could hear was their breathing. Then she remembered what she'd looked like in that mirror and pulled away. She didn't want him seeing her this close up when she looked and smelled like she did.

She put the papers back in the box and moved it over to reveal the one underneath it. She pulled the lid off to find a box of old record albums that had likely belonged to her father. They'd probably fought about them long ago, and her mother had hidden them from him just because she could. Good for you, Mom, Violet thought. For the first time in weeks, she felt proud of her mother.

"You go through this one," she told Micah, pointing at the albums. "I doubt there's anything in here, but we might as well look just so we know."

He mock saluted her. "Yes, ma'am."

She sneered at him and moved out of the way so he could lift the box and begin. The next box held travel brochures, lots of them. She riffled through them, taking note of the many destinations her mother had been interested in: Hawaii, London, Australia, China. How interesting that this box existed in the same stack with the legal papers. How sad that even as she'd been fighting to keep her house and support her daughter, she'd been dreaming of escaping to someplace far away.

Micah, done with the albums, closed the box and looked over her shoulder, dangerously close again. "Does your mom like to travel?" he asked.

"No," she said. "We never really went anywhere."

"Well, she must've wanted to. At some point." He reached into the box and held up a handful of brochures. "I'm getting some ideas for future trips." She let him look through the brochures while she hurried through the last box, full of old fan magazines from when her mother was a kid: *Teen Beat* and *Tiger Beat*. From the looks of things, her mother had had a pretty big crush on Tom Cruise back in the day.

She put the lid back on the final box and turned to Micah again. "There's nothing in this box, either," she said. "We should probably get going."

He put the lid back on his box, too, and stretched. "Yeah."

"I'm sorry we didn't find anything," she said.

He pressed his lips together. "I mean, part of me is relieved we didn't, but part of me just wants to know. Knowing is better than not knowing. Ya know?"

She nodded, her eyes on the box that held the divorce papers—yet another secret her mother had kept from her, a secret that had helped Violet understand a little better what had driven Norah to do what she'd done. Violet took one last glance at the warped mirror, finding the reflection of the person Norah had done it for.

Polly

The house was so quiet she could hear the ice settling in her glass, could hear Barney dream-running on the floor nearby, could hear her phone not ringing. Which was almost as bad as ringing. It was the anticipation of what surely was coming that set her teeth on edge. She could feel Calvin circling like a shark, eyeing her life raft, waiting to strike. She didn't like being left alone to think such things. She wished Violet were there to distract her, but Violet was off with that boy from across the street, the handsome one with the sad eyes.

She hadn't anticipated being alone like this when she'd agreed to take care of Violet. She'd thought that her granddaughter would be with her, or at least around more. Not shut up in her room behind closed doors, sneaking out to meet a boy in the middle of the night, and then disappearing with him for a whole day to who knew where. Violet was secretive, and Polly didn't feel she had the right to press, which made for a bad combo. She was in unfamiliar territory here, in more ways than one. This was not what she'd pictured when she had arrived at Norah's house. She'd had something else in mind—something warmer, something that felt redemptive. She'd thought she'd stand in Norah's house and feel her life coming full circle.

The sound of Violet's key in the door was a relief. She jumped up to greet her, probably a little too eagerly. She saw Violet step back at the sight of her broad grin, wide eyes, and open mouth, ready to ask questions. Teenagers were like wild animals: sudden or energetic movements could scare them off. Better to move slowly and show very little emotion. She'd learned this when raising Norah, but she'd forgotten. She was like a beginner, learning all over again.

She took a step back and, in an easy tone, simply said, "Oh, you're home."

Violet put the bag she always carried—some cross-body backpack thing—down on the desk in the kitchen. "Yeah," Violet said, then went to the refrigerator to get a bottle of water, downing it like she'd spent the day in the desert. With Violet's eyes averted, Polly took the chance to study her. She looked pretty grubby, like perhaps she had indeed spent the day in the desert. She wanted so badly to ask where Violet had been, but she knew better than to do so. She hoped Violet would stay in her presence for just a few minutes, that she'd get the chance to talk to her granddaughter. She didn't dare say the wrong thing and send her running.

"So, is that boy—what's his name again—your boyfriend?" she ventured, sounding dumb on purpose.

Violet spit out her water in response, laughing. "Micah?" she asked as water dripped down her chin. "Hardly."

"Well, I don't think it's *that* out of the question," said Polly, then watched as Violet rolled her eyes and finished her water.

Polly looked at Violet, feeling simultaneously envious and sympathetic. So much lay ahead of her, things she couldn't envision yet. Polly had been in Violet's shoes once. Would she want to be in them again? So many times she wished she were young again, but to be young meant to not know what she knows now. It meant having to make those same mistakes again and live with the consequences. It meant looking in the mirror and seeing a beautiful young woman, yet not being smart enough to know it at the time. She wanted the young body, but she didn't want the young mind that came with it.

"Did your mother ever tell you about the Beaucatchers?" she asked, blurting it out before she lost her gumption. She didn't expect that Norah had ever told Violet about the family legacy. But she wanted her granddaughter to hear it because it was part of Violet, whether Norah liked it—or believed in it—or not. Polly believed. It had been the case for her grandmother, her mother, her aunt, herself. In truth, Norah's current situation could be attributed to it. Not that she would ever admit that.

"What's a Beaucatcher?" Violet asked. Polly could tell by her face that she was intrigued, though trying to pretend not to be. Teenagers are practiced at the art of nonchalance.

Polly smiled, because she was happy to be sharing this with her granddaughter, and because she wanted Violet to see the legacy as a good thing. Norah never had. In its own way, it had come between them. Norah had run from it as much as she had run from Polly. She did not want to admit that it was part of who she was. She'd rejected the legacy, and in doing so, the line of women who had carried it before her. She had called it silly and stupid and, ultimately, false. She had forbidden Polly to ever bring it up in her presence again. "I don't believe in your backwoods fairy tales," she'd pronounced. And as far as Norah was concerned, that had been that.

"It's the legacy of all the women in our family," Polly said to Violet. "We are Beaucatchers."

Violet knit her eyebrows together in response. "And what does that mean?"

"Do you know what a beau is?"

Violet shook her head.

"It's an old-fashioned word for a boyfriend." She paused to make sure Violet absorbed what she said. "So, in our family at least, a Beaucatcher is a woman who literally catches beaus, or boyfriends. She doesn't try—she doesn't really even know she's doing it. Men are just drawn to her, like magnets. They can't help themselves. It's been true of generation after generation of the women in our family. It was true of my great-grandmother, my grandmother, my mother, my aunts—her sisters—and me and your mother. And it's true of you."

Violet smirked at her. "Doubtful," she said. In her voice was the slightest warble. She couldn't believe it could possibly be true of her. And wasn't that what it was to be a woman, to feel that you were the exception to everyone else's rule?

Polly understood this. She'd said as much to her own mother when her mother had shared the legacy with her. Polly had stood before her lovely mother, awkward and uncertain, slow to develop, late to understand what other girls seemed to inherently know. But like the tortoise and the hare, she'd eventually left those other girls behind and won the race. Though, of course, winning that particular race meant losing, too. Men *were* drawn to her—that was true. But that didn't mean they were nice men, or honest men, or considerate men. With each man, she learned a little more, but there were hard, painful lessons along the way. That was the sour that went with the sweet, the yin that followed the yang, one step up and two steps back, as it were.

"You'll come into your own," her mother had said to her back then, a promise that kept coming true, even all these years later. Coming into your own, Polly had learned, was an ever-changing thing.

"You'll see, Violet," she said, making a promise like her mother had made her. Because one thing Polly knew: sometimes just the promise itself was enough. Sometimes the promise alone could keep you going. "There's still so much good ahead of you, honey."

There was bad, too. But she didn't say that. There was no need. That part of the family legacy each woman had to discover for herself. Was the legacy a blessing or a curse? Polly didn't know. Her beauty had been both. It would be the same for Violet, someday. Polly hoped she would still be in Violet's life when that became true. She hoped this time together would, by some miracle, extend.

She wanted to reach out and hug her granddaughter, but she didn't dare. It would scare the child. So she just said, "You have to believe me, because I'm old and wise."

Violet cocked her head and studied her for a moment. "You're not that old," she said.

Polly winked at her. "I'm not that wise, either." They both laughed, and, for a moment, she felt OK about things. She felt capable, like maybe she was coming into her own yet again. And maybe her estranged daughter's house was the place to do it.

"I need to ask you something," Violet said, and alarm bells went off inside Polly, disturbing the peace that had, for the briefest moment, settled in her heart.

"Sure," Polly said. She tried for her kindest, warmest voice, but she could hear the shakiness under the word.

"Can we go see my mom?"

Go see Norah? It was a normal thing for a child to ask. In fact, now that she thought about it, she wondered why Violet hadn't asked before. Children want their mothers. When she'd considered coming to watch Violet, she'd assumed she wouldn't see Norah. If Norah was released, she'd leave before Norah walked in the door. The two wouldn't cross paths, the way she'd figured it. But if she took Violet to see her mother, then Polly would have to see her daughter. There'd be no escaping it.

"I need to ask her about something," Violet continued. "It's important. It's . . . for a friend."

Polly could guess which friend it was. She wondered again what Violet had been doing all day. But she didn't dare ask. Violet would tell her if she felt comfortable, and until then, Polly wouldn't pry. She would be gentle, proceed with caution, let the girl warm to her. She wouldn't do what she'd done with Norah: expect that love was a natural byproduct of blood. Love, she'd learned too late, came only by decision, when it was earned. Love that was demanded was not love at all.

But that didn't mean she wasn't going to call that Bess person and ask her what she knew about this boy Violet had been spending time with. Just as soon as possible.

"I'll see if that can be arranged," she said. "I'll call Jim Sheridan right now. Not sure what they'll allow, but if anyone can make it happen, he can."

Violet's smile was but a flicker, there and gone like a shooting star, beautiful in its fleetingness. Polly found herself wanting to grasp it, to bring it back to her face. Another sign that Violet was a Beaucatcher. Men would feel that way about her for the rest of her life, would go to great lengths to put that smile back on that face. She saw her granddaughter's future, and she felt both fear and excitement. She could not change it; she could not save her from it. But she could maybe teach her how to navigate it. She just had to stay in her life.

"Thank you," Violet said.

"You are so welcome," Polly said, and watched as that elusive, lovely smile returned, there and gone, once again.

Casey

She opened her eyes to unfamiliar surroundings. She blinked a few times, expecting her field of vision to clear and things to look familiar again. Instead she saw a brown-paneled wall, an old clock radio with the red LED display showing a time that couldn't be right, a poster of the twin towers with a corner ripped off. For a moment she feared she had traveled back in time. She sat up to find herself naked, the back of a dark head on the pillow next to hers. Her mind raced to orient itself, to tell itself a story that was somehow acceptable even though her surroundings were not. She scanned the room, willing herself to figure out what had happened, relaxing a bit as it slowly came to her.

She'd gone to lunch with the cop, whose name was Todd. They'd had a nice time. He'd asked her to go back to his place to watch a movie. She'd gone along. He'd made them a cocktail, something with vodka in it. It had been strong. She remembered that. He'd made her another as soon as she'd finished the first. She'd drunk them too fast. He'd kissed her. She'd told herself not to freak out. She was fine. This was fine. This was life. This was men and women. It would always be this way. She had to get past what had happened with Russell Aldridge. Todd wasn't Russell. He meant her no harm. He was a cop, for crying out loud.

She kissed him back, throwing herself into it thanks to the alcohol and because she wanted to feel normal with a man she was attracted to. She wanted to enjoy it, so she told herself she did. One thing led to another, and she went with it. She was in control of this situation. She was making these choices. It felt good to be making the choices, to be in control. He told her she was the coolest girl he'd met in a long time. But she knew that wasn't because she was actually cool. It was because she wasn't stopping him like another girl would. She wanted to tell him she wasn't a girl at all. She was a cyborg, devoid of normal human response and feeling. She was a shell of what used to be a girl. But of course she hadn't said those things. She had kept silent and, when it was over, they had both passed out, curled on their sides, with their backs to each other.

He slept on as she crawled out of the bed and scrounged around on the floor for her clothes, tears leaking from her eyes as she did. She told herself the tears were because it was late and she was having trouble finding her clothes in the fading light of the setting sun. It was because her mom was going to question her when she got home, eyeing her with that knowing look she had, the one that seemed to see right into Casey's very soul. Her tears were proof she still had a soul.

She gripped the doorknob, then froze at the loud squeak of its turn. Over her shoulder she saw him sit bolt upright in bed, blinking at her, feeling around on his nightstand. He kept his gun there, which she'd told him was hot, but which really scared her. He stopped fumbling around and jumped out of bed, naked, and moved toward her. Casey averted her eyes, turned back to the door, and opened it.

"Hey, hey," he said. Casey suspected he'd already forgotten her name. "Where ya running off to?" He grabbed her shoulder to stop her from leaving.

"I have to go," she said. She tried to shake his hand from her shoulder, but his grip tightened. She felt the fear come roaring back, once dormant, now wide awake. She felt the panic in her throat, the urgency to flee. She looked at him, into his dancing eyes. He was enjoying this, seemingly oblivious to her fear.

"Don't go just yet," he said, and gave her a lazy smile, one she suspected worked on girls like her. She was one of many. She'd held no illusions about that. She thought, painfully, of Eli, of how he'd feel if he knew about this.

"I need to get home. My mom's expecting me."

He laughed, and she could smell his sleep breath, dark and musty. His eyes went from warm and amused to hard and cold. She'd seen that happen before with Russell, but at the time she hadn't known then what could happen next. Now she did.

"Your mommy's expecting you?" He said it with a sneer in his voice. Rejection brought out the anger in him. She was finding that to be true of most men.

She took a step back, right into the door. It banged against the wall, the noise loud in the tiny apartment. She straightened her back, willing courage to replace the fear. She didn't have to be afraid, she reassured herself. He was mad, but he wouldn't hurt her. If he did and she reported it, he'd lose his job. She just needed to appeal to his rational side.

"Could you let me go, please?" she asked. She wished he'd put on some clothes. The room smelled of sex and sleep and adrenaline. The smell made her nauseous. She feared she would vomit right in his doorway, right on his bare feet. "Maybe we could see each other later?" She threw the hope out to distract him. "But right now I just need to get home."

He stepped back. She stifled a relieved exhalation. He turned his back to her and walked over to the bed. She looked away when he bent over to retrieve his boxers from the floor. He talked as he put them on, but she kept her eyes averted. "I should've known better," he said, "than to mess around with you."

She heard the mattress springs squeak and looked up to see him half-clothed, sitting on his bed. Their eyes met, and his gaze narrowed like he was trying to figure something out. "You're just a little girl," he said. "A little girl playing grown-up games."

She shifted under his gaze, considered just turning and running, but something made her stand her ground.

"The problem with little girls who play grown-up games is that they end up getting hurt," he continued. He lifted his eyebrows. "You should be more careful. So you don't end up hurt."

A wave of anger surged through her, hot and red. It burned through every vein and muscle and organ, searing all the fear away. The burning felt like its own kind of power. She wanted to jump on him, pound her fists into his chest, and scream in his face: What do you know about little girls who get hurt?

Instead she just said, "Too late." Then she turned and walked calmly out of his apartment, leaving his front door wide open behind her.

Bess

Bess dialed Polly's number and listened to it ring, thinking as she did that this was *Norah's mother* she was calling. Sometimes the way life worked out didn't seem possible. For a long time she'd assumed Norah's mother was dead, because Norah had never mentioned her—even around the holidays or Mother's Day. She never took an obligatory trip out of town to visit her or made a last-minute scramble for a gift with a coordinating lament about how hard mothers were to buy for. (Bess's own mother was quite easy to buy for. She just sent her the most expensive bottle of gin for her martinis. As her mother said, "Well, I can always use it!" And use it, she did.)

But none of that from Norah. Bess had assumed she'd lost her mother tragically, and it was just too painful to talk about. Until one of their wine-soaked nights out when, out of the blue, Norah had spilled it about her mother, Polly, who *was* lost to her, but not due to death. Just to a roaring argument and a lifetime of resentment over her mother's poor choices with men. The bottom line: Norah's mother had never been without a man, whether that was best for Norah or not.

Her dependence on them was, according to Norah, clinical. Polly had moved Norah in the middle of the school year for one husband, dragged her to church and made her get baptized for another. She'd changed careers, hair colors, and political parties in the name of whatever man she'd hitched herself to at the time. It made sense that Norah had grown up to see men as commodities to be traded, pawns to be moved around on her board, a means to an end. They were always, in her world, interchangeable. Accessories more than humans.

Polly's voicemail came on, and Bess left a message, making her voice sound cheerful and upbeat. Bess didn't hold the woman's prior sins against her. Polly wasn't her mother. And she was doing the right thing by offering to help in this hard time. It was the least she could do. "Hey, Polly," she said. "I've made too much dinner and thought maybe I'd bring some over to you and Violet. Thought maybe that would be one less thing to worry about. Let me know if that sounds good!"

She put the phone down and peered out at the shed, willing Jason to step out of it now while she was home alone—Casey was off doing whatever with whomever, Nicole was at play practice (she hadn't gotten the lead role in the fall musical and was hell on wheels to live with, so Bess preferred when she was gone these days), and Steve had a dinner with a client and wouldn't be home till late. So she was home alone. Never mind that she'd put a whole chicken in the Crock-Pot that morning with carrots and potatoes and onions. The food smelled delicious, and there was no one there to eat it.

She wished Jason would show up. She'd feed him the meal she'd made, sit across the table and watch him eat, will herself not to give away how much she'd thought about that brief, chaste middle-of-the-night kiss. She'd all but convinced herself it had never happened. That she'd dreamed it just the same as she'd dreamed her daughters were in that body bag. She shuddered at the recollection, reached for the phone to text them both, just to make sure they were OK. As she grabbed her phone, it rang and she jumped. It was just Polly calling her back.

"Hi, Polly," she said. "Guess you got my message."

"Yes," the older woman said. "Sorry I didn't answer. I didn't recognize the number, and I was afraid you were—"

"Afraid I was who?" Bess asked, curious.

"Oh, just afraid you were that damn detective. He keeps nosing around," Polly said.

Bess heard the lie in her voice, but she said nothing. If she could talk to Norah, she would tell her that her mother was not with a man this time, nor had she mentioned one. Maybe, she'd say to Norah, your mom has changed.

"So you think you could use the meal?" she asked Polly.

"That would actually be a lifesaver. I'm about to head out to take Violet to visit her mother." She paused, then added, "In the jail," in case Bess was not clear on where Norah was.

"Wow, I'm surprised they're allowing it. I thought she was on complete lockdown."

"Yeah," Polly said. "Technically she is. They're acting like they're doing this for Violet. Some good deed." Polly sighed into the phone. "But to be honest, I think they're allowing it because they want to listen in, see if Violet gets Norah to open up."

Bess tried to imagine shy, reticent Violet entering a jail, facing her mother who'd lied to and betrayed her. Once, on one of their moms' nights out, Bess had been complaining about her daughters. Nicole was morphing into a mouthy teen; Casey was demanding. The usual stuff. It had surprised her when Norah, who rarely said a negative word about Violet, joined in, admitting that her daughter was not what she'd expected. "I wanted a hell-raiser," she'd said. "A ballbuster. Instead I got a shrinking Violet." She'd laughed at her own joke, and Bess had felt sorry for Violet, a sweet child she'd always liked. Bess had a feeling Violet wouldn't always be shrinking, and that Norah might not know what to do with her daughter when that day came.

"I called her attorney," Polly continued, "just so I could tell Violet I'd asked, and he said he'd have to get some special permission but not to count on it. I told him I wasn't counting on it at all, but the kid was asking and just to try his best. The next thing I knew he was calling back and telling me where to be and when."

"Well, that's good for Violet. Right? I mean I'm sure it'll be good for her to be able to see Norah after all this time."

Polly sighed. "I guess. I just feel like that damn detective's got something up his sleeve. They got back to me way too fast."

Bess thought about this. She'd met the detective twice, but she doubted he recalled the first time, when she'd dropped a meal at his missing brother's home. The other time was when he'd come around to ask her questions. He'd done his homework and knew that she and Norah had once been best friends, but not anymore. He'd fished around, trying to find out if there might be more to the story of their breakup, but Bess had assured him that wasn't the case. She'd told him that, looking back, she saw that their breakup had probably been Norah's way of keeping Bess from finding out what she was up to. He'd said that that made sense.

She'd smiled warmly and sent him on his way, relieved he was gone. Cops made her nervous. Whether she drove past one and panicked that she was accidentally committing some traffic violation or stood on her porch and watched one leave her home, her heart pounded just the same. She'd stayed on her porch, watching until she was sure he'd driven away. She could see why Polly didn't like him. He seemed to presume everyone was guilty. Which she guessed was true. Everyone was guilty of something. It didn't take a detective to figure that out.

"I'm sure it will be fine," she said.

Polly chuckled. "Well, I'm glad you're sure." There was a long pause, and Bess heard Polly sigh.

"Everything OK?" she asked.

"I don't know," Polly said, and in her voice Bess heard the long exhalation of the exhausted and confused. Bess was familiar with the feeling. "Violet's outside talking to that boy who lives across the street? The good-looking one? Micah? I can't remember his last name."

Bess knew all too well who she was talking about. "Micah Berg," she supplied.

"Should I be worried?" Polly asked. "She's been spending a good bit of time with him."

"Eh. Not gonna lie to you. There's a little controversy around him. He was involved with a tragedy last spring," Bess said. "His girlfriend died under mysterious circumstances, and he's been accused of having something to do with it. The rumors still swirl. But there've been no charges made," she was quick to add. She knew Micah's parents, Bob and Jane Berg, as gentle, kind people. They didn't deserve what had happened. The whole family had been swiftly ostracized, judged and condemned by the people they had once called friends.

"Do you think he really did do something to her?" Polly asked. Bess could hear the fear in her voice, that her granddaughter could be in harm's way.

Bess pondered this for the briefest of moments. She'd heard Casey rail against Micah all last spring, blaming him for her friend's death with no real evidence to go on. But Bess had also bumped into a sad, bewildered Jane in the grocery store this past summer. Jane Berg had had dark circles under her eyes, and she had looked remarkably thinner. Bess had coaxed the story out of her neighbor next to a display of Campbell's soup. Jane had explained what they understood to have happened, not absolving her son, yet not vilifying him, either. Bess had gone home and told Casey that perhaps Micah had a legitimate side, one that deserved to be heard. Bess sympathized with the Bergs in a way that she could not readily explain.

"I think he's a good kid," she said to Polly now, believing it as she said it. "A kid who did something stupid, to be sure, but not malicious. He wouldn't hurt someone on purpose." She almost added, *I don't think*, but decided not to. It would only plant doubt in Polly's head. The poor woman had enough to worry about without adding to it.

"Why don't I bring the dinner over about six thirty?" Bess said, to change the subject. "We could talk more about it then. Think you'll be back by six thirty?"

"Sure," Polly said. "They're only giving us thirty minutes with her, and you'd think they gave her the damn crown jewels when they allowed that." Polly paused. "But if we hit traffic . . . maybe you could let yourself in? Do you know the code for the door?"

Bess pressed her lips together as tears pricked her eyes, surprising her. There had been a time when she'd just walk into Norah's house and call out "It's me!" without a second thought. She'd had that, then she'd lost it. She'd grieved it when it was gone. She'd thought she was way past grieving, but she wasn't sure that was ever the case with grief. It was always lurking.

She ran the code she knew from way back when by Polly, and sure enough, it was the same. "So if you get there before me, just let yourself in. And then you can get on with your evening."

"How about I bring a bottle of wine over and wait for you? Sounds like you might need it," Bess said, on impulse. But as she said it, it felt like the right thing to do.

She could hear Polly smile in response. "That sounds perfect. I'll see you when I get home."

"I like the sound of that," Bess said. Because she did.

Violet

Violet no longer needed Barney as an excuse to go over to Micah's. She just walked across the street when she saw him outside, yelled his name over the sound of the basketball drumming against the cement. He looked up, saw her, and stilled the ball. When she got close, he put it down, using his foot to keep it from rolling away.

"Hey," he said, and smiled. Even though they hadn't found the list, he still seemed glad to see her. She told herself it was just because he was lonely, and beggars couldn't be choosers. They were united in their outcast status, and it was as simple as that. Boys like him didn't like girls like her. She thought again of what her grandmother had said, about the family legacy, about what it meant to be a Beaucatcher. The beau she most wanted to catch stood right in front of her.

She intended to ask her mother about the legacy as soon as she could. She wanted to know why Norah had never told her something so important. It was a family legacy, after all.

"I'm going to see my mom today," she said to Micah. Though this didn't really involve him, she needed to tell him. She found herself often thinking of things she wanted to tell him. Needed to tell him. It was amazing how fast it had become that way. Sometimes she thought his willingness to talk to her might not last. At any moment his friends could decide to forgive him, and he could be right back in the fold, forgetting all about her. If she revealed what she knew, it would happen for sure. So to care about him meant telling the truth, but to tell the truth was to lose someone she cared about. She didn't like to think about this dilemma too long. It made her brain—and her heart—hurt.

His eyebrows shot up toward the brim of his ball cap. "Really?"

"Yeah," she said. "It just got approved. So my grandmother said we should go before they change their minds."

"How long's it been since you've seen her?" Micah asked.

She acted like she had to think about the answer, but really she knew to the day, almost to the minute: eighteen days. For some reason she didn't want to say that. "Almost three weeks," she said.

"One summer I spent a month away from my parents, but that's as long as I've ever gone," he said. He looked at her sympathetically. She didn't want his pity, so she changed the subject.

"I'm going to ask her, if I can. About the list." She knew he was thinking about the list but would never ask. She was starting to be able to tell what he was thinking, which was nice, but also scary. She didn't want to know him like that if she couldn't keep him.

"You don't have to do that," he started to argue. He'd told her several times they should just drop it. But she couldn't. Not if there was a chance she could help him. And not if there was a chance she could help her mom, too. Or instead. She hadn't yet decided what to do about that dilemma, either. She hoped it wouldn't come to that.

"My grandmother said not to get my hopes up about being able to talk to her much, or for very long. She said they'll be monitoring every word she says." She leaned forward and lowered her voice. "But I've been thinking of ways to talk in code."

He laughed. "So you're James Bond now?"

She raised her eyebrows. "You shouldn't underestimate me."

His smile softened to an amused grin. "You're a funny girl, Violet Ramsey," he said for the second time in their short relationship.

"Funny how?" she asked, feeling bold because she knew she was about to leave. Still, her heart picked up speed as she said it. She was learning that sometimes love felt more like standing on a cliff and looking over the edge than feeling safe in someone's arms.

He cocked his head, considering his answer before he spoke. Across the street she heard her grandmother call her name, but she stood still.

He shook his head. "You're just different. From other girls. From any I've known."

She wanted so badly to ask, *Different good or different bad?* But her bravery had nearly run out, and her grandmother was waiting for her. So instead, with the last scrap of bravery she had, she supplied an answer to her own question.

"Some people say different is good," she said, and started walking away.

"Is that so?" he called after her.

She turned around and shrugged, grinning. "Just what I've heard."

He picked up the basketball, spun it around in his hands as he grinned at the ball instead of her. "I'll take that under advisement," he said.

She started walking away again, wondering if this was flirting, and if she was any good at it.

"Call me and tell me how it went?" he called out one more time. She hadn't expected that.

She turned around, gave him the thumbs-up sign, and hurried across the street that had once been the division between their two houses, a gap so wide no one dared cross it. No one would've thought it possible, least of all her.

On the drive over to the jail, she and her grandmother remained quiet. It was not unusual for Violet to be quiet, but it was uncharacteristic of Polly. Violet took it as a bad sign that Polly wasn't talking, which made her feel even more nervous about the visit. With each mile they traveled, the butterflies in her stomach sprouted more butterflies, and the swarm of them beat their wings inside her until Violet nearly felt nauseous.

The jail was all the way uptown—a long way from their house in the suburbs. As they drove, Violet tried to imagine her mother riding in the back of the police car all this way, her hands cuffed. It must've been uncomfortable, not to mention humiliating. Violet was glad she had not been home when her mother was arrested. She would not have liked to witness that. She probably would have cried, and she did not like to cry in front of other people. She especially wouldn't have liked to cry in front of that horrible detective. She hoped he wasn't there for this visit, but knowing him, he would be. Lurking around, looking at them suspiciously like he always did, and just generally being annoying.

Finally, Polly spoke up, and, though she would not admit it willingly, Violet was relieved. She'd come to count on her grandmother prattling on about something. Her voice had started to feel familiar, comfortable. Sometimes she worried about Polly going away when her mother came home. Violet *would* admit willingly that she would be very sad if that happened. When the time was right, she planned to tell her mother just that. Though she feared what her mother would say, Violet had some opinions of her own. The most important one her mother couldn't argue with: Polly had been there for her when literally no one else had. The thought brought tears to her eyes, but she blinked them away.

"Cat got your tongue?" Polly asked.

Violet realized she'd missed something Polly had asked. Just because she liked the sound of Polly's voice did not mean she always listened to every word she said.

"Sorry," Violet said, going with the truth, "I didn't hear the question."

Polly sighed like she was frustrated, then grinned to show that she wasn't. "Off in the clouds, are you? Not paying your old grandmother a bit of attention. I bet you're thinking about that boy across the street."

"Micah?" Violet played dumb.

"As if there's another boy across the street you spend all your time with." If grandmothers said *duh*, Polly would've said it. "Yes. Micah. The cute one."

"You think he's cute?" Violet asked. She found herself wanting to talk about Micah. She'd not had anyone to talk about him with, longing to hash it all out like she would've if this had happened when she and Nicole were friends. But the truth was, if she and Nicole were friends, this probably wouldn't have happened. Because she would've lived with Nicole while her mother was in jail. And then she never would've had occasion to talk to Micah Berg. She glanced over at Polly. Her grandmother never would've had to come to her house, either.

"Oh, he's more than cute, Violet. He's handsome. *Movie-star* handsome. He looks a little like Paul Newman. You know Paul Newman?" Violet shook her head. Polly glanced over at the movement and shrieked, her voice loud in the enclosed space. "You don't know who Paul Newman is?"

Violet laughed at the outburst. "No," she said.

Polly looked up toward the roof of the car. "Kids these days," she said. "Well, you should look him up on your precious phone. Use the Google to find pictures of him, and you'll find out what handsome really means. None of those girly men you see so much of nowadays." Polly's voice sounded wistful, like she was off in the clouds, too, thinking about Paul Newman.

Violet left her alone with her thoughts. They were getting close to the jail, the city skyline looming just ahead. Violet assumed they'd both be silent until they reached their destination. But then Polly spoke again. "He likes you, too, you know."

Violet shook her head in denial even as a thrill raced through her entire body. It felt like the time she was on a roller coaster with her dad: the dropping sensation and the rising sensation all happening in tandem.

"He doesn't like me," she said. Because to think anything else was crazy. Violet was a lot of things—smart, sarcastic, uncoordinated, a procrastinator—but crazy wasn't one of them.

Polly only smirked in response.

"What?" Violet wanted to know what the smirk meant. Especially if Polly was going to say that she was wrong. She wanted to be wrong about Micah's feelings for her. She wanted to be wrong about that more than anything.

Polly gave her the side-eye. "Now we're getting close," she said. "I've got to concentrate on where we're going. These city streets can be confusing."

Violet slid closer to the passenger-side window and rested her head on the glass, turned cool from the air-conditioning inside the car. Her grandmother wasn't going to play. She wasn't going to make another encouraging speech about how Violet was going to be beautiful some-day, that men were going to chase her down the street the way they did her mother. She wasn't going to give her something to look forward to. It was not the time for that, she scolded herself. It was time to see her mother. That's what she should want more than anything.

"Except," Polly said.

Violet picked her head up, looked over at Polly's profile. She loved the word *except*.

Polly gave her a smile before turning her attention back to navigating. Still, she spoke. "Except I think he does like you. I just don't think he's ready for it. Something's going on with him?"

She wondered if Bess had told Polly about Micah, if she'd believed the worst about him without bothering to get the full story. Of course, no one knew the full story. Except Micah. And Violet.

She nodded her assent but didn't give any more details. Maybe later she'd tell her grandmother the *whole* whole story. Maybe Polly would be the first person she'd tell. She was starting to think she'd be the best person to tell. She felt a momentary pang of betrayal at the thought, as though she were cheating on her mother. But hadn't her mother cheated on her? Wasn't that why they were going to a *jail* to visit her?

To Polly's credit, she didn't press for more. She just went on. "But he does like you, as much as he can like anyone right now."

Violet sighed and banged her head on the headrest. "No offense, Polly, but I think you might have this one wrong. He keeps telling me I'm a funny girl. Like, funny odd. That's hardly the stuff of great romances."

Polly laughed out loud as she made a left turn, then drove a few more feet, concentrating on the directions with her mouth pinched and her eyes squinted. She made one more turn, and Violet saw that they were entering a parking deck designated for the jail. Her stomach twisted inside her.

Polly drove past several parking spaces that Violet thought looked just fine till she found one she liked and pulled the car in, killing the engine. She turned to Violet. "He calls you funny because he doesn't know how to describe you. He doesn't know where to put you, because you're different from other girls. But once he figures it out . . ." Polly's voice faded away, and she looked out the driver's side for a moment. Violet thought she was trying not to cry.

"What happens once he figures it out?" Violet prodded.

She heard Polly sniff. Then she looked back at Violet. "He'll have a hard time letting go." Polly opened her door, signaling that the conversation was over, at least for now.

Violet tried to imagine a world where Micah Berg had a hard time letting her go. It was a nice thought, albeit unlikely, a distraction from what she was about to go do. She was glad her grandmother had talked about Micah because it was fun to talk about him. It was fun to get someone else's opinion about whatever this thing was between them. Whether Polly's opinion was right or wrong, it was fun to speculate. Mostly the conversation had been good to pass the time as they rode to the jail, helping her forget where they were going, and why.

Violet kept her seat and watched Polly climb out of the car, realizing her grandmother had probably known that, and that was exactly why she had done it. Polly leaned back in the car, a concerned look on her face. "You coming?" she asked.

Violet nodded yes, tugged her own door open, and followed her grandmother's lead.

Polly

After all the rigmarole of getting into the jail, they were ushered into a small, windowless private room and left to wait. They took seats at the lone table in the room and sat silently. Polly stared straight ahead at a glass wall. She'd seen enough cop shows to know someone likely stood on the other side, observing them, listening, hoping they'd say something incriminating. Polly shifted under the perceived person's gaze. She didn't want to say anything to Violet lest she say something wrong. Though the room was cool—she wished she'd thought to bring a sweater for both of them—she felt beads of sweat forming on her skin underneath her clothes.

She glanced at Violet, who gave her a brave smile in return. This is for you, kid, she thought. She didn't want Violet to feel guilty for wanting to see her mother. But if it'd been up to Polly, she'd have put off seeing Norah indefinitely. She relished the time with Violet, but the thought of seeing Norah rattled her. And she was rattled enough already. The threat of Calvin was plenty to be rattled about. She had thought she saw his truck drive down their street just that morning, but it hadn't been the right make after all.

Calvin had gone silent recently, and his silence scared her more than his incessant phone calls and texts. She didn't dare think the silence meant he'd given up. No, the silence meant he was devoting his efforts in a new direction, with the same intended outcome: getting at the money he felt he was entitled to. She'd changed its hiding place again just before they left to come to the jail, as if moving the money around Norah's house would render it invisible. Mostly she just wanted to do something to make herself feel safe, like she was at least *trying* to protect herself. Still, she felt Calvin out there somewhere.

The door opened and a man walked in. She'd seen his picture in the news articles about Norah, but they'd not had occasion to meet. It was Norah's attorney. He thrust his hand at Polly. "I'm Jim Sheridan," he said. "Norah's attorney."

Polly shook his hand. "I'm Polly Ca—" She stopped short of giving her last name, which was Calvin's last name. She waved her hand in the air like it just plain ole didn't matter who she was. "I'm Norah's mother."

"Good to meet you, Norah's mother," the attorney said. He turned to Violet and greeted her with a wide, genuine smile. "Hey, Violet," he said, and squeezed her shoulder. "You OK?"

Violet nodded even as she looked stricken. "Is my mom coming?" she squeaked out.

"Oh yes. She's about to come in. Just wanted to go over the ground rules before she does." He pointed at the glass wall. "This meeting will be monitored, and Norah's been instructed not to say anything pertaining to the case, as it could be held against her later, and, depending on what you guys say, you could be subpoenaed to testify about this conversation in court if it comes to that." He clapped his hands together, the loud sound resounding in the small room. "So, what I'm saying is, it's best if we avoid any and all mention of the case. Use your twenty minutes together to catch up on other things." He looked from Polly's face to Violet's and back again. "Capiche?"

They both nodded in unison. Jim Sheridan looked at them both again and smiled. "Man, the family resemblance is uncanny. It's like I'm looking at different versions of the same person."

"Thank you," said Polly, though she didn't know why, especially since, in his scenario, she was the old version.

He clapped his hands together again. "OK, let's go get your mommy," he said to Violet and gave her shoulder one more squeeze before darting out of the room.

Violet looked at Polly. "Mommy?" she said.

Polly laughed. Under the table, she reached for Violet's hand, resting on her lap, and gave it a squeeze. She waited for Violet to let go, but she didn't. So Polly didn't, either. And so it was that Norah shuffled in, the chains on her wrists and feet making a jangling noise not unlike Barney's collar. Startled by the noise, they let go of each other in an instant, as if they'd been caught doing something wrong. She wondered if Norah had even realized that her mother and her daughter had been holding hands. And if she did, if she cared. There was that litany running through Polly's brain lately: the one that said Norah should be grateful to her for coming to stay with Violet. Just grateful, and nothing else. But it was never that simple with Norah.

She took the seat across from them, and Polly was struck by two things: One, that Norah's bottom lip was trembling, which meant she was holding back tears upon either the sight of her daughter or the emotion of being reunited with her mother in this way, or some combo thereof. And two, that she looked awful. A far cry from the glamorous photos shown in all the news articles. In those photos, taken at various society events and fundraisers through the years, Norah had looked beautiful, radiant, expensive. But now she looked wan, drawn, and cheap. Her roots were showing. Her eyes had bags under them big enough for an overseas flight. Her complexion verged on a yellow-green color.

"Are you sick?" she heard herself ask, the first one to speak. Because once a mother, always a mother, she guessed.

Norah forced a smile. "Hello, Mother." She looked over at Violet, "Hi, Vi."

Beside her, she felt Violet relax at the sound of her mother's voice. Had her voice ever done that for Norah? She hoped so.

"And yes," Norah added, turning back to Polly. "I am sick." She looked over at Violet. "Sick of being in here." She gave a little laugh, intended to put her daughter at ease. She was probably thinking, If I can still joke around, then I must be OK, no matter how things appear.

"Are you coming home soon?" Violet asked, sounding much younger than Polly had ever heard her sound.

"We're working on that," Norah said.

"No you're not." Violet's response was wounded and automatic.

Across the table, Norah inhaled sharply. "Violet, yes, we are. Mr. Sheridan and I are doing everything we can to get me out of here."

Violet had a response at the ready. "I've read the articles just like everyone else. I know you're not telling them where your client list is. I know that if you did, they'd let you out. So, no, you're not doing everything you can. Because you could turn that list over." She crossed her arms and glared at Norah, daring her to disagree. The thing was, the child was right. Except she didn't totally understand. Not like an adult would. Not like Polly did. To Violet it was cut and dried. Turn over the client list and come home.

But Polly understood that to Norah it was more complex than that. Turn over the client list and make some very dangerous enemies, expose some people who would go to great lengths to avoid exposure. Mostly because a charge of this kind would open them up to further investigation. And if there was one thing Polly had learned, it was that men who were involved in a nefarious activity usually didn't limit it to just the one thing. There would be repercussions for that kind of exposure. To give up the client list was to potentially put Violet in harm's way. She and Norah looked at each other, and Polly understood: by staying in jail she wasn't protecting just herself; she was protecting those she loved.

She spoke up. "Your mother has her reasons. She's getting good counsel from wise folks about all of this. And this wasn't what we came here for anyway."

Violet, cool as a cucumber, turned to look at her. "This is exactly why I came here," she said. "To tell her to tell me where the list is. Is it on a drive? Or is it a printout? Is it, like, in a spiral notebook, old-school style? What?" Violet rose from her chair and leaned across the table. She lowered her voice to a whisper, and Polly wondered if the microphones in the room could pick up sound at that level. "Tell me and I'll go find it. I'll be the one to turn it in, and then those men can't blame you."

Polly watched as Norah flinched like she'd been slapped. She began to cry. "No, honey, it's not about who gets blamed. It's about doing the right thing. For everyone involved. It's not just me, honey. There are other people—"

"What about me?" Violet's raised voice made them both jump. She pounded her fists on the table, and Polly couldn't help but think of when she had been a baby in a high chair doing the same thing. "I thought I was the only other person who mattered to you. That's what you used to say. Remember? You said you'd never let anything come between us. You said you'd take care of me. But you didn't!"

"I know I did, baby. I know I did. I was wrong, OK? I was wrong to tell you that. I made promises to you that were impossible to keep." Norah looked over at Polly, desperation and something else that Polly couldn't read on her face. "That's what mothers do." And then she knew what it was she saw on her daughter's face: absolution. Somehow, in that jail cell, Norah had found it in her heart to forgive her. In the face of her failings as a mother, Norah had found the room to forgive her own mother. "The best I can hope for is that someday you'll find it in your heart to forgive me. For letting you down. For not being honest with you. For making mistakes."

Polly spoke up. "It's unavoidable."

Norah looked at her, her face impassive. But then she nodded, one quick dip of her chin.

Violet glanced over at the two of them, taking in what was happening. "You should thank Polly," she said. "I'm not sure what I'd have done without her."

Norah ducked her head, chastised. "I am thankful to her," she said to the table.

"She's a good grandmother," Violet said, and in her voice was a challenge, a bit of the defiance Polly wanted to see in the girl. That was the one thing she hadn't seen to remind her of Norah or herself. But Violet's life had been different from both of theirs. She'd been cared for, even coddled, by a doting mother, never lacking for anything. It had created a passive complacency that said less about her personality and more about her situation. Without the coddling, Polly could see that Violet would find the pluck she needed to survive. She looked at her granddaughter and, once again, was reminded of herself. Usually she didn't like what she saw when she saw herself. But when she saw herself through Violet, she felt proud and pleased. She felt hopeful for all of them.

Jim Sheridan stuck his head in the door, startling all three of them. He made a pained expression. "We should probably be wrapping things up. Saying any final words."

"Could I have a moment with my daughter alone?" Norah asked, looking from Jim to Polly, asking for permission from them both.

Polly rose in answer to Norah's question. "Yes, but make it quick," said Jim. Together, the two of them left the room. They stood outside the door awkwardly. Jim Sheridan looked at a door just down the hall. She knew what he was thinking.

"Do you want to get back in there so you can listen in on them? Make sure she doesn't say anything to hurt her own case? You don't have to stand here with me."

He looked at her gratefully. "Do you mind?" he asked.

"Not at all," she said. She gestured in the direction of the door, like a maître d' saying "Right this way."

"I hope this was beneficial," he said. "Seeing her."

"It was. For Violet."

And because he was a defense attorney and was used to being lied to, he nodded along, then gave her shoulder a squeeze just as he'd done to Violet. He walked away and disappeared behind the door into a room where he would listen in on Polly's daughter and granddaughter in their last few minutes together till who knew when.

Violet

When the door closed behind them, her mother wasted no time leaning forward, talking rapidly in an urgent tone. "Are you really OK with her? Tell me the truth."

"With Polly?" Violet asked, as if there could be another *her*.

"Yes, with Polly. Is that what you're calling her?"

Violet raised her eyebrows. "It's her name." She was being insolent on purpose. She wasn't going to hand over the keys to her kingdom to a woman who'd betrayed her, even if she was still hoping her mother would give up the client list and she'd have a chance to help Micah, or Norah, or both.

Norah ducked her head again, but the penitent look didn't suit her. Violet missed her strong, confident mother. This one scared her. It was like someone else pretending to be her mother. She looked like her, but she wasn't her. "I don't like you with her," Norah said to the table, her voice low. "That's the worst part of all this, that your flake of a father called her instead of doing his part."

Violet thought about all the things she'd wanted to tell her mother about being at her dad's, about her ridiculous stepmother and spoiled half siblings. She recalled how, when this had all begun, she'd truly believed that her mother would come home and they'd laugh—laugh!—about all of it. It would just be another amusing family anecdote. But of course, when this had all begun, Violet had believed they were a real family. She didn't believe that anymore. But if they weren't a family, then what were they?

"How come you never told me about the Beaucatchers?" she challenged, sensing that her mother wouldn't like it and wanting to punish her for staying in jail to protect other people instead of coming home to care for her.

She saw Norah bristle in response and felt the little thrill of hitting her mark. Their relationship hadn't been like that before, but, as Violet was coming to understand, their relationship had changed forever. She wondered if she'd ever trust her mother again, or if she was fated to feel about Norah the way Norah felt about Polly. If losing trust in your mother was part of the legacy just as much as attracting men.

"She told you about that?" Norah asked. She sounded tired. She looked beaten.

Violet nodded and Norah sighed, long and loud.

"Don't listen to that, Violet," she said. "Please. It's nonsense. It's not true. Just a bunch of Appalachian hillbillies making up their own kind of fairy tales. They told themselves something to make them feel better about where they were in life, which was nowhere. She raised me on that malarkey, and I vowed I'd be the last female in my line to have to hear it." Norah shook her head and closed her eyes. "I can't believe she told you that. I bet she couldn't wait to poison you same as she poisoned me."

Violet was quiet as she studied the woman who resembled her mother but was not her mother. Her voice was smaller than she wanted it to be when it came out of her mouth. "I liked it." She sounded like a child, but she wasn't a child anymore. She'd grown up in the last few weeks. She wanted to show her that. She cleared her throat, spoke louder. "I wish you had told me. I wish I had known Polly all along. I like being part of a line of women who are special."

"It's a fairy tale."

"People love fairy tales, Mom."

"But they don't come true." Norah looked around the room they were in, as if it were all the proof they needed.

"That legend didn't get you here," Violet said. "You got yourself here."

Norah's nostrils flared; her eyes went squinty. Violet had seen that look before. When she didn't clean her room. When she wore grubby clothes out to dinner. When she didn't listen to Norah. She saw the look flare, then die on her mother's face. A calm look replaced it.

"You're absolutely right," Norah said. "It didn't. But it did inform some things I believed about myself growing up. Things that weren't so good for me. I want you to be different from me, than Polly." She closed her eyes. "It was all I ever wanted. And I know you'll never understand this, but it was why"—she stopped, considered her words, probably remembering that the police and her attorney were listening—"it was why everything that has happened has happened. I was always thinking of you. Trying to make things better for you. So you didn't have to be like me."

"You mean a prostitute?" Violet countered, feeling smug and satisfied as once again, her word arrow hit its mark. She saw it go into her mother, and she pushed away the guilt that came after.

Norah hauled her bound wrists onto the table, settling them uncomfortably with a clang. She leaned forward. "When I was a little girl," she said, "my mother used to take me to visit her mother and aunt. They were just country bumpkins to me. Old ladies who baked biscuits and grew tomatoes in their garden. They certainly didn't seem like Beaucatchers, like my mother claimed they were. The only thing I could tell was that they'd both been married several times but now lived together with no man in sight. And all they seemed to want to ask me was, did I have a boyfriend? They didn't care if I had hobbies or interests. They didn't seem to care about current events or learning new things. They only cared about men. They made me a bride doll, gave it to me like that was the epitome of my existence. It had a beautiful lace dress with a matching slip underneath." Her mother tapped on the table with her finger, once, twice, three times, and looked at her. "I gave it to you, remember?"

Violet nodded, her mind racing as it processed what was happening. "It gave me the creeps. I felt like it was staring at me at night." She forced herself to say it lightheartedly. To act like this was just a fond memory, a family story—nothing more, nothing less. People were listening, after all.

Her mother laughed at the recollection. "So you hid it. Remember?" she said, leaning forward, eyebrows raised.

"I remember," Violet said.

"I gave you that doll not because I wanted to pass on some stupid legacy to you. But because I wanted it to be a symbol of what I didn't want you to be. Being a bride—some man choosing you for his own—isn't the be-all, end-all of your existence. It doesn't say nearly as much about you as you can say for yourself." Her mother swallowed and their eyes met. In that moment, Violet knew she would forgive her. Maybe not right this minute, but soon enough. She would be mad—she should be mad—but she would come to understand what it was her mother had tried to do for her. And what her mother had just done for her.

Violet nodded her understanding, both of what her mother was saying and of what she wasn't. Her mother slid her hands forward and Violet did the same in response. They weren't supposed to touch but did anyway. Their fingers had barely made connection when the door opened and Polly stepped into the room with an apologetic look. It was time to go. In one guilty motion, they both pulled their hands away, the chain of Norah's handcuffs making a scraping noise across the table, a sound that would echo in Violet's head long after they had left the jail, and her mother, behind.

Nico

After they were gone, he went into the room where the mother-and-child reunion had taken place. He could still smell the grandmother's perfume, floral and cloying, the kind of stuff older women wore, the only thing that gave a hint as to her age. It had been a study in genetics, watching the three of them together. It wasn't just looks or body types that were similar, but speech and movement. Sometimes he'd forgotten to pay close attention to what they were saying because he was paying closer attention to how they were saying it. They were quite a trio: they made him uneasy enough one at a time, but all together was almost too much to take.

He stood in the small, windowless room and collected himself as he waited for the smell of Polly's perfume to evaporate. He had to get it together so he could go after them. He'd picked up on something there at the end of their conversation. It was the story Norah had told Violet. She'd been trying to be sneaky. She thought she was smart—smarter than him—but his spidey senses had gone off. (It was a pleasure to know they still could.)

He suspected there was subtext to what she'd said to her daughter. It hadn't been just a heartwarming story meant to comfort the child. It had been a clue. He'd give them time to get home. Get dinner going. Be lulled into a false sense of the coast being clear. Then he would show up, ask to see the bride doll she'd mentioned. He'd tear the thing apart if he had to, pull the stuffing out of it till he found what Norah was hiding.

In his pocket, his phone buzzed. Matteo's autopsy results were due back at any moment. He pulled the phone from his pocket and frowned at it. It wasn't the medical examiner. It was an alert from his security system, signaling that the cameras had picked up movement in his driveway, which didn't make sense. Earlier he'd watched Karen, Lauren, and Ian all arrive home. Maybe one of them was leaving. He opened the app to see who it was.

But the person in his driveway wasn't related to him by blood or vow. He wasn't related to him at all, save the fact that they'd been neighbors for years, sharing bits of news, garden tools, and the occasional beers. If pressed, Nico would've called him a friend. When Matteo went missing, Mike had brought over a six-pack and offered to sit with him on the deck and drink it. It had been spring, and normally Nico would've done it. But he'd declined, saying he wasn't up to it and that he wasn't good company, all of which was true.

He couldn't imagine passing the time with anyone but his brother. Mike Lewis was a poor substitute. He'd accepted the beers, though, drinking them alone out on the deck, getting drunk as he watched his family pass by the windows inside, getting ready for bed without him. He'd waited till they were all asleep to go inside.

Now Mike Lewis knocked on Nico's door, unaware or unconcerned that he was being recorded. As he waited for someone to answer his knock, he whistled. Nico tried to place the song. Mike whistled a few more bars, and, for a blissful moment, Nico thought that no one was going to come to the door and Mike Lewis would go back where he came from, back to his homely wife and hellion twin boys. Mike Lewis had been coming around more and more, making lame excuses, which Karen fell for, offering his help in Nico's absence, playing the concerned neighbor. He'd had to refrain from telling Karen, "Listen, about Mike

Lewis. No man is that concerned about a woman without having some sort of motive."

Then Karen would know he was watching. And he wasn't supposed to have this app on his phone anymore. He'd gone as far as to delete it in front of her when she had asked. So he had to play it cool now, only make a move if it was truly necessary. He took a deep breath and spoke out loud in the small, windowless room. "Turn around and go home, asshole." No, Mike Lewis was not, and never had been his friend. He was glad he'd turned him away that night.

Karen answered the door, stepping out onto the porch. She smiled when she saw him. She'd showered since she got home; wet strands were visible. She'd put on lipstick. She was wearing a skirt. He gripped the phone tighter, squeezing it so hard he wished it would break. Nothing good came in on his phone anymore. The device was an interruption, a nuisance. He'd like to throw it away. Yet he could not be without it. It was his only remaining connection to his family.

"So, you still want to go?" Mike Lewis asked, and smiled nervously.

"If you do," Nico's wife said to his adversary, smiling that adorable grin that Nico had thought until this moment she reserved just for him.

Mike Lewis held out his hand to Karen. She took it. "You need to say goodbye to your kids?" he asked.

"Oh no, they know I'm going out with a friend." She giggled. "They couldn't wait to get rid of me."

"I'll have to thank them later for being so shortsighted," he said. And then Mike Lewis pulled Nico's wife away from the camera's eye, away from the home they'd shared, away from him. Off camera, Mike Lewis started whistling again. And this time Nico recognized the song. "Carolina in My Mind," by James Taylor. Karen had always liked that one because her name was in it. He couldn't believe she'd told him about that. What else had they shared? Nico sank into a chair and listened as, off camera, the whistling stopped, two car doors slammed, and the car started up and drove away.

He let himself sit and absorb what he'd just seen. He'd sit there for as long as it took to calm down. He had to be on his A game when he went to Norah's to see about the doll. He had to be OK. He'd deal with Karen's infidelity later. But was it infidelity if they were split up? It was for Mike Lewis. As far as Nico knew, he was still very much married. Maybe he'd call Mike Lewis's wife from the station, give her a tip. But not now. Now he had to get to Norah's before that kid did something with that doll. There was no time to waste. He rose from the chair and walked out of the room.

He was almost out of the station when his phone buzzed again. If anything could deter him from following up on the doll, it was the results of the autopsy. He stopped in the lobby and pulled his phone from his pocket. But again, it was the security camera, not the autopsy. His heart lifted. He smiled. Karen had come to her senses, told Mike Lewis it was a bad idea and to take her home. He clicked on the app to watch the scene unfold.

But instead of seeing Karen going back inside their house, looking guilty and ashamed of herself, he saw the smirking faces of those two thugs he'd seen his daughter talking to before, back at his door. Though he couldn't see her from the camera angle, he could hear as Lauren opened the door wide and greeted them happily.

"We got here as fast as we could," one of them said.

Off camera, Lauren giggled. "Come on in," she said.

And they did. He heard the door shut behind them, and the camera kept recording nothing and no one. He watched for a bit, waiting for Lauren to remember the rules and kick the boys out. A bird flew by the camera. A breeze blew, rustling the branches of the azalea bush, long devoid of flowers. An adventuresome squirrel scampered along the rail of the porch. But no sign of the boys. Karen was gone. Ian was likely in his room with headphones on, lost in a world of animated gun battles, oblivious, leaving Lauren alone with two older boys wearing matching leers.

He looked up suddenly, remembering he was standing in the lobby of the police station. Candace, the receptionist who occasionally flirted with him (harmlessly), glanced nervously away. But he could tell she'd been watching him, likely wondering just what he had stopped to see on his phone. He shoved it back into his pocket and tried to catch Candace's eye. But she busied herself with *looking* busy.

He walked out of the lobby, looking sheepish and feeling worried. And torn. Should he go to his house and interrupt Lauren and the delinquents? Or should he head to Norah Ramsey's house as intended? Should he do his job, or protect his daughter? His hunch about the doll was just a hunch, after all. No one would know if he didn't follow up. No one but him. Which would he regret more? If he didn't catch Norah Ramsey, he might never know what happened to Matteo. But if he didn't check on Lauren, something bad could happen, something that he'd regret forever.

Matteo was dead. No investigation was going to change that. When there had been a chance Matteo was alive and just in hiding, then the detective work—the dedication—had been worth it. He had had the hope that he could save his brother. But Matteo didn't need saving. Not anymore. His daughter, however, did—even if she didn't know it. Nico got into his car and sat there for a moment just to be sure exactly what his gut was telling him. Could he even trust his gut anymore? He could feel the pull toward home, toward his family, acutely. It was like the moon pulling the tides. And the tide had turned for him, just like that. He backed out of his parking space and turned in the opposite direction of Norah Ramsey's house. For the first time in a long time, Nico had something—someone—else to save.

Bess

She let herself into Norah's house, just like she used to, remembering the code in the same way that she could still remember her childhood phone number. Some things just stayed with you. Behind her, Casey carried the rest of the dinner. She'd thought that maybe she and Casey would just stay and eat with Violet and Polly. It had to get lonely, just the two of them rattling around this house.

Bess wondered what they talked about. Did Polly tell her what Norah had been like as a child? Did she tell her about herself? Ask Violet questions about her life? Bess couldn't imagine being estranged from one of her daughters for so long. She wondered how Polly had withstood it. She knew that Polly hadn't had much choice in the matter. Bess knew how stubborn Norah was, how long she could hold out once she committed to something.

"I guess they're not back yet," she said to Casey as they trooped through the house toward the kitchen in the back.

"Back from where?" Casey asked, sounding bored. She was asking only to make conversation. Bess was still shocked she'd agreed to come along and help transport the meal.

"They went to visit Norah," she said. She tried to make her voice light as she said it. What was it the kids said in their texts? NBD: no big deal. She wanted to make it sound like Polly and Violet's errand was just that, an errand.

But Casey wasn't falling for it. "In jail?"

Bess nodded and began unloading the food. She'd brought too much; she always did. She smiled at Casey as she set the salad down on the kitchen island. "Thank you," she said. She truly was thankful for the help, but more than that, she was thankful her daughter had agreed to spend one-on-one time with her. Casey had been even more wary of Bess since the whole scene with Eli. Bess wanted her to know she was forgiven, but she didn't want to bring it up and embarrass Casey anew. But maybe now, here, she could try to smooth the waters.

She opened her mouth to speak, trusting the right words would come out. She would tread lightly, she would speak gently, she would begin making inroads to her daughter's heart. "I . . . ," she got out.

She watched Casey's face change, a panicked look registering as she glanced around the empty house. Clearly Casey had counted on Polly and Violet being there to act as buffers. She'd not counted on being trapped in an empty house with her mother while they waited for them to get home.

Still, this was Bess's moment and she was going to take it. "I . . . ," she started again.

She watched as Casey's face changed again, but this time it filled with relief, her eyes training on something just over Bess's shoulder. She glanced behind her to see Violet letting herself in the back door. Bess exhaled, not with disappointment, but relief. She was off the hook for a little while longer. But soon, she told herself. Soon she would confront her daughter. She'd find out what had happened to bring her home. She'd make Casey tell her. Somehow, she would.

Polly bustled in after Violet, looking beleaguered. It had to be hard, seeing your daughter incarcerated, no matter how long you'd been estranged from her. Bess reached into the bag on the counter and extracted the wine, holding it up to Polly with her eyebrows arched in question.

"Bless you," Polly said. She held up her index finger. "I'll be right back." She disappeared into the back bedroom suite. Bess turned to the girls, who were surveying each other warily. For a day or so, Bess had thought that the two of them were becoming friends, which she'd found sweet. But now something seemed strained, like a thread pulled taut in the air between them, dangerously close to breaking. Again, Bess wondered what she didn't know about her older child. Again, she found herself wishing she could break through the barrier Casey had erected to keep her from gaining access.

Instead she just asked if the two of them would like to help her assemble dinner. When in doubt, cook. That was her philosophy.

"I think I'll go upstairs. I'm not very hungry," Violet said.

Bess looked at this girl she'd watched grow from preschooler to teenager, seeing all the iterations of her at once, like she was partly hers, like she had claim, too. Which, in a perfect world, would be true. That's what she and Norah had said; that's what they had promised: to be there for each other all the time, through all the years. Back then they'd never imagined it working out any other way. But it had.

"Sure," was all Bess said in response. "Of course."

After Violet left, she and Casey blinked at each other, like *What now?*

The answer came in the form of Polly breezing back in, looking less worse for wear. She'd even managed to put on a smile, albeit a weak one. When Bess handed her a glass of wine, the smile widened, the dog at her heels. Bess had forgotten all about him. He sniffed Bess, and she scratched his head. "Hey, boy," she said to him. She hoped she'd remembered correctly that he was a boy. Polly opened the back door to let him out.

Casey saw the moment as her opportunity to take her leave. "I'm just gonna go check on Violet," she said as she backed out of the kitchen.

"Don't get your feelings hurt," Polly called after her, "if she doesn't talk much. Didn't say a word on the ride home."

Casey disappeared up the stairs, and Bess poured herself a glass of wine. "I'm sure that was hard on her," she said.

Polly let the dog in and went straight to her glass, taking a large gulp. "I'll say."

"Hard on you, too," Bess said, taking her own, more judicious sip.

Polly shrugged. "Norah's just so damn stubborn. Wouldn't cave about that damn list even to her own daughter. She says it's for the best—and maybe it is; who knows what she's gotten herself mixed up in—but to sit there in front of her daughter and tell her she won't do what needs to be done so she can come home. I mean, even if just to her face, just to comfort her somewhat. It just . . ." Polly shrugged and sank into one of the bar stools lined up along the island.

"I remember how stubborn she is." Bess laughed, trying to lighten the mood, to distract her.

Polly looked at her quizzically, like she was just remembering that they'd once been good friends. "How long has it been since you . . ." She faltered in trying to find a good way to say that Norah and Bess's friendship had come to an end.

Bess took another, larger sip of wine. Maybe she and Polly would just sit there and get good and drunk. "How long has it been since we parted ways?" Bess asked, filling in Polly's blank.

Polly smiled. "Yeah."

"Well, when did *Iron Man Three* come out?" Bess asked.

Polly wrinkled her brow. "*Iron Man?*"

"We went to see it. That was the last thing we ever did together."

Polly gave her a bemused smile. "That's kind of specific."

"Well, we both felt pretty strongly about Robert Downey Jr." Bess smiled like it was nothing, but in truth that night stood out against all the others she'd ever had with Norah. She remembered it with clarity: the movie, the conversation, the way things unfolded from there.

"Did something happen? That night? I mean, for it to be the last night . . . ," Polly asked.

Bess shook her head. "Nothing specific," she lied. She didn't know Polly well enough to go into detail. And even if she knew Polly better, she wouldn't go into what she and Norah had talked about that night. "We just sort of drifted apart after that. She started pulling away. I let her, figured she was busy. I figured she'd come back around. But she never did." Bess shrugged. "She just never did."

"She lets people go," Polly said, sounding sad.

Bess nodded, thinking how easy it had seemed for Norah, how hard it had been for Bess. She stood up to fetch them both more wine. It was going down easy. She felt the head rush that came from drinking too much, too fast. She welcomed it.

Her movement disturbed the dog. He got up and followed her, sniffing around her feet hopefully. "No wine for you, buddy," she said to him. "What's his name again?" she asked Polly, grateful for the subject change. She didn't want to reminisce about Norah anymore.

"Barney," Polly said.

"Hey, Barney," Bess said to the dog. "Where'd you get him?" He didn't look like any certain breed, though he could've had some Labrador retriever in him.

"He's a rescue. I used to volunteer for a rescue society. He was the last puppy left in a litter. He just cried and cried when they all left him behind. I caved and took him home."

"Did he come with the name?"

"No, I named him that," said Polly. She took another sip and smiled to herself. "He's named after Barney Rubble. Remember *The Flintstones*?"

Bess took a sip, too, then smiled as well, like they were playing the copycat game the girls used to play. "Big *Flintstones* fan, are you?" she asked.

Polly shook her head, but her smile didn't fade. "I brought him home and sat down on the couch holding him, just thinking, What have I done? I clicked on the TV just to distract myself. And *The*

Flintstones were on. And there were Fred and Barney on the screen. And for some reason it was like I was noticing Barney for the first time. Like Fred always gets the attention. He's the bigmouth, the blowhard. And Barney is just the sidekick, right?"

Bess realized that Polly expected an answer. "Right," she said.

"And I thought about how"—Polly shook her head—"never mind."

"No!" Bess protested. "You have to tell me!"

Polly rolled her eyes, looking for all the world like Violet. "OK, but it's going to sound stupid."

"I don't care," Bess said.

"So I thought, OK, yes, Barney is a caveman. But he's a caveman with a heart. He's not like Fred. He tries to do the right thing. He tries to talk sense to Fred. He thinks about Betty and Wilma. He knows he's a caveman, but he doesn't have to act like one. It was this kind of—I don't know—revelation for me." She fell silent, thinking about what Bess didn't know.

"So there are some good cavemen out there in the world, is what you're saying," Bess piped up.

Polly lifted her glass as if in toast. "At least I thought so that day."

Bess lifted hers as well. "To the Barneys of the world," she said. "And to those of us who like to believe they do exist."

"To the only Barney I know," Polly said. At their feet, the dog heard Polly say his name and lifted his head, sniffing the air for something that wasn't there, but certain that it was coming.

Casey

She didn't knock before entering Violet's room. She should've, but she didn't. She didn't know why except that something told her not to. The element of surprise worked to her advantage. She saw Violet on her bed, messing with a doll. She'd caught Violet, doing what, she did not know. But the shocked and guilty look on the younger girl's face told Casey that Violet was up to something. Violet put the doll down.

"People are supposed to knock," she said, scolding Casey.

Casey recognized the tactic: find the wrong someone else had done in order to take the spotlight off yourself. She herself had used it before. But what had Violet been up to with that doll? Casey studied the thing, now tossed aside, its cold china eyes staring blankly at the wall beside Violet's bed. It wore an old-fashioned bridal dress, layers of stiff lace and fabric, a high collar. The doll was entirely white, save the two blue eyes and the round pink circles painted on its cheeks.

The same feeling that had told Casey to walk on in told her not to press Violet about the doll. She had just come from seeing her mom in jail, after all. Maybe the doll had been some sort of sentimental gift from her mom or a prized family heirloom. Casey looked from the doll to Violet and back again, thinking about the irony of a bride doll belonging to a prostitute. But of course, Norah Ramsey hadn't been accused of prostitution; she'd been accused of running a prostitution ring. She'd arranged the services, put her administrative skills and business acumen to use. Nothing Casey had seen in the news asserted that she'd performed the services herself. Casey tried to imagine the same woman who had once cut up apples for their snack and slathered sunscreen on their shoulders going to bed with a stranger for money. She couldn't. And what if she had? Casey had gone to bed with a stranger and hadn't gotten a thing out of it except a scary encounter when she tried to leave afterward. She shuddered at the recall.

"Polly says when you shiver like that, it means someone just walked over your grave," Violet said.

Casey squinted at Violet. "That's bizarre, Violet."

Violet looked down, embarrassed. "Well, it's what Polly says."

Casey was sorry for what she'd said. She was older than Violet. The kid looked up to her. "Sorry," she apologized. "I've just never heard that before."

Violet shrugged. "Neither had I. Polly says lots of things I've never heard before." She cocked her head. "So if it wasn't someone walking over your grave," she countered, "what was it?"

"What was what?" Casey asked.

"What made you shiver? It's not like it's cold in here." Violet watched her, her gaze like a laser cutting through Casey's resolve to keep it all inside. Casey tried to dodge the question, wanting to tell Violet that everything was fine. To lie. Again. But the same thing that had led her to walk into this room unannounced now told her that she should be honest with the kid, that now was finally the time to tell someone what was going on, and that, surprisingly, Violet was the person she should tell.

"Did you find anything the other day? When you went with Micah?" She would ease into it, give herself a way out of the conversation if she chickened out.

"No," Violet answered. A funny expression crossed her face when she said it, one that told Casey that if she wanted to distract Violet, she could by probing for what Violet wasn't telling. Casey wasn't the only one keeping secrets in this room. But Violet's secrets were hers to tell when she was ready.

"Too bad," Casey said, still hedging, still circling around what she needed to say.

"It was for Micah," Violet replied with a shrug. "Not me." Violet tried to sound nonchalant, but Casey wasn't buying it.

"How'd it go with you two?"

"It was fine," Violet said. "He's nice. Not like you think."

"That's good," Casey said. She moved over to Violet's desk and pulled the chair out. She perched on the edge, took a deep breath, then went for it. "I shouldn't have blown you off the other day. When you asked me to go with you guys."

Violet sat up a little more. "No," she agreed. "You shouldn't have. Micah's not a bad guy. There's stuff you don't know. Stuff only Micah and I know."

Casey narrowed her eyes, tempted again to go down a different conversational path, one also about secrets, but not hers. It would be so easy, and yet, it was not what she needed to do. She'd scared herself the other day with the cop; she'd gone too far. The only way to keep from doing it again was to talk about it, to tell someone the truth. And poor Violet had drawn the short straw.

"There's stuff you don't know, too," she said. "Stuff about me."

Violet's hazel eyes widened, turned greener than Casey had ever seen. Casey looked at the girl as if seeing her for the first time. Was it possible that in a few short weeks Violet had changed enough that it was visible, even to her? Casey had always thought of Violet as a child, but she saw now that she wasn't anymore. She had to repress a sudden urge to wrap her arms around the girl, shelter her from harm. The same kind of harm that had been done to her. But maybe, in telling Violet what she was about to tell her, she would be doing just that. In knowledge, she thought, there is power. In relationship, there is strength.

"I slept with the guy I had lunch with."

Violet sucked in air. "You cheated on Eli?"

"This isn't about Eli," Casey said. She had to stop herself from laughing at the absurdity of this having anything to do with Eli. Granted, Eli would be hurt if he knew—and she supposed he probably had a right to know, since she once loved him and probably, deep down, still did. But this was more than her and Eli. More than her and that cop. It was about what was broken inside of her. And who broke it. Russell Aldridge.

"I did it because I was trying to convince myself I was OK. That what happened to me didn't matter."

Violet's words were a whisper. "What happened to you?"

Casey felt her body start to shake, but this time, instead of an outward shudder, it was a tremor inside her, building like an earthquake.

"I came home," she said. She forced herself to look at Violet, who nodded in agreement. She knew Casey had come home. She'd gone on a walk with Casey the day she had arrived, the day Violet's mother had been arrested. That seemed like a long time ago now, but really it had been a matter of weeks.

The dean had called Casey again today, urging her to return to school, pleading with her to file a statement alongside the other girl, the one Russell Aldridge had also assaulted, the one who'd upset her so much the night before, she'd fled. Perhaps this was the real reason that Casey was talking about it now, because she knew it was time to stop fleeing. She'd run home. She'd run into Eli's arms. She'd run into a stranger's arms. She'd even run here, to this house, to avoid telling her mother. But no matter how much she ran, it kept catching up to her.

So now here she was, blurting the truth out to a fifteen-year-old kid. Casey didn't know if this was fair to Violet, but she couldn't stop now that she'd started. She had to unburden herself, finally. And besides, Violet was the toughest kid she knew. She could still picture Violet announcing that it was probably best she leave their house after Nicole was such a bitch to her. She'd handled that. She could likely handle this.

"I left school after a girl told me that she knew that I'd been assaulted by a guy we both knew. He assaulted her, too. And she wanted us to go and report what had happened to the school officials. She wanted to make it public. She didn't want him to do it to anyone else. She wanted us to stop him from hurting anyone else. She wanted . . ."

Inside of her, the shaking intensified. Her jaw began to quiver as she went on, making it hard to talk, but she forced herself to keep going. "She *still wants* justice. But I hadn't allowed myself to think of what had happened in that way. I didn't think of it as a crime. I'd been telling myself it was my fault. I dressed too slutty that night. I agreed to go alone with him to his apartment to get more beer. I told myself that going with him like that was the same as consent. I'd been drinking too much. I'd brought it on myself. And when it was happening, I froze. I didn't fight back. I let it happen. So I told myself it wasn't really an assault. I convinced myself it was no big deal. Just something that happened—that happens to a lot of girls in college who are stupid. Then they learn, and then they get smarter. I tried that the other day, with that guy. I tried to be smarter, to be in control." She inhaled deeply, needing the oxygen.

As she did, Violet's voice was quiet but clear. "And were you in control?"

Casey felt hot tears leaking from the corners of her eyes. She shook her head. "I'm starting to think there's no way to control it. For anyone."

"My mom tried," Violet said with a sigh. "And it didn't work for her."

The two of them looked at each other, and for a few seconds, neither of them said a word.

Violet broke the silence. "Maybe the other girl has the right idea. Maybe justice *is* control."

Casey slowly blinked. She'd considered this. It was certainly better than what she'd tried already. Hearing Violet say it out loud made it feel real, close. Possible. "I think—"

Violet threw up a hand to stop Casey, hearing an angry, unfamiliar male voice erupt from downstairs. "You'd have respected me like a good wife!"

Polly

She'd been so distracted by her conversation with Bess, so delighted to have someone to talk to after that disconcerting meeting with Norah, that she hadn't locked the door behind Barney when she let him back in. Calvin just opened the door with the turn of a knob, strolling in like he lived there, with that shit-eating grin on his face and a gun in his hand. Barney, the dumb-ass dog, got up and went to greet Calvin, his long-lost master. With his free hand, Calvin reached down and scratched Barney's ears as Barney wagged his tail. The traitor.

"Calvin, what are you doing here?" She yelled as if she were startled, but really it was so that Bess would hear her. Bess had just stepped into the bathroom, so Polly didn't know if he realized anyone else was there. She hoped Bess heard her yell, hoped she knew not to show her face. She hoped it also alerted the two girls upstairs, and that they were smart enough to sense the danger and stay out of sight. She would handle this herself. She would keep everyone safe as best she could.

"I got tired of waiting for you to come home," he said.

She thought of lying, but she figured if he was there, he knew the rest. She had banked on him never finding out she had a daughter. She wished she knew how he had found out, but she wasn't going to ask and anger him further.

"I had to come here," was all she said in response.

"Not with our money you didn't," he countered.

"You were spending it without my per—" No. *Permission* would be the wrong word choice. That would set him off. "Without my consent." She swallowed. "It's my money, too. We should be discussing where it's going."

"Then you should've stuck around and discussed it," he sneered, punctuating the sentence by jabbing the air with the gun, like dotting an exclamation point.

"I had to leave in a hurry. I was needed here."

He looked around at the setting, the sheer domesticity of it. The flowers on the table, the dinner heating in the oven. The plates on the counter. The two glasses of wine. Two. He knew someone else was here. "Where's your friend?" He gestured to the wine, drawing a line in the air between the two wineglasses. "Is it a male friend, or a female one?" He sniffed the air as if to discern perfume or cologne in the air.

"Female. She had to leave." Polly pointed toward the front door, insinuating that Bess had gone out the front as he had come in the back. "She had to take her daughter to soccer." She hoped she looked believable. Thankfully Bess and Casey had walked the food down, and Polly had moved Norah's car into the garage weeks ago, so there was no car in the drive to disprove her statement.

He gestured at the glasses of wine. "She shouldn't drink and drive," he said. As if he were the bastion of sound judgment and good decisions.

"It wasn't much. She forgot, actually. She just ran out of here real quick as soon as she remembered." She was still talking loudly, hoping the others in the house heard and figured out that someone was here. Someone dangerous.

But Calvin didn't seem to be listening. Instead he moved out of the kitchen and farther into the house, his eyes darting around as he took it all in. The fact that Bess hadn't returned encouraged her. Polly hoped she'd heard. She hoped the girls had heard. She hoped she could get rid of Calvin quickly, appease him, distract him, whatever it took. She squeezed her eyes shut as if when she opened them he would be gone;

this would all be a terrible hallucination. She'd never been much of a drinker, and this would prove why she should stay away from the stuff. The worst thing about it was that she and Bess had been having such a nice time. She'd actually been having—as strange as it was on the heels of that hard encounter with Norah—fun.

She watched the back of her husband's head and wished she had a gun in her own hand. She'd shoot him dead right that moment. For the first time since he'd walked in, she wondered if she would survive this, if he would decide to let her live. She felt her pulse rate pick up, felt the fear rise in her throat like bile.

"I'll give you the money," she said. "If that's what you really want. I'll give it to you right now. You can just take it and go."

He turned around. "You make it sound so nice, sweetheart. So civil." He smiled coldly at her. "But if it was that easy, you'd have already done that. You wouldn't have taken our money and run off and left me with no explanation. You would've answered when I called you." His voice grew louder. "You wouldn't have lied to me all these years that you didn't have a child when you most certainly did. A granddaughter, too." He narrowed his eyes, held the gun up, and roared, "You'd have respected me like a good wife!"

"I'm sorry, Calvin." Her voice sounded small and weak. She cowered, afraid of the wild energy rolling off his body and the darkness he seemed to have ushered into the room with him. She wished she had the strength to stand up to him, to not be paralyzed by the threat of his anger paired with that gun. But she knew this: she had to live. Because if she died, Violet would have no one. She couldn't let that happen. She'd rather placate him and lose some dignity than have her granddaughter find her lying dead in her den. The child had experienced enough.

"I'll give you the money. I'll give you all of it. I made a mistake," she said evenly and calmly. "I reacted badly to the news about my daughter. I wasn't thinking straight. I've been consumed with things here. I haven't handled it well." She could hear herself begging, and she hated it. But she had to do what she must do. Pride, in this case, really would go before a fall. A fall she wouldn't stand back up from.

He yelled at her again. "You think you can just buy me off? You think that you can hand me money and make up for the disrespect you've showed me? You and your *whore daughter?*"

At that moment, she heard the footsteps on the stairs, four feet running. She dropped her head in defeat. If Violet and Casey showed their faces, things would only get worse. But she couldn't stop them. Once they saw the gun, they would realize the danger. Once they saw the gun, it would be too late. She thought again of Bess, hoped that wherever she was, she was calling the police. But then she remembered, Bess had left her phone on the island, right beside her wineglass. And Norah didn't have a house phone that Bess could go to.

At the sound of the girls' arrival, Calvin turned toward the stairwell with a smirk, the gun pointed. "Hello," he said. "Which one of you is Violet Ramsey?"

Casey stepped forward without missing a beat. "Me," she said. "I am." Violet looked at Polly with questioning eyes. Polly gave her a barely perceptible shake of the head. *Just go with it,* she willed her granddaughter while silently thanking Casey for doing such a brave—albeit crazy—thing.

She saw Calvin look from one girl to the next. She saw his gaze linger on Violet, and she wondered if, when he saw her, he thought of the framed photo Polly had kept on her dresser. It was of her, her mother, grandmother, and beloved aunt. "Peas in a pod" was written along the bottom of the photo in her grandmother's chicken-scratch handwriting. That was why she'd kept it. Because of that caption. Because it reminded Polly of where she had come from, of who she was. Which wasn't this. It wasn't any of this. She was deeply ashamed of herself for where she had ended up, deeply ashamed of how far she had not come. She had a broken picker. That was clear. So why did she keep on picking?

She hoped that Calvin didn't see Polly's younger face on Violet, hoped he wasn't that bright. Thankfully he didn't. He just waved the gun at the two of them. "Then who's this?" he asked Casey.

Casey started to answer, but Violet broke in. "I'm Casey. I'm a neighbor. I was here to help Violet study."

"Well, isn't that just peachy?" Calvin singsonged. He stood there for a moment, keeping his eyes on Casey, who he thought was Violet. "You're a pretty thing," he said to Casey, who bristled as he said it. He looked over at Polly. "You always said you were a late bloomer, but this one's not a bit late. I'd say she's right on schedule." He laughed, his laughter ringing through the silent house.

In the kitchen, Barney roused, aware that perhaps things weren't OK. He trotted over to Polly and sat down beside her, nervously watching Calvin.

"You in the same business as your mama?" He turned back to Casey.

Casey stood completely still, but Polly could see she was working hard to keep from trembling. Don't worry, Polly thought, I will throw myself on that gun before I let him touch you.

"Not gonna tell me, huh?" he asked. He looked again at Polly. "This a family business?"

Polly also said nothing. Barney made a low warning growl. She patted his head, uselessly trying to comfort him. Barney wasn't a spring chicken. He would be no match for Calvin's gun if he tried to fight his former master.

"Huh?" He pointed the gun at Polly. "Answer me when I ask you a question, you bitch!"

"No," she said.

"Well, I think you're lying. I remember when I asked you how you came into all your money. I remember you saying you made a good investment a long time ago and it paid off. And I figured it was something one of your former husbands did for you, something I shouldn't go nosing around in. Not looking a gift horse in the mouth, so to speak." He laughed, even though it wasn't funny. Calvin always did think he was funny when he wasn't. "But now it makes sense. The money came from her, didn't it? You're the one they're looking for. You're the silent partner. The one who was washing the money for the hos. Wasn't ya?"

Violet—the real Violet—blurted out, "Wait, you're Lois?"

Polly shushed her so that Calvin wouldn't figure out who the real Violet was. If he figured out that Casey had lied, that would make things worse. She looked at her granddaughter and wondered how much she knew about Norah's operation—whether Violet had figured things out for herself or whether Norah had told her. She wondered again what they had talked about when they were alone in the jail.

"Casey," she said to Violet. "I told you you've been reading too much about the case. I told you not to worry about it. Be a kid. Don't worry about grown-up stuff." She turned to Calvin. "In fact, I think you should let the kids go. This has nothing to do with them. Especially Casey, here. She's a neighbor. She should go on home." She raised her eyebrows at Violet, daring her to say any more. If he lets you go, she thought, run like hell to that kid across the street and get some help.

But Calvin shook his head. He tucked the gun into his waistband. "I don't think her going home right now is the best thing. I think we need to get things settled here first. And I ain't gonna hurt 'em," he said. "Unless they do something stupid. And they don't look like stupid girls to me." He looked from Violet to Casey, watching as they confirmed that they weren't stupid.

Satisfied, he strolled into the kitchen and opened the refrigerator, searching, Polly knew, for a beer. Norah didn't keep beer in her fridge, though. So he was shit out of luck. She heard him close the fridge and wondered for a frantic second if she could herd the girls out the front door. She could see the door from where she was standing, but would they make it before he could round the corner and start shooting? Would he start shooting? Or was the gun just a prop intended for intimidation? Polly didn't want to risk finding out. So she kept still.

He came back with one of the glasses of wine topped off from the bottle sitting on the island, where it was tucked into one of those fancy things that kept white wine cold. Bess had explained the gadget to Polly. At the thought of Bess, she glanced around, wondering where she was and what she was doing. Perhaps she was just hiding, hoping they would be rescued. But by whom? No one could possibly know that Polly's ex-husband had invaded their house. She'd told no one here that she was even married. She hoped that kid across the street happened over, sensed something was wrong when no one came to the door but the car was there. She hoped for something. From someone. Hell, she'd welcome that detective at the moment.

Calvin sipped the wine as he made his way across the room to stand in front of Casey, who he thought was Violet. He held the glass up to Polly, the wine sloshing slightly as he did so. "Fancy," he said. And in that one word was recrimination, accusation, and a reminder that she didn't belong here, in this world of finer things. That no matter what kind of life Norah had made for herself, Polly wasn't good enough for it.

She didn't need Calvin to tell her that; she had always known where she belonged, and she'd tried to stay within the boundaries. Even when she had the money to leave—after Norah had tracked her down and proposed a business deal, an arrangement that, as Norah had said then, would ensure Polly never needed a man again. On some level she understood that Norah had been trying to help her, to free her from dependence on a string of terrible men. And yet she'd stayed with Calvin. Right inside those self-imposed boundaries.

She watched in helpless revulsion as Calvin leaned closer to Casey, reached out, and fingered a lock of her hair as he took another sip. He was downing the wine fast, like he usually drank beer. Desperate, she hoped that the alcohol would make him clumsy, foolish, vulnerable.

Calvin was always a sloppy drunk. Just keep drinking, dumb-ass, she thought. Go get a refill. And get away from that child.

But Calvin stayed where he was, leering at Casey, occasionally glancing at Polly just to watch her squirm. He was toying with them, enjoying it. Who knew how long this would go on and where it would lead. And then Polly saw movement in the hall, just off the den, behind Calvin. Bess moved with the sinewy stealth of a panther, silently creeping closer to the action. Polly had no idea how long Bess had been inching her way down the hall. Probably since the first time Calvin had gone near her daughter. She looked over and saw in both girls' frozen faces that they'd spotted Bess, too, that they knew what was about to happen.

And then it did.

Bess

She'd spent months in that self-defense class preparing for a moment like this, training, drilling, practicing. She'd learned all the moves and countermoves. She'd developed her strength and her reflexes. She'd been a star pupil, getting praise from her instructor. Just like everything in life, she'd strived to be the best. But now, faced with the real possibility of fighting a man holding a gun, she feared she'd forgotten it all. She feared she would fail. And she would die. But she couldn't stay hidden any longer, reviewing her strategy in her mind, avoiding putting it into action because she was afraid to move. She'd been afraid to move all her life.

But when she heard the man talking to Casey, who'd so bravely said she was Violet, Bess sprang into action, her body moving even before her mind registered what was happening. Forget waiting for a rescuer; she was going to be one.

She didn't know what had happened to Casey at school. All she knew was that something had happened, and she hadn't been there for it. But she could be there now; she could show Casey: *I will fight for you no matter what. I will fight for you when you can't fight for yourself.* She hadn't done a good job of that since Casey had come home. She hadn't done a good job of that ever. She'd stayed hidden her whole life, doing what was expected of her instead of what she wanted. Norah, she thought, Norah had always challenged her to be bolder, to live bravely. But Bess had continued to stay hidden. Not anymore.

As she approached the man, she reviewed her advantage: he couldn't see her, so she had the element of surprise on her side. And her disadvantage: he had a weapon, and she did not. He was also bigger than her. "Your disadvantages are not your determiners," she heard her instructor say in her head. She tried to believe that as she prepared to attack.

She would use a combination of a takedown and a sealed choke hold—something they'd spent a whole day drilling in class. She'd done this successfully before, and with an instructor larger than her. As she moved down the hall, she recalled that day, running through the motions like a highlight reel. She knew what she had to do: jump on his back and lodge her feet behind his knees, pulling back with her arms at the same time. This would cause them both to end up on the ground, with him flat on his back, his head on her lap. Then she needed to instantly get her right arm around his neck, her left hand behind his head, wrap the fingers of her right hand around her left elbow to create a choke hold, and squeeze. With no more than ten seconds of applied pressure, she could render him unconscious.

All I need is ten seconds, she thought. The girls and Polly can run out the front door as soon as I have him down. And once I've choked him out, I can run, too. Ten seconds is all that stands between this menace and safety. She stood right behind him. It was time.

As she jumped on his back, she yelled "Run!" and all three of them did just that. If nothing else, she thought as the two of them hit the ground, the others will be safe. The surprise attack worked: she heard his gun clatter to the floor, the wineglass hit the ground and shatter. She felt liquid splashing her leg. "Bitch!" she heard him yell, but it sounded far away, the sound dulled by the roaring wind blowing in her head. She no longer felt like a woman; she felt like an animal: a lion or a bear, something fierce and ferocious. She got him into a choke hold, using every muscle in her upper body to create the seal. She had him.

His punch caught her off guard. He aimed for her elbow, his knuckles connecting to her funny bone. Her arm lurched forward, breaking the seal she'd just created. He tugged on her forearm, loosening his head from her grasp, and scrambled away toward the gun. Her instincts took over, and instead of choosing flight, she chose fight. They both lunged for the gun, hands flailing and grabbing. She felt pain in her arm, but in a distant way. It seemed more like a dream of pain.

And then he prevailed. He grabbed the gun and their eyes met, both wild, both angry. He saw her realize she'd been beaten; he saw her run toward the front door, left open by the three who had gotten out. At least they are safe, she thought as she ran toward the open door. She heard shots ringing out behind her, saw one hit that huge pumpkin on Norah's porch as she neared it, watched it explode. He'd missed. Perhaps the wine had made him a bad shot. Just make it to the porch, she thought. He won't shoot you in the front yard, in plain sight. By now the girls will have called the police. They'll be on their way.

She reached the threshold when she felt a force knock her forward. She was falling. As she fell, she saw Jason running toward her, something shiny clutched in his hand. She smiled at him, grateful that his was the last face she'd see instead of the man trying to kill her. Then Jason's face faded, and she saw colors swirling before her eyes, all the colors of the rainbow. The colors ran together like alcohol ink, shimmering and undulating. It's so beautiful, she thought. And then she thought nothing at all.

Nico

He pulled into his driveway so sharply that the tires squealed, announcing his arrival. So much for the element of surprise working to his advantage. He didn't care. This was his house. He still paid the mortgage. And if he didn't want two walking hormones in his house, he had a right to show up and say so. As he climbed out of the car, he doubted that his daughter or his wife would agree. But he was ready for the confrontation. He'd been nice—and quiet—too long.

He marched to the door, his phone buzzing in his pocket, letting him know someone had pulled into his driveway. What was it the kids said? It was very meta. If he said that to Karen in ordinary circumstances, she'd laugh at his attempt to keep up with the culture. He missed Karen's laugh. He missed Karen.

He stopped short, the pain of loss—both of Matteo and of his family—hitting him in the chest. He looked around at the familiar surroundings, seeing them as a visitor might. Because that's what he was now: a visitor. There was the tree they had planted the week they brought Ian home from the hospital. There was the fence post that needed to be replaced. There was the firepit he'd made with his own two hands. In the fall they roasted marshmallows and made s'mores there, eating until their stomachs hurt. But he wasn't there to make s'mores.

He looked back at his car, debated going back to work, leaving his family to it. Let Karen deal with whatever Lauren was doing when

Karen got home from whatever she was doing. He wasn't supposed to know anything. Karen would be furious if she knew that he did. He wouldn't be the only one spoiling for a fight. He saw that, in his haste to get out, he'd left his car door open, like an invitation to just climb back inside.

He walked back to the car, stood there for a moment, trying to decide what to do: admit defeat and retreat, or stay and fight. But was it too late for a fight? Had he ruined things for good? Karen was off with friendly neighbor Mike, and Lauren was entertaining thugs. And who knew what Ian was doing. None of them missed him. None of them seemed to notice his absence. But was that their fault—or his?

He went to shut the door and heard his police radio go off, the dispatcher sputtering out codes for a shooting with a possible fatality. His pulse spiked at recognition of the location. He'd been to that house enough, after all, barked out that same address to plenty of people as he coordinated the investigation and search. He'd done it thinking it would bring his brother back. But Matteo was already lost to him. The ME had said he'd likely been in that water since he'd gone missing. All that searching, all that time away from his family. And for what?

He looked back at his house. Then at the radio. Then back at the house, his feet frozen in indecision. He should go to the scene. This was his case. He likely knew the shooting victim. He worried it could be Norah's daughter. If something happened to that kid, he'd have one more thing to feel guilty for. It would be another disaster fueled by his obsession with Matteo's disappearance. If his brother hadn't gone missing, he wouldn't have investigated Norah Ramsey. At least not to the degree that he had. He'd lost sight of everything else. And then he'd lost everything else.

He put his hand on the car door just as he heard the back door open and his daughter call out. "Dad?" Lauren asked. "What are you doing here?"

He looked at her, guilt deepening the lines on his face. He wanted to cry, to run to her, to hold her until she squirmed out of his grasp. But he held his ground as he debated how to answer her question. He supposed that when you didn't know whether to fight or flee, sometimes holding your ground was all you could do.

She watched him warily, wondering, he knew, if she was busted. "I was afraid you were in trouble," he finally said. "I came to . . ." He didn't want to admit what he'd come to do. He'd come to yell at her, to demand an explanation, to rage at the injustice of being expelled from his home just because he'd tried too hard to find his brother. But it wasn't Lauren he should be upset at. It wasn't Karen, either. It wasn't Matteo. It was himself.

"Daddy?" She hadn't called him that in so long.

He felt wetness on his face, tasted salt on his lips, saw his daughter through a sheen of tears. Her blurry form moved toward him, rocketing into his arms. Behind him, he heard the radio alert again. And for a moment, he felt that tug, the one that compelled him to go where the danger was, to protect and serve as he'd always done. Away from here, things were happening: bad things, to innocent people. But they weren't his people. His people were here, and they needed him. He couldn't save those people. He probably couldn't save his own. But he could start trying. He could start trying right now.

Violet

After they had asked her a few questions, they forgot all about her, which was what she needed them to do. They were too concerned with the emergency situation at hand. So when heads turned toward the victims, she sidestepped out of the den, crept up the back staircase, and made her way to her room as fast as she could. It hadn't been that long since she'd tossed the doll aside, feigning nonchalance, when Casey had walked in.

It hadn't been long, yet so much had happened. Later, she would let herself think about it all: the man with the gun, how heroic Casey had been. She'd let herself recall Bess bleeding on the doorstep. The scary man—Polly's husband, she knew now—lying in the backyard, stopped by the bearded stranger who'd chased him down after he had shot Bess. Polly wringing her hands and pacing, mumbling to herself about how it was all her fault. Casey shrieking over her unconscious mother, begging her to wake up. But not now. Now she had one thing she needed to do—and fast—before that detective showed up, because surely he would. She clicked the lock on her door and went back to get the doll.

She fished around under the doll's dress, recalling, as she did, the confused look on Casey's face when she'd walked in on Violet. She knew that Casey had wondered what she'd been doing to that doll. She grinned to herself as she once again found the lacy slip under the dress, the little inner pocket, meant to hold a brooch or handkerchief for a real bride, something blue or borrowed, nestled close to the heart.

Instead, hidden in the tiny pocket, there among the folds of lace and fabric, was the rectangular piece of plastic, the jump drive she'd been searching for. Violet carried it reverently over to her desk, fired up her laptop, and inserted it. She waited for the answers it would hold while at the same time wondering what her mother had intended her to do with the drive. She had cued Violet with the three taps on the table in the jail. It had been their code. When they were around someone else and she wanted Violet to listen, her mother needed only to tap three times to say *This is important*, to make sure that Violet was paying attention.

But paying attention to what? Had she meant for Violet to hand the drive over to the authorities? Or had she meant for Violet to just know that, even though she wouldn't give it to anyone else, she'd trust her with it? Violet didn't know. And she couldn't ask her mother. So she decided to look at what was on the drive first, then make up her mind. If she found Micah's father's name on the list, her decision would be even harder.

She watched as the list loaded onto the screen, leaned forward to decipher it. In this document, she thought, I'll find the names of men who've done despicable and dishonest things, powerful men and ordinary men alike, who don't want anyone to know what they've done. This document, she thought, could ruin lives, whole families. She thought about Micah's face that night they'd talked in his kitchen. He'd wanted to protect his family. But she wanted to protect her mom.

She knew her mom had done something wrong, something illegal, but she was still her mom, the same mom who watched *13 Going on 30* again and again with Violet even though she had to be sick of it; the same mom who ate pepperoni on her pizza even though she didn't really like it but knew that Violet did; the same mom who let Violet crawl into bed with her anytime she didn't feel well or had a bad dream. It was just the two of them, they used to say, against the world. Violet didn't like facing the world without her. She thought about the scene in her backyard right now, the emergency personnel and police scurrying around. The world was a scary place.

The names were arranged alphabetically, most of which she'd never heard of. News articles surmised that there would be athletes and politicians, CEOs, and local celebrities on the list—men for whom exposure like this could mean the end of their careers, their marriages, their good reputations. She understood why they wanted to protect themselves; she knew what happened to a family when something like that came out. She'd lived through it herself. But she'd lived. It had changed her, sure. But she would go on from here; she'd take what she'd learned and apply it in the future, the good and the bad. And so could these men.

She didn't find Micah's father's name on the list. She double-checked, just to make sure, and, once confirmed, she ejected the drive with a sigh of relief. She stood up and pocketed the drive, humming to herself as she walked out of her room. The humming distracted her from the bloody scene downstairs, the weight of the tiny thing in her pocket. As far as she knew, she held the only copy of her mother's client list in the world. She could take a hammer to it and throw it away, and no one would ever know what she'd done. But if she did that, her mother would stay in jail.

She walked down the back stairs, prepared to tell anyone who stopped her that she'd simply gone up to use the restroom. But no one noticed her. She was invisible in her own house. She wondered what her mother would think of the scene: the blood tracked through the house, the flashing lights reflected in the front windows, her poor exploded pumpkin, another casualty of the evening. Violet wondered if her mother would think this was all her fault, if she would blame herself like Polly did. Really it was Polly's husband's fault. But she could see how one thing had led to another. If Bess hadn't been at their house, she wouldn't have gotten shot. If Polly hadn't been at their house, he wouldn't have shown up with his gun. If Norah hadn't been in jail, Polly wouldn't have come to stay with Violet.

Violet saw the series of events like dominoes falling. She felt herself growing angry with her mother and decided not to think about that, either. Later, after Norah was home, she would tell her how she felt; she would demand an apology. And she knew Norah would give her one, every day for the rest of her life if necessary. It would take a while, but eventually Violet would forgive her.

She went outside and stood at the edge of the backyard, surveying the circuslike atmosphere. Polly was talking to a cop. Out front, the ambulance carrying Bess, with Casey riding along, was pulling away, the siren's wail building as the engine picked up speed. Several cops gathered around the bearded man, now handcuffed and sitting on the little garden bench, just a few feet away from the body of the man he'd killed. Violet didn't like looking at the body, and yet her eyes kept straying back to it. It fascinated and disgusted her at the same time. She wasn't sorry the man was dead. Even though he was dead, she was still afraid of him.

She heard barking and looked around. She'd forgotten all about Barney. She scanned the yard until she spotted a cage. She could just make out his brown nose poking out, protesting as he struggled uselessly to escape. She ran over and squatted down to make eye contact with him. He stopped barking and panted when he saw her. "Hey, boy," she said in the most soothing voice she could muster. "It's OK." She slid her hand between the bars till it reached his velvety muzzle, stroking as best she could.

She felt someone standing over her and looked up to find an officer looking down at her. "You can't let him out just yet," he said. "Sorry," he added. He squatted down beside her and, together, they studied the captive dog. "He yours?" he asked.

She shook her head. "No. He's my grandmother's." She gestured over at Polly. "But I take care of him sometimes." She grabbed the cage wire and Barney sniffed her fingers hopefully.

"He's had a hard night," the officer said. "I guess you all have."

He gave her a sympathetic smile. He was young and handsome. He seemed like someone she could trust, someone who would do the right thing. With her free hand, she reached into her pocket and let the drive fall onto the grass. She glanced down to make sure it hadn't disappeared underneath the leaves that had been steadily blanketing the yard in the past few weeks. It landed in an open spot of grass right between them, but the cop didn't notice. He kept talking to Barney, promising the dog he would get out soon.

"I'm gonna go check on my grandmother now," she said. She stood, her heart racing. If she didn't say anything, he likely wouldn't see the drive; she could still take it back. She waited for him to stand up, too.

"I'll let you know just as soon as he can get out, OK?" he asked. "It's no fun being cooped up like that, is it, boy?" he asked Barney. And Violet thought of her mother, and freedom.

"I think you dropped something," she said, and pointed at the ground. She hoped he didn't notice her finger shaking.

She watched him spot the drive, shining white against the dark grass, and bend down to pick it up, a curious look on his face, before she walked away, leaving him to figure out what he'd found, hoping he realized what he had.

Casey

She sat on a hard chair in the emergency room waiting area, dialing her father again and again, wishing he'd answer. But he was MIA. He was supposed to be working late, but if he was, he would've answered by now. Nicole was at a friend's, waiting for their dad to come get her and bring her to the hospital. Whenever Casey got ahold of him, that was. Casey had spoken with her little sister only briefly, but it had been the most pleasant conversation they'd had since she'd come home. She wished it didn't have to be like that, wished everything could've been different. Mostly she just wished for her mother to be OK.

She tried not to think about how pale Bess had looked, how much blood she'd lost, how scary the ambulance ride had been with the technicians working on her the whole way. "Your mom will be OK," they'd assured her, but Casey feared that they told everyone that, whether it was true or not. She feared whatever was happening to her mom back in that trauma room, feared the moment they would come out and tell her that Bess was dead. She would be all alone. She had come home to not be alone, yet she'd ended up that way anyway.

She looked up from her phone and scanned the room, then turned and looked at the doorway to the waiting area, willing her father to appear. But the doorway stayed empty. The lady behind the registration desk watched her. They exchanged glances, then the lady pressed her lips together and closed her eyes. The lady felt sorry for her. She was a victim, the object of someone's sympathy and concern. She was tired of being a victim.

Suddenly someone waved a can of soda in front of her eyes. She looked up to see who it was, maybe Polly and Violet. Instead she saw a familiar set of eyes, brown and kind and also sad. But not sad *for* her, like the lady behind the desk, sad *with* her. Eli sat down in the empty chair beside her. "I came as soon as I heard." He tossed his arm around her. The movement was casual, friendly. She didn't feel threatened or uncomfortable. She just felt comforted. It wasn't her mom or her dad or her sister. He wasn't related to her in any way. But he felt like family.

She wondered if that was what love was: not sex and not attraction and not romance—not any of those things. She wondered if it wasn't just this: sitting in a hospital together, showing up without being told you were needed. Knowing that Sprite was what you always wanted when you were upset. She popped the top and took a long pull.

"I was with someone else," she blurted out. Because if he was going to leave her, she needed him to go before she got too used to his presence.

He shrugged and gave her shoulders a squeeze. "I don't care," he said.

She looked at him, confused. "You don't?" Maybe she'd mistaken what he felt. Maybe he'd been using her as much as she'd used him. If that was the case, she guessed she deserved it.

He grinned. "I mean, of course I care. But we're broken up. We were"—he sighed—"I don't know what we were. But I figure . . ." He shook off his confusion.

She looked up at him, and she could see it there, in his eyes. He could act nonchalant, but she saw the love she'd come to expect. The love, she realized, she still counted on.

"I figure we'll figure out what we were"—he stopped, corrected himself—"what we *are*. In time. Right now, if you don't mind, I'd just like to sit here with you and wait for news about your mom. I'd like to be with you when they come out to tell you. If that's all right with you, that is."

She rested her head on his shoulder and felt relief fill her entire being. "It's all right with me," she said. "It's all right."

◆ ◆ ◆

She stood over her mother, watching her sleep. They'd said her mother was still unconscious but that she could see her, for her reassurance. They knew she'd seen her mother get shot, had held her till the ambulance arrived. Even now, though she'd changed into some of Violet's shorts and a T-shirt and washed her hands, she could still see blood under her nails. She could still smell the ironlike scent of the blood, the burned air from the gun firing. The smell would not leave her any more than the images of Bess taken down by the bullet would.

"Eli's here," she said, hoping that would stir her. Hoping she'd get angry and wake up, demand to know why he was there and what he wanted. "He's been sitting with me since he heard. He brought me a Sprite."

She pulled a chair over to the bedside and sat down. She felt so tired. But she didn't want to sleep. She wanted to be awake if something changed, wanted to be the first person Bess saw when she opened her eyes. Bess had lost a lot of blood, had had to have surgery to repair her shoulder where the bullet had hit. She would need physical therapy for a long time, but she'd regain use of her shoulder. That's what the doctor had said when he came out to talk to them. Her father had finally shown up with Nicole. The two of them sat side by side in the waiting area, looking shell-shocked and afraid, uncertain what to do. They looked at Casey with a wariness, like they wanted to ask her questions but were holding back. They seemed afraid of her, of what she'd witnessed. She felt apart from them, separated even more than before. But this time she enjoyed the distance. She wanted to stay on the other side of whatever gap existed now because her mom was on that side, and when she woke up, they would stand together, connected by what they'd experienced. She thought of the girl at the party that night saying that Russell Aldridge had raped Casey, saying it had happened to her, too. That connection had terrified her. But maybe, she thought, it didn't have to.

She kept chatting, and her mom kept sleeping. She told Bess about the homeless guy who killed the man who'd held them hostage. The cops said the man had been stealing things from people's storage sheds and garages—food and beverages mostly. They said he'd probably been canvassing the neighborhood for where to hit next and just happened to be in the right place at the right time. He'd stabbed the man with a knife he carried for protection. He was a hero, albeit an unlikely one. She told her mother she planned to track him down somehow so that she could thank him. Who knows what would've happened if he hadn't come along. "I bet you'll try to rehabilitate him or something," she said to Bess. "Knowing you."

Casey waited hopefully, but Bess didn't respond. So she kept on talking, as much to keep herself awake as to communicate with her mom. She babbled on about Eli, about school, about whatever popped into her head. The longer she talked, the more she revealed. She told her mom about her conflicted feelings about Eli, about the cop, about how badly she'd handled everything lately. "I've messed everything up," she admitted.

And then Bess opened her eyes. She looked at Casey and reached out to her. The two grasped hands, and she saw Bess take in the surroundings, seeming to understand where she was and what had happened, no explanation needed. "You didn't mess everything up," Bess said to Casey through tears. "You were so brave today. What you did for Violet. You didn't even hesitate." She squeezed Casey's hand, and Casey was surprised by the strength she still had. This was her good hand now, her good arm.

Casey squeezed back. "So were you," she said. "I didn't know you knew how to do that."

Bess tried to shrug, then winced. "Well, I didn't do it all that well. Obviously." She dipped her chin in the direction of her bandaged shoulder.

"Mom, you were a hero. You got us out of there."

Bess closed her eyes for a moment. "I don't remember all of it," she said, and opened her eyes again.

"I do," said Casey. "And maybe someday I'll tell you whatever you don't remember."

"You'll fill in my gaps," Bess said.

Casey smiled. "Yes."

Bess's face grew serious. "There are other gaps I'd like you to fill. You promised me you would when you're ready. Think you're ready now?"

Casey gave her a scolding look. "Using your injury to guilt me into spilling my guts." She tsked in mock disapproval. "That's low, Mom."

Bess gave a little laugh. "Trust me when I say I wanted to get you to talk somehow, but this wasn't what I had in mind."

"If you were brave enough to tackle a large man with a gun, I guess I should be brave enough to tell you what happened at school. Why I came back. You've waited long enough."

Bess gestured to the bed with her good arm. "And, hey, I've got lots of time."

Casey nodded. "That you do," she said. "That you do."

And then she repeated what she'd told Violet in her room just hours before. It had been a dress rehearsal of sorts, she supposed, a practice run for this moment. She was glad she'd had Violet to talk to then. She was glad she had her mom to talk to now. She had fled school and run home. But the journey to actually get home had taken far longer than she had anticipated. She was glad to finally arrive.

Violet

Instead of her life returning to normal, it just kept getting stranger. She was in Micah Berg's house, spending the night in his sister's old room. Polly stayed in the room down the hall, the one Violet was pretty sure Olivia Ames had died in, but she didn't mention that to Polly. They'd had enough talk of death for one night.

Violet sat on the edge of the bed, too nervous to crawl under the covers, too keyed up to have any hope of falling asleep. A light knock on the door startled her, but she composed herself and said "Come in" just loudly enough to be heard. It was probably just Polly, checking on her yet again, or Micah's mom, who'd come over and invited them to spend the night, considering all the cops streaming through their house, which was a crime scene once again. Or—she dared to hope—maybe it was Micah, responding to the text she'd sent him: I've got something to tell you. In person.

The door opened and she saw his shape fill the doorway, like a wish granted. She'd hoped he would respond to the text, but this was too quick. Micah Berg sauntered. He strolled. The only time he hustled or rushed was when he chased a hockey puck down a frozen rink or rebounded a basketball. Or, she thought, when he hoped that the girl across the street had information about his father. Before she spoke, she reminded herself that that was all she was to him: the girl across the street.

She beckoned for him to come in, motioned for him to close the door. He took a few steps forward but stopped at the midpoint between the doorway and his sister's bed as if there were a mark there, like actors have on stages. He looked stricken, as though he were balancing on a tiny raft and surrounded by hot lava he might fall into. She and Nicole used to play that game all the time.

"I found it," Violet said.

Micah looked down at her hands to see they were empty, then raised his eyes back to meet hers. "Well, where is it?"

"I . . . must've dropped it. When everything happened," she said. It was just a little lie, a necessary one. Everyone had to believe that a cop had found the drive on the scene, not that it had been turned over by the accused's daughter. For her plan to work, no one could know what she'd done. It was this secret thing that would remain solely hers. Her mom wasn't the only one who could keep secrets, she reminded herself.

Micah's face changed from hopeful to devastated in a flash. "Then what did you have to tell me?" he asked, impatient and exasperated.

"Before I lost it, I checked it. I checked it twice." She waited a beat, then added, "Like Santa." She grinned at him, and as she did, he saw that she had good news to deliver. He exhaled and smiled. "He's not on there, Micah. He's not on there anywhere." Micah bridged the gap between them in two steps and swooped her up, hugging her so tight she could barely breathe. But she didn't mind. She didn't mind a bit.

"Thank you," he said, and kissed her cheek. Shocked by the unexpected contact, she pulled back, a reflex she instantly regretted. Micah's face became all circles: round dots of color on his cheeks, round eyes, round mouth. He set her down and took a step back.

"I'm sorry," he said, holding his hands up. "I shouldn't have done that. You've been so nice to me these past few weeks. You're practically the only person who has been nice to me in this whole freaking town. I didn't mean to overstep." He lowered his head. "No one wants to be this close to a girlfriend killer." He said it low, but she heard it.

The silence between them swelled until she finally spoke, her words quiet, but clear. "You didn't kill your girlfriend," she said.

He gave her a sad smile. "You're sweet, Violet," he said. "But I know what everyone thinks. Trust me, you don't have to try to save me from that. You've done enough, just with what you've done."

He took a step back, ready to move toward the door. She could just let him go, let him and everyone else keep thinking what they'd thought since that night last spring. Or she could finally tell her secret. There were only so many secrets Violet could carry. She'd picked up a new one tonight, so this was as good a time as any to lay the old one down.

"I saw you," she said, and watched as his face changed from resigned to curious. "That night. Of your party. I was . . ." She searched for a less incriminating, less embarrassing way to say what she had to. "I was watching the party from my window." She pointed in the direction of her house. "I had the window up, and I could hear everything."

She waited for him to grasp what she was saying. He frowned at her, perplexed. "You heard? You heard what?"

"You broke up with her. And she was crying. She'd cheated on you, and you'd caught her."

"That part everyone knows. Lizzie McCoy told everyone that she saw Olivia kissing that other dude." He gave her a half smile, like she was cute trying to be in the know.

"But not everyone knows what I know," she said. "It's the part you didn't tell anyone." She waited for him to realize what she was referring to, watched as the flicker of knowledge crossed his face like a fluorescent light, coming on in phases. "I always wondered why you didn't tell."

He raised his eyebrows, still unwilling to admit anything. "Why I didn't tell what?"

"She told you she was going to kill herself. She said she was going to drink enough to die. She said she was going to drink herself to death and make sure you got blamed for it. She said if you broke up with her she was going to ruin your life."

Micah winced, though Violet knew it wasn't because of what she said. It was because he was recalling it. "It worked," he said. "She ruined it." His shoulders slumped.

"But why didn't you tell that part? That it wasn't an accident? That she said she was going to do it? Why did you take the blame like you did?"

"Because I blamed myself. I was hard on her that night. Things hadn't been good with us for a while. We were basically over, but we were kind of both hanging on. Hell, that's why she hooked up with that guy. But she was scared for us to really be over. So she threatened me. And I thought that was all it was—just a threat. She was always being dramatic, saying shit like that. So I ignored her. And I went inside and got drunk myself, and I never even looked for her again." He looked at Violet, and she saw tears pooling in his eyes.

"I just pushed it out of my mind and went and had fun. I didn't see her again, so I thought she left. Come to find out, she did exactly what she said she was gonna do." He shook his head. "It was her last words—those texts she sent—against mine. And I'm not one to speak ill of the dead. I figured, sure, people would think it was lousy, but I thought . . . I thought my friends would know me. They'd know I wasn't the type of person who'd do something like that. I thought they'd ask me. They'd give me the chance to explain."

"But no one did," Violet said.

One tear escaped and trickled down his cheek. Another followed close behind. "No one. They all just condemned me, and it was like, once they did that, I didn't want to try to explain. I just, like, went inside myself, so no one could get to me. I figured it was easier that way. I'd finish out my senior year and get the hell out of here."

Violet nodded her understanding. Feelings like Micah's made her into the girl at the window, watching the party but never daring to join it. She found it easier to keep her distance. There was less risk of getting hurt that way. She thought of her father—her own father—sending her away, her mother lying to her for years, her best friend pushing her away because Violet wasn't cool enough. She understood being misunderstood, being rejected. She just never dreamed someone like Micah Berg might understand, too. She saw him smiling at her and gave him a quizzical smile back.

"What?" she asked. She couldn't fathom what he'd find to smile about after a speech like that.

"And then one day," he said, "I find the girl across the street hiding with Casey Strickland in my bushes. And everything changed." He laughed.

"So you don't hate me? For keeping quiet all this time, for not coming forward?"

He shook his head. "No." He paused. "Actually, I—"

He stopped short, clapping his lips together like a drawbridge closing. She wanted to know what he was about to say so badly, but something inside her told her not to ask. All in due time; she felt the words more than heard them. And for a moment she wondered if this was what her grandmother had been talking about, about being a Beaucatcher. Maybe this sense of knowing had lived inside her all along—an instinct, something that would grow over time, its own kind of power, gaining strength.

There in that room with Micah Berg standing before her, working out what he would say next, she understood for the first time that she had more ahead, so much more. She felt herself straining toward this unknown future, not afraid anymore. The anticipation felt like she imagined riding in a convertible with the wind rushing through her hair would feel. She'd never done that before, but she had the sense that she would, someday. She would do it all.

Nico

Nico stood in front of the mirror and knotted his tie with the practiced efficiency of a man who'd done so every day for many years. But this time he did it in front of the mirror on his dresser, in his bedroom, in his house. He pulled the knot firmly and thought about friendly neighbor Mike and the casual conversation he'd had with him the day before. He'd pretended to need to borrow a posthole digger to fix that post. He'd used the opening to let Mike know he had moved back in the house, and to clue Mike in on what he knew had been going on. He made sure to point out that Mike's wife was the only one of the four of them who was clueless. Nico had built his career on clues, he'd told Mike, then watched with satisfaction as the other man nodded his understanding, looking stricken.

Karen came into the room holding a cup of coffee, still wearing her nightgown. He pulled her to him and planted a kiss on the top of her head, inhaling the smell of her sleepy self, something he'd never thought of missing till he didn't have it. There was an intimacy in knowing what someone smelled like first thing in the morning. It was a privilege to be the person who got to experience it, who knew that part and not just the part they showed to the world.

"I missed you," he said for the hundredth time.

She smiled at him, still wary. She'd let him back in the house, but it would take a little longer to let him back into her heart. She had to know he wouldn't abandon them ever again, not for any case, not for anything. That would take time. But he would wait as long as it took.

"Big meeting today, huh?" It was not really a question, but she posed it as one.

"Yeah," he said, sitting down on the bed to slip on his shoes. He needed new soles.

"I hope it goes well."

"I think I'm going to stop by and see Maria on the way in," he said. He'd been putting it off, but he couldn't anymore.

"I'm sure she'll appreciate that."

He turned to look at Karen. "It scares the hell out of me."

She sat down beside him. "So do it scared."

He grinned. "I guess I'm gonna have to."

"Are you going to tell her, about that last day with Matteo?"

He was quiet for a moment, thinking it over again. He looked at Karen. "Should I?"

Now it was her turn to think it over. "I don't know. It's the truth. But it's also a hard thing for her to know about her dead husband."

"I thought I'd just ask her if she has any questions about the autopsy report, make sure she understands that it was likely an accident. He was drinking in his car. Probably had the car running. Passed out and somehow the car went into the lake. And that was it."

"But why was he at that lake drinking on a Wednesday evening?" Karen mused. "That's what she's got to be asking herself."

"Because his brother had just sent him away," Nico said, sadly. "He'd chastised him, and sent him away."

"He'd just confessed he'd been with a prostitute. You had a right to be angry."

Nico nodded, thinking about that day. Matteo had been in agony over what he'd done. But he'd also been concerned about what he'd seen, more importantly about *who* he'd seen, a man he said he recognized but couldn't place. "I'm telling you it's someone I've seen before, like in the papers. Some government official. He didn't like that I saw him. I wasn't supposed to." Matteo's eyes were wild, darting around the room.

Nico hadn't handled it well. He'd called his brother an idiot. He'd told him he didn't have time for his shit that day. He had a huge case in court the next day and needed to go over his testimony. "You got yourself into this. You get yourself out."

Then Matteo said the thing that Nico could never—would never—forget. "But I need you." And Nico had turned his back on him. He'd never seen him again.

The truth—the whole truth about what had happened with Matteo—had gotten him back into the house. Once he had explained to Karen why he'd been so dogged in his search for his brother, why he'd thrown himself into investigating Norah Ramsey, Karen understood much more. She still didn't like the decisions he'd made, but she gave him the chance to make better decisions going forward. It was all he could ask for.

Now, Karen planted a kiss on his cheek. "You'll do the right thing," she said. "You always do." She raised her eyebrows. "Eventually."

He laughed, grateful for the bit of humor. Grateful for his wife. Grateful for the life he'd been given back, a second chance to do the right thing. He didn't intend to ever need a third.

Polly

She'd done this before, of course. With Norah when she was a kid. But that had been many years ago. Now they had fancy gadgets to make it easier. She spread the newspaper out on the table and placed the pumpkin in the center of it. She'd bought a new pumpkin to replace the other one, a casualty of Calvin's rampage.

Bess sat at the island watching her spread the paper out, drinking wine with her good arm. "This is all the lifting I can do these days," she quipped, and raised the glass to her lips.

"Well, cheers to that," Polly said. She went back to arranging the paper so not one bit of Norah's table showed. "You said Casey's dropping by?"

"Yeah, she's busy packing to go back to school, but she said she'd come supervise for a minute. She says she's an expert pumpkin carver, but I think she just wants to keep an eye out for Violet, make sure Micah has the best of intentions."

Polly rolled her eyes. "Well, according to Violet he has no intentions at all. But you should see the way he looks at her. I give it a coupla months, and they'll be an item."

Bess smiled knowingly, then changed the subject. "You doing OK?" she asked, her voice tentative.

"Yeah," Polly said. "It gets a little easier each day. I'm not having as many nightmares. You?"

"Physical therapy is gonna be a bitch. And I worry I'll never have mobility in my arm like I used to. You don't realize how much your shoulder controls what your arm does." She sighed. "Funny how one thing can affect so much." She ran her good hand through her hair. "But mentally, I'm doing OK. I'm not as scared as I thought I'd be. Course I'm militant about the security system being on."

Polly raised her eyes heavenward and nodded an emphatic agreement to that. She felt much the same about their security system ever since "the incident," as she'd come to call it. Sometimes she replayed that moment of letting Barney in, her eyes straying to Bess pouring the wine, forgetting all about locking the door behind her in the process. She'd always regret leaving it open for Calvin to walk right through. But that was the past, and there was nothing that could be done about it. And, as Bess said, she'd apologized enough.

"You'd think I'd be freaked out now that it's just me and the girls," Bess continued. "But I'm weirdly OK with it."

"Your ex giving you any trouble about splitting up?"

Bess pursed her lips. "Kind of hard to when he was MIA for hours after I'd been shot because he was *with another woman*." She and Polly both laughed at this, even though it really wasn't funny.

"And besides, you've got Jason," Polly teased. She'd given Bess a hard time about that as soon as Bess confessed that she actually knew the homeless man who'd saved them, that she'd been helping him out for a while and they'd actually become friends, of sorts. Bess insisted she didn't have feelings for him, but Polly wondered. She'd seen him when he had come by to visit Bess after she got home from the hospital. He'd showered and shaved and had on new clothes. He cleaned up good, as they say.

"Oh, I do not," Bess groused. Then she smiled. "But he did get a job. And he's looking for an apartment."

"And how do you know that?" Polly asked, a teasing tone in her voice.

"Wouldn't you like to know," Bess teased back.

The doorbell rang, and Polly went to let Micah in. He was right on time. She threw open the door with a flourish, nearly hitting herself in the face with the wreath she'd hung on the door, festooned with fall leaves and gourds. She'd bought it at the same time she'd bought the pumpkin. The new pumpkin wasn't as big as the one Norah had bought, but it was good enough. It was all they needed.

The man on the porch wasn't who she'd expected to find on the other side of the door. It was a man she honestly thought she'd never see again, which would've been fine with her. She had to repress a sneer at the sight of the detective. "Yes?" she asked, making herself be cordial. He was a cop, and she didn't make a habit of being rude to cops.

"Ma'am," he said. "I don't want to take up too much of your time, but I came by because I wanted to personally deliver some news. Some good news." He smiled. She'd never seen him smile before. She didn't even know that he could.

"We've had some new information come to light and, because of that, we were able to offer your daughter a plea deal. I just came from a meeting in which she accepted the deal. Her attorney was going to let you know, but I wanted to be the one to tell you."

Polly clapped her hands together. "She's coming home?" she asked, barely believing what she'd just heard.

His face darkened slightly, then went light again, like the sun emerging from behind a cloud. "Well, not right away. We negotiated a three-year sentence, including time served, with the possibility of parole after eighteen months. So in, say, a year and a half, it's likely she'll be home."

"Well, that's not nearly as bad as I feared," Polly said.

"Yes, sooner than it would've been, had one of our men not found that drive on the grounds. We think she dropped it out there when she saw us coming for her. Not sure how we missed it the first time. But it's what's getting her home faster now," he said. He reached out to shake her hand, but she pushed his hand out of the way and gave him a hug instead.

"You give me news like that, and I don't settle for a handshake," she teased him. He blushed and took a step back. He stood there and looked at her for a moment, studying her face, like he was trying to figure her out, trying to see what made her tick. She saw him give up, like so many men had through the years. He bid her goodbye and took his leave.

As the detective went down the front porch steps, Micah came bounding up. The two men passed each other with a nod. Polly greeted Micah much more warmly than she had the detective, calling out for Violet, shooing him into the kitchen to wait there. "Go get yourself a drink out of the fridge. Whatever you want."

Polly shut the door as Violet came down the stairs. "Was that Micah?" she asked, not bothering to restrain her eagerness. "I thought I heard another voice down here, too."

"Yes," Polly said. "Micah's here. He's in the kitchen. That detective came by as well." Better to go ahead and tell Violet the news.

The joy drained out of Violet's face, quickly replaced by fear. "Did something happen to my mom?"

"Apparently they had a meeting, offered her a deal, which she took." She smiled at Violet. Though Norah wasn't being released, she wanted Violet to understand that, based on Norah's crime, her sentence was light, and they should be grateful.

"Is she coming home?" Violet asked, her voice quavering, caught in the space between hope and disappointment.

"Not right away. She'll have to do some time in prison. Because she broke some pretty serious laws. But it's not as bad as I feared, Violet. It could've been worse."

Polly felt the guilt that had been her constant companion since Norah's arrest swell inside her. Though she felt guilty that the authorities hadn't discovered her role in Norah's business, leaving Norah to pay the price alone, she understood Norah had wanted it this way. If Norah was caught, she wouldn't take anyone down with her. That had been Norah's plan, and it had mostly worked. Besides, Polly had consoled herself, if she'd gone to jail, who would've taken care of Violet?

"How long?" Violet asked. Their eyes met, and Polly could've sworn she saw Violet change before her eyes, aging years in those two words.

"Up to three years, but likely just eighteen months."

"I'll almost be a senior in high school by then," Violet said. "She'll miss everything."

Polly pulled Violet to her, wrapping her in the hug she'd been wanting to give her ever since the first moment she saw her. "Not everything, honey," she consoled her, smoothing her hair as she spoke. "She won't miss everything. We'll make sure of it."

Violet pulled back and looked at Polly. "We?"

Polly smiled. "Well, sure, we."

"You'll stay with me? For that long?"

Tears filled Polly's eyes as she looked at her granddaughter. For the first time she didn't see herself when she looked at her. She saw someone else, someone different, changed by all that she'd been through. Someone stronger, smarter, tougher. Someone who didn't need the Beaucatcher legacy to define her. Violet, Polly understood, would write her own definition.

"I will stay for as long as you'll have me," she told her.

Violet smiled and her eyes shone with unshed tears. In the kitchen the alert signaled the back door had been opened. That sound still made Polly jump. Each time she heard it, she recalled Calvin walking through that door with the gun in his hand. She shuddered at the image.

Violet squeezed her shoulder. "It's OK, Polly," she said, understanding without explanation. "He's gone now."

"I know," she said, and gave Violet a brave smile. They started to walk toward the kitchen to see who had arrived, but Violet stopped short and looked at her. "Can I ask you one thing?" Violet said. "About that day?"

Polly's heart picked up speed. Violet hadn't talked much about what had happened, and Polly had let her process things at her own pace, in her own way. But she'd known that, eventually, Violet would have questions. "Sure," she said.

"When he talked about the money. It's money from my mom's business, isn't it?"

Polly wanted to lie. Telling the truth—if Violet ever told anyone—could undo all that Norah had done to protect her and the others. But she wouldn't lie to her granddaughter. She'd have to trust Violet to keep the secret. "Yes," she said.

"But I thought you and my mom didn't speak?"

Polly laughed in spite of herself. "We didn't," she said. "And then one day she contacted me. Found me on Facebook and asked to meet. So we did, and she told me her plan. Asked me to join her. She wanted . . ." Polly felt the words swell in her throat, choking her. "She wanted to help me become financially independent so I could stop relying on men. Because she'd seen me do that her whole life. It was part of why she was so angry at me. She thought it was only because of money that I kept a man around. But with me it wasn't that simple. It wasn't just about money. If I didn't have a man, I felt like half of a whole."

"That's why you stayed with Calvin even though you had all that money," Violet said, taking it in and, Polly hoped, learning a thing or two.

"Yes," Polly said. "I thought he made me better, more valid somehow." She thought about it. "Well, I used to think that. When I got the call from your dad, I'd been thinking about leaving Calvin, was figuring out my next move." She winked at Violet. "Then you came along and gave me just that."

Violet grinned. "So you're Lois?" she asked.

Polly raised her eyebrows. "Actually, I'm not. I have no idea who Lois is. That was by Norah's design. She wanted anyone associated with her to have no further knowledge of the operation. Then if we were ever questioned, we'd have plausible deniability. So whoever Lois is, she got off, and she's somewhere living her life, I guess. Which was the way your mom wanted it."

"So you and my mom have been in touch all this time?" There was a note of accusation, and hurt, in her voice.

Polly shook her head. "No. That was also part of what Norah called 'the beauty of it.' Since we were estranged, I was the last person anyone would suspect. It was hard, knowing it meant we weren't going to reconcile, but I was glad just to be in her life to whatever extent. I was always hopeful that one day it would lead to more."

"And now it has," Violet said.

"Now it has," Polly said, and squeezed Violet's hand. In the kitchen their guests laughed, reminding them of their hosting duties.

"Why don't you go rescue Micah from making awkward small talk, and I'll be right there. Just going to make sure I locked the front door." Violet threw her arms around Polly for a quick hug, then darted away, leaving Polly to stand there stunned, and thrilled, for just a moment.

In the kitchen she heard Violet greet Micah and Bess. She heard Casey's voice and realized that must've been who had come in the back door. They were all there. They were all OK. She exhaled and walked back to check the front door. She was headed back to the kitchen to deliver the good news about Norah to everyone else when she heard Casey pose a question, "So are we doing a scary face or a funny face on this pumpkin?"

"Scary," said Micah.

"Funny," said Casey, Bess, and Violet in unison.

"Hey," she heard Micah concede. "That's three to one. The ladies win."

Indeed, Polly thought, they do.

Bess

Two Years Later

Bess took off the headset and put it on the desk. She reached up and finger-combed her hair, resisting the urge to put it into a ponytail like she often did. She still needed to get used to her long hair. Her girls loved it and begged her not to cut it back into the pixie style she'd had for all those years.

"It's a new you," Casey always told her.

Bess agreed that it was. She was still getting used to the new her. She gripped the extended hand of Bill Parsons, creator and host of the *Nosy Neighbor* podcast, grateful the recording was over. She'd gotten through unscathed, which had been her goal. Bill and his producers had hounded her to do the podcast until she finally had given in, with the stipulation that he not bring up the shooting, which had nothing to do with Norah's case and wasn't something she relished discussing. It was in the past, and Bess preferred to leave it there.

"Were you pleased," Bill asked, "with how I handled everything?"

"Yes, thank you," Bess said. "It was tasteful. I appreciate the chance to tell the real story. There were too many rumors flying around. Rumors that implicated people I care about—people who were innocent. It was important to us to set the record straight."

"Us?" Bill's eyebrows flew up toward his hairline.

"I mean to those of us who were involved. Neighbors and such."

He smirked but didn't press for clarification. "Glad we could do our part. I don't know how far-reaching the podcast will be, but hopefully it will help."

"Three million downloads is a good start," she said.

"You did your research," he said, preening a bit at her mention of his record.

"Why else did you think I agreed to do this?" She smiled to soften her words.

He smiled back, unfazed. He shifted on his feet, glanced toward the door, and lowered his voice. "I couldn't help but notice while we were recording that you weren't wearing a ring, and I wondered . . . if maybe . . . you'd be interested in grabbing lunch with me." He made a point of looking at his watch, as if his offer were an afterthought. "I mean, it's lunchtime."

Bess smiled sweetly. She was slowly getting used to being asked out. It didn't happen all the time, but it happened enough. "I've actually got someone picking me up. I have to be somewhere."

He looked crestfallen but recovered quickly, resting his hand on her bad shoulder. It still hurt from time to time, but nothing a little ibuprofen wouldn't take care of.

"Well, the offer's open. You know how to get in touch with me if you ever change your mind."

Bess nodded. "I certainly do." In her head she could hear Nicole's voice saying, *As if.* She'd starred as Cher in a production of *Clueless* for her senior play, and, for better or worse, the phrase had become part of the whole family's lexicon. "Well," she said, "I better go. My ride is waiting."

She made her exit before he could ask her anything else, hurrying out of the studio and down the sidewalk to the parking lot. She made a visor out of her hand and scanned the lot for the car, an older-model blue Ford Explorer. She spotted it and hurried over, tugging the door open and jumping inside with a relieved sigh.

"You survived," Norah said.

"I survived," Bess replied, and smiled at her best friend.

"No surprises? He didn't spring anything on you that you didn't expect?"

"Nope," she said. "It went exactly as we discussed in the preproduction meeting."

Norah backed the car out of the parking spot but kept talking as she drove. "Was he a complete blowhard? He seems like he's impressed with himself."

"Just another guy with a superhero complex, thinking he's saving the world in his own special way."

"A captain of industry," Norah said.

"Leaping tall buildings in a single bound." Bess gave her customary response.

"Looking for a Pepper to his Iron Man," Norah said.

"Looking for a Lois to his Superman," Bess replied, and they smiled at each other at the stoplight.

Norah launched into one of her diatribes on the male species again, but Bess tuned her out. She was only repeating the things they'd said on that night long ago, when it had all begun, the night Norah had confessed to Bess how she'd found a "growth opportunity," as she'd called it, one that could make them both financially secure. "You could leave Steve," she'd said. It had been one of those nights where the wine was flowing liberally. They'd both been drunk.

"Leave Steve," Bess had repeated. And the rhyme had seemed hilarious. Though her life with Steve had been far from funny. At the time, leaving him had seemed impossible. She had no way of supporting herself. Her daughters were still young. How would she work and care for them, too? She admired Norah, but she didn't think she could be like her.

Norah laid out the plan that night, an idea that had taken shape thanks to two of her marketing clients—one launching an online dating service and one opening a spa. The dating service owner told her she was getting more requests for escorts than dates—"company for the evening," the men called it. The spa owner said that a male customer had insinuated she could make a lot more money by "branching out" into other services besides the massages she offered in the back rooms. Norah connected the two conversations in her mind, hatching a plan that ultimately the two business owners had gone along with. They could make real money, Norah said. And all they would be doing is what they'd been doing in one form or another for years for free: making a man feel important and good about himself.

"You want me to sleep with men I don't know for money?" Bess had felt her happy buzz replaced with the sobering reality of what Norah seemed to be seriously considering.

"No," Norah quickly reassured her. "We won't have to do that. Though, trust me, there are women who will. I've already got some lines in the water. It would surprise you who."

"Who?" Bess couldn't resist.

Norah waved away the details. "We'll get into that later. But it's women you'd never suspect. That's the beauty of it." Norah had raised her eyebrows. "No one else will, either."

Was this foolhardy, or too good to be true? Either way, it wasn't for her. She hoped this would just be a get-rich-quick scheme for Norah, something she'd forget about next week.

But Norah kept talking. "All we have to do is run the administrative side. Coordinate things. I'll handle most everything. I just need someone who knows what to do so that if something happens to me, that person can step in and shut the operation down quickly and efficiently. And no one's more efficient than you." She gave Bess the side-eye.

"So you need a Pepper to your Iron Man, is what you're saying," Bess teased, still trying to keep things light, to pretend this wasn't happening.

Norah nodded and smiled. "A Lois to my Superman."

"I wouldn't want to deal with actual money," Bess said, going along with it. Later she intended to tell her an emphatic no. But later never came.

"You won't have to." Norah had thought of this. "I've got someone in mind for that."

"Who?"

Norah waved away her question a second time. "Someone from my past. You don't know her. But she's like you. She could use a little help making her own way so she doesn't have to depend on a man anymore. She's got some previous experience I could put to use for what I've got in mind."

Of course, now Bess knew that the someone from Norah's past had been her own mother. A few months ago, Bess had worked up the courage to ask Polly how she'd known how to launder money. She'd said that a long time ago she had worked for an attorney with some shady clients, then she'd winked at her and refused to say more, and Bess didn't push. The details didn't matter. Not anymore. They'd each made good money off that crazy-sounding scheme from that long-ago night. And thanks to Polly never being discovered, they'd managed to hang on to most of it, enough to find the freedom Norah had wanted for all of them.

Now the three of them, along with Casey, Nicole, and Violet, had become their own kind of family. They'd made it work. They'd been there for each other, through Norah's incarceration, through Bess's recuperation, through Polly's guilt over what had happened with Calvin, through Bess's divorce, through Casey's fight to get Russell Aldridge expelled and prosecuted. And they'd done it without help from any men, which was what Norah was still babbling on about. The mention of the podcast guy had gotten her all riled up, which predictably launched her into a diatribe about the detective, the men who'd tried to keep her quiet, and any other man who might've wronged her.

"When are they going to learn?" she was saying. "They don't save us. We save them."

Bess didn't give her an answer, because Norah didn't expect one. They'd had this particular conversation countless times. Instead Bess rested her head on the window and thought about Jason risking his life to stop Calvin, and Steve surprisingly being an involved dad even though they were divorced now, and Eli faithfully driving Casey to counseling when she came back from school, and Micah keeping silent about Olivia instead of clearing his own name. She thought about Barney the dog, named after a caveman who did have a good heart and tried to do the right thing. She thought about love blooming and growing, taking root in unlikely places. Just last week she had seen a lone flower growing up through the asphalt in a parking lot. Unlikely things are possible, sometimes.

She decided to interrupt Norah mid-rant. "Maybe," she said. "It's not about them saving us or us saving them. Maybe," she ventured, "we're all just supposed to save each other."

Norah pondered that for a moment. She glanced over at Bess, then looked back at the road. "I like that," she said.

"I do, too," Bess replied.

A Motown song came on the radio, and Norah cranked it up, the conversation over, for now. At the crossroads, they turned in a different direction than they once would have—to Norah's new house. The radio played and the two of them sang together as they took the new way home.

POPPY-SEED CHICKEN CASSEROLE

(For when you or those you love need some comfort food)

4 chicken breasts

1 (14.5-ounce) can cream of chicken soup

1 1/2 cups sour cream

1/3 cup chicken broth (reserved from cooking the chicken)

2 tablespoons poppy seeds

2 sleeves Ritz crackers, crushed

1/2 cup (1 stick) butter, melted

Preheat the oven to 350 degrees F.

Boil the chicken in water seasoned with salt and pepper till tender (15 to 20 minutes). Save 1/3 cup of the broth from cooking the chicken. Remove the chicken from the water and shred with two forks.

In a large bowl, mix together the soup, sour cream, broth, and poppy seeds. Fold the chicken into the mixture. In a separate bowl, mix together the crackers and butter. Press half the cracker mixture into a lightly greased Pyrex baking dish (8 by 8 inches). Add the chicken mixture on top of the cracker crust. Top with the remaining cracker mixture. Bake for 30 minutes, or until the crackers are lightly browned.

DISCUSSION QUESTIONS

1. The Beaucatcher legacy was a connection point for Violet and Polly but a breaking point for Norah and Polly. Why do you think that was? How would you feel about having a legacy like that in your family? How much do you think it would or wouldn't inform your self-image?

2. Bess says that Jason was a secret that was just hers and "wasn't hurting anything." How was that true for each character? Did their secrets really not hurt anyone?

3. Was Norah's reduced sentence fair? Why or why not?

4. Discuss Casey's reaction to her assault. While this isn't "normal" by some people's estimations, did you find it understandable? Does it make you more or less sympathetic to her?

5. Was there a character you felt connected to more than the rest? Why do you think that character stood out to you?

6. How is each character struggling at the opening of the novel? By the end of the novel, have they overcome—or at least come to terms with—what they were struggling with?

ACKNOWLEDGMENTS

It might be my name on the cover of this book, but no novel is produced solely by the author. There's a team of awesome people behind that title. So I'd like to thank my agent, Liza Dawson, and her wonderful staff, especially Kayla Lightner and Havis Dawson, who help me in big and small ways in all of my writing pursuits. I'd also like to thank my gracious, talented editor, Jodi Warshaw, and the team at Lake Union, who work so hard behind the scenes to put a quality novel in front of readers. (Special thanks to Gabriella Dumpit, who does such a great job of keeping the channels of communication wide open. And to Laura Barrett for being a production editor extraordinaire.) Finally, a special thank-you goes out to my developmental editor, Blake Leyers, who made writing this novel a less solitary pursuit than novel writing normally is and encouraged me every step of the way. Thank you for understanding and believing in this story.

My inspiration for this story came from several directions. Most notable: The song "Torchlight" by Missy Higgins was one I could always play to get in touch with what Casey was going through. The book *Missoula* by Jon Krakauer directly informed Casey's reaction to her assault. The song "Woman in Chains" by Tears for Fears (featuring Oleta Adams) is the song I repeatedly played anytime I needed inspiration. And, though it sounds odd to say, I'd also like to thank the real suburban madams in the US, whose situations and motives informed Norah's character. I'd also like to thank Fred Silva from the Lucas Lepri

Brazilian Jiu Jitsu studio, who patiently helped me block the fight scene even though I was a stranger who walked in off the street claiming to be a novelist. He helpfully answered my questions, though it was apparent that he was not convinced I wasn't crazy. Fred, I'm not sure this is proof that I'm not crazy, but it is proof I am a novelist.

Ariel Lawhon, another book means another moment to publicly thank you for the private kvetching and meltdowns you've graciously listened to, not to mention the abundance of shared laughter, albeit sometimes inappropriate. We've done this journey together every step of the way, and I treasure the gift of your friendship.

I'd also like to thank my wonderful neighbors and friends for their tireless encouragement and willingness to show up for me and my family in countless ways (see my other books to find the list of their names—they know who they are). And to the many readers, book clubs, and bookstagrammers who've read and shared my work—a mention or encouraging review never fails to come along at the "just right" moment and is immensely appreciated.

Most of all, I'd like to thank my family. To my mom: You're the model of intelligence and strength that I continue to aspire to. Any of the spunk and wit that is in my characters comes from who you've been to me all my life. To my husband, Curt: Your patience, love, and encouragement throughout this process was just what I needed, and your belief in me never fails. Thanks for those long walks and talks on the beach. And to my children, Jack, Ashleigh, Matt, Rebekah, Brad, and Annaliese: Being able to write novels is a gift, but the greatest thing I've ever created is you guys. I pray you'll all go out and become every bit of who you were meant to be.

And, speaking of prayer: Jesus, You are truly the friend who sticks closer than a brother. I don't know what I'd do if I didn't have You to talk to. Thank You for always listening, and for the big and little amazing things You bring my way. Apart from You, I can do nothing.

ABOUT THE AUTHOR

Marybeth Mayhew Whalen is the author of *Only Ever Her*, *When We Were Worthy*, *The Things We Wish Were True*, and five previous novels. She enjoys speaking to women's groups around the US, sharing how the power of story informs our own lives. Marybeth and her husband, Curt, have been married for a very long time and are the parents of six children, ranging from elementary age to young adult. Marybeth divides her time between the shores of Sunset Beach and the suburbs of Charlotte, North Carolina. She is always at work on her next novel. You can find her at www.marybethwhalen.com.